SHORT
INVESTIGATIONS

OTHER BOOKS AND AUDIOBOOKS
BY CLAIR M. POULSON:

I'll Find You
Relentless
Lost and Found
Conflict of Interest
Runaway
Cover Up
Mirror Image
Blind Side
Evidence
Don't Cry Wolf
Dead Wrong
Deadline
Vengeance
Hunted
Switchback
Accidental Private Eye
Framed
Checking Out
In Plain Sight
Falling
Murder at TopHouse
Portrait of Lies
Silent Sting
Outlawyered
Deadly Inheritance
The Search
Suspect

SHORT INVESTIGATIONS

A
SUSPENSE
NOVEL

CLAIR M. POULSON

Covenant Communications, Inc.

Cover images: *Old Red Barn* © timnewman; *Crime Scene Do Not Cross* © JaysonPhotography, courtesy istockphoto.com

Cover design copyright © 2018 by Covenant Communications, Inc.

Published by Covenant Communications, Inc.
American Fork, Utah

Printed in the United States of America
First Printing: August 2018

24 23 22 21 20 19 18   10 9 8 7 6 5 4 3 2 1

ISBN 978-1-52440-693-6

To Kent and Marie Poulson

"I THINK WE HAVE WHAT we need," Max Fisher said to his best friend and cousin, Sammy Kist. The two men were taking the day off to go fishing. It was their favorite pastime, and since neither of their wives liked to fish, the two of them did it together.

They paid for their purchases and stepped out of the sporting goods store. They had come in Max's green Chevy pickup, and even though he'd had it for five years, it was the first new vehicle he'd ever purchased and was his pride and joy. The men got into the truck and drove to their favorite fishing hole on the Provo River.

The two men parked the truck and walked down a narrow path to the river and then hiked a short distance before beginning to fish. There were two other men just a short distance away also fishing in the popular river.

After just a couple of minutes, Max caught a large fish. Then Sammy caught a nice one, and within a half hour they each had a couple more. Max grinned at his cousin. "Good fishing today," he said.

Suddenly the other men were right beside them, towering over them. Sammy and Max were both a shade under five feet, but the other men must have been six feet or taller.

"You're in our spot, runts," one of them growled. "Move."

Sammy stretched himself up as tall as he could and told them to get lost.

That was a mistake. One of the men punched Sammy in the gut, causing him to bend over in pain. Max shouted, "Hey, buddy, what do you think you're doing? Sammy didn't do anything to you guys."

The second man then punched Max in the face without uttering a word. Max and Sammy attempted to defend themselves, but they didn't have a chance. The larger men delivered a brutal beating. Max's attacker grabbed him by the front of his shirt and held him with a beefy fist while he pummeled his face. Then the beefy man dropped him and began to kick and then stomp on him. The last thing Max remembered was the man saying something about teaching him and Sammy to hog a good fishing hole. Then, as another blow struck his head, he blacked out.

Max woke up in a strange environment. There were two people standing over him wearing scrubs. He noticed a stethoscope around one man's neck. The lights were bright. And he became aware of machines buzzing around him. He struggled to sit up, but a gentle hand restrained him. "Where am I?" he asked.

"You're in the hospital," the man with the stethoscope said. "I'm Dr. Daryl Springman. I operated on you and patched you up a bit." The doctor smiled. "Can you feel anything yet?"

"Just pain," Max replied. "Why did you operate on me?" he asked as his head began to clear. "Wait! I remember. A couple of guys attacked us while we were fishing. Did you operate on Sammy too? Can I see him?"

The doctor and a pretty young nurse exchanged glances.

"What?" Max demanded. "Where is my cousin?"

"I'm sorry, Max, but Sammy didn't make it," Dr. Springman said.

"Didn't make it? You mean he's . . . he's dead?"

"I'm sorry," the doctor said again. "He was dead before some fishermen found you both. You're lucky to be alive. You'll recover, but you will be in the hospital for quite a while."

"But . . . but . . . Sammy," Max said, his eyes burning. "I . . . we were just fishing, minding our own business when these other guys came along and told us to leave, that we were fishing in their hole. We disagreed, and they attacked us." He fell silent, trying to make sense of what had happened.

"That was on Wednesday," the doctor said kindly. "You have been in a coma for five days." The doctor went on, explaining more to Max about his injuries and the treatments he'd need as he recovered, but Max didn't hear much of it. All he could think of was Sammy.

Shortly after that a couple of officers came into his room. He told the cops everything he could remember. He described his and Sammy's attackers in detail. He described the fishing gear they were carrying and the clothes they were wearing, right down to the kinds of boots and hats they wore.

Detective John Gravitt of the Utah County Sheriff's Department raised his eyebrows. "You have a pretty good memory for someone who has been in a coma. Are you sure you're right about all this?"

"I have a photographic memory," Max explained. "If I ever see those men again or even hear their voices, I will recognize them."

Despite the detailed descriptions, the police never found the men or the fishing gear they had stolen from Sammy and Max. The killers must have even taken their fish, because the officers said there were no fish or fishing poles where the cousins were found.

The next three months were a nightmare for Max Fisher. As Max lay in the hospital recovering, his wife, Hallie, a pretty woman who was a half inch taller than him at an even five feet, was constantly by his side. And as often as possible, his daughter, Patches, came to visit him. She was a beautiful girl of eleven with wide eyes, an oval face, and a pouty little mouth. Her green eyes shone with intelligence. But whenever Max spoke with her, he could feel the anger that filled her soul.

"Patches, you've got to get over this," he said one day. "What's done is done. Daddy will get well, and I'll be able to go back to work."

"Daddy, they hurt you. And they killed Cousin Sammy. And all over a stupid fishing hole! Someone has to catch them," she sobbed as she clung to his clammy hand and peered into his eyes.

Max blinked back a tear. "The police are doing the best they can," he said. But their best was not good enough. Hour after hour, day after day, Max lay recovering, thinking about the men who had committed this crime just because they were being outfished. At least that was the only reason he could think of when he thought about the attack. He honestly didn't think they'd meant to kill anyone but had simply gotten carried away. But they had killed, and he wanted them brought to justice.

As those days crept by, Max made himself a solemn promise. No one would ever be able to hurt him so easily again. He vowed to do whatever it took to learn to defend himself. And as he looked into those loving, pain-filled green eyes of his daughter, he realized that not only should he be able to defend himself but his wife and daughter should also be able to defend themselves.

When he was finally well and back to something close to normal, he took steps to fulfill that promise. He enrolled all three of them in a karate class, and they all began taking firearms training. Max and his wife and daughter were strong and highly motivated. They worked hard and learned fast. And they continued to improve as time passed.

Never once did Max Fisher forget the faces or voices of the men who had killed his cousin, his best friend.

CHAPTER ONE

Ten years later

"THERE'S A BODY IN THE barn," the caller told the dispatcher, Karen Wilton.

"What kind of body?" Karen asked.

"A dead one. Are you stupid?"

Karen recoiled at the caller's cruel words. But she did not speak back in the same way. "What *kind* of dead body?" she asked. She suspected it was human, but she had to be sure before she sent an officer to the barn.

"Stupid woman," the caller said with a growl. "It's a female. A human being. A dead lady. Got it?"

Karen felt her face heat. She wished she could reach through the phone and throttle whoever it was. But she was a professional. So she calmed herself before she asked, "What barn? Where is it located?"

"That little bull rider's barn," the caller snarled.

"What's his name?" she asked.

"Figure it out. He killed a woman."

"Who are you?" Karen asked next.

There was a click on the line. The call had come from a blocked number. She sat back for a minute, deep in thought. Then she called an on-duty deputy on the radio. When he answered, she instructed him to give her a call as soon as he could.

The call came within a minute. "Hi, Karen," Deputy Clayson Lebow said. "What have you got?"

"This could be a prank, but we need to check it out," Karen began. "Somebody called in. Whoever it was wouldn't give me his name and acted like a real jerk. All I was told was that there's a dead woman in the barn of 'the little bull rider.'"

"Did the informant name the bull rider?" Deputy Lebow asked.

"No, just that there's a woman in the barn and that the bull rider killed her."

"Do you have any idea who the bull rider is?"

"Not a clue."

"Well, I think I just might. My first guess would be Rhett Ketchum," Deputy Lebow said darkly. "He's a national champion bull rider—of sorts. I'm sure he cheats to win. That's the kind of guy he is. People call him Shorty."

"I know Rhett," Karen said. "He's a great guy. He'd never hurt anyone, let alone kill them. Who else could it be?"

"Karen, apparently you don't know Shorty like you think you do. I, on the other hand, know him only too well. I'll take a ride out to his place," he said. "I know where it's at."

The call ended, and Karen sat there wondering why Deputy Lebow hated Shorty Ketchum so much and why he would jump to such a crazy conclusion. Even if there was a body in Rhett's barn, which was a huge stretch, she was quite certain it wasn't his fault. She shook her head and then took another call.

***

Deputy Clayson Lebow parked in front of the house at the Diamond Bar Ranch and shut his gray Explorer off. He glanced at the ranch-style home where Rhett and his widowed mother lived. He couldn't see Rhett's dark-gray Ford F350 pickup. Sarah Ketchum was a slender woman of about fifty. She'd lost her husband less than a year ago to a brain tumor. Rhett had moved home to take care of the ranch. He had three sisters, but none of them lived at home anymore. All of them had married and left the Heber Valley. So when Rhett was gone from home on the rodeo circuit, Sarah managed the ranch by herself. Clayson knew all this, but his hatred for Rhett dulled his sensitivities toward the cowboy's widowed mother.

He was certain there was a body in the Ketchums' barn, and it made him smile, for then he could arrest Shorty for murder.

With the grin still on his face, he got out of his vehicle. He approached the house and rang the bell. Rhett's mother answered the door as he wiped off the smile.

"Why, hello, Clayson. If you're looking for Rhett, he's out of state at a rodeo. Is there something I can do for you?" she asked sweetly.

"Why would I be looking for Shorty?" he asked curtly. "Have you been in your barn today?"

She gave him a strange look and said, "Why do you ask that?"

He stared hard at her and said, "You need to answer my question."

"No, I haven't been in the barn today," she said. "What seems to be the matter?"

"Why don't we go take a peek. You don't have a problem with that, do you?" the deputy asked snidely.

"Of course not, but I don't know what you expect to find there," Sarah said as she stepped out of the house, bristling at the way Clayson was speaking to her. "The barn's behind the house and yard, but I guess you already know that."

"I do," he said as he headed that way at a brisk walk. Sarah, who was only about five-foot-two, had to jog to keep pace with him.

The big door at the north end of the barn was open, and Clayson stepped right in and then stopped and asked Sarah where the light switches were located. She stepped past him to the left of the doorway and flipped several switches. The place was immediately flooded with light.

"I need to have a look around," he said. "You stay right here."

"I'll walk with you," she insisted. "You still haven't told me what you're looking for."

"I'll tell you when I see it," he said brusquely and started up the alley, which was lined with stalls on both sides. She followed. He turned to her and repeated his order. "Go back and wait at the door, Mrs. Ketchum. This is a police matter, and I am telling you to let me do my job."

Sarah stepped in front of him, put both hands on her hips, and glared up at Clayson. "This is my barn, mine and Rhett's. You have no right to be in here without our permission," she said. "I've changed my mind. You should go get a warrant if you think there's something in here that shouldn't be. Otherwise, you can just stay out of here!"

Clayson returned her glare and said, "So you know what's in here, do you? The fact that you won't let me look is evidence you are trying to hide a crime and obstruct justice. But if you insist, I'll call for backup and get a warrant while another officer makes sure you don't disturb anything."

Sarah looked flustered, and she said, "I'm not hiding anything, Clayson. But I don't like your attitude. I know you and Rhett don't get along, but you are an officer of the law. I would expect you to treat me with some courtesy."

Clayson's anger was building. He said, "Come back to my truck with me while I call for another officer."

"Clayson, I don't know why you are being so stubborn. You are welcome to look around in here, but only if I accompany you," she said. "But first you need to tell me what you're looking for."

"Come along then," he said, exasperated—he didn't want to wait for a warrant. He once again started deeper into the barn. "I was told there was something dead here in your barn," he lied. "Let's start by looking in each of these empty stalls."

"Something dead?" Sarah asked, taken aback. "I don't smell anything dead."

"That's what I was told," he said again. Even though he had not been told it was *this* barn, *he knew*. He approached the first stall on the west side of the barn. He looked in it and found nothing.

He crossed the alley and checked the first stall on the east. It too was empty. Sarah stood in front of the next stall, barring his way. "Are Rhett and I suspected of poaching deer or elk?" she asked.

"We'll see about that," he responded, letting her think it was a big game carcass he was interested in.

"Then let's finish. We never have and never will poach. We kill our own beef and pork when we need meat," she said as she stepped aside.

There were a dozen stalls in the barn, a tack room, an office, grain storage areas, and a small round arena. It was in the very last stall on the east side that Clayson found what he was looking for. Lying on the floor of the stall was the body of a woman. She was lying facedown, her arms bound behind her back, and her legs bound together with duct tape. She had on tan capris and a flowered brown blouse. She wore no socks but had white running shoes on her feet.

Sarah screamed. "Who is that?" she cried as she stumbled backward to the center of the aisle, her hands over her mouth. She slowly crumpled to the concrete floor.

Clayson stepped into the stall and over to the body. He stooped and felt for a pulse, knowing there would be none. The body was still. It had been there long enough for rigor mortis to set in. Clayson was intent on telling the world who Shorty had killed. And, in his mind, there was no doubt he would prove Shorty had done it. He looked back to the door of the stall. Rhett's mother was sitting with her head between her knees, sobbing. She did not appear to be paying any attention to what he was doing.

He quickly reached down and turned the body over. He knew this girl. For a moment, his anger almost consumed him, but then he got it under control. He carefully turned the body back over. No one need ever know he'd moved her at all.

He slowly stood up, and then, so softly that no one, even Sarah, if she was listening, could hear him, he vowed, "Charity, my love. Shorty will pay for what he did to you. I swear he will." He backed out of the stall and glanced at Sarah, who looked up just as he did. "I'm calling the sheriff," he said. "You are to wait in the house. There has been a murder in your barn. And we both know your son did it."

"Rhett would never hurt anyone," Sarah protested as she finally made her way to her feet.

"So says a mother blinded by her son's charm," he said, unable to keep the anger and hatred from his voice.

Sarah Ketchum gave him a scathing look but said nothing more as she left the barn, in apparent shock over what she'd seen and Clayson's accusation.

Clayson looked back at Charity's lifeless form, memories flooding him. When he and Rhett were in high school, they had both dated Charity Simmons. But she had soon picked Rhett over Clayson, and he hated Rhett for stealing her from him. When Rhett had left to serve a mission, Clayson supposed that was his chance to gain Charity's affection.

But it wasn't to be. Charity had turned him down several times when he asked her out, stating that she was waiting for Shorty. She always called him Shorty as if it were an endearing name. Clayson called him Shorty thinking of the nickname as derogatory, even though he was only two inches taller than Shorty.

Even when Rhett broke off the relationship with Charity early in his mission, she refused to go out with Clayson. She ended up marrying Gene Gaffey, a fellow several years older who was into drugs and drank heavily but had always charmed women. By the time Rhett returned from his mission, the newly married couple had left Wasatch County.

For years Clayson had pined for Charity. And even though she'd married Gene, Clayson still blamed Shorty for Charity's spurning him. He'd heard recently that Gene and Charity were divorced. He had hoped she would return to Heber and that he would finally get his chance to win her affection. He'd already called her several times, and she had turned down his every invitation to take her to dinner. It irked him terribly. She had no right to reject him like that. It was all Shorty's doing, and Clayson would make him pay.

***

Rhett Ketchum pulled his ringing cell phone from his pocket. He'd been looking into a livestock pen filled with rodeo bulls, one of which he'd be riding that night. They were excellent stock. He was excited. He looked at the screen of his phone. It was his mother. He hoped she wasn't having trouble. He hated leaving her alone like this, but she'd always understood. In fact, she insisted he continue to ride bulls. The two of them needed the large purses he won to keep the small ranch in the black. And she had faith in his ability even though she feared for his safety, praying constantly for the Lord to watch over him.

"Hi, Mom," he said cheerfully. She didn't respond, but he could hear her sobbing. "Mom, what's the matter? Are you hurt?" he asked as his heart began to hammer at his ribs.

"Rhett," she said. Then he could hear her clearing her throat. "There is a dead woman," she began and started to sob again.

"Mom, what's going on?" he asked as gently as he could with the sudden rush of adrenaline that hit him.

He waited while she composed herself. Finally, she was able to speak again. But this time, he could detect anger in her voice. "There is a dead woman in the barn. The deputy says you killed her."

Rhett was stunned. "Mom, what in the world are you talking about?"

"Someone killed a woman. Her body is in one of the horse stalls in the barn," she said, more in control now.

"And who accused me of doing it?" he asked, shocked at the very thought.

"Deputy Clayson Lebow," she said angrily.

"Why would he accuse me? I'm not even in Heber. I'm not even in Utah."

"Apparently he hates you," Sarah said. "I know you were going to ride tonight, but I think you need to come home as soon as you can."

"And let that creep Lebow throw me in jail?" he asked as his shock was displaced by anger.

"He can't do that, can he?" his mother asked. "You've been gone for three days."

"Of course not. Okay, Mom, you just try to relax. I'll come home. I'll forfeit my ride tonight. But it'll take me several hours to get back from Reno. In the meantime, you need someone with you. Call one of the girls. I'll bet Susie would come. She's not that far away."

"Okay, Rhett. Drive carefully."

"One more thing, Mom. Don't say a word to Clayson or anyone else until I get there. Not the sheriff, not anyone," he told her. "Tell them I'll be there as soon as I can."

"But they will want to ask me questions," she said. "I should answer them. I don't know how that body got in the barn. I can tell them that."

"Mom, if Clayson is intent on blaming me, then he'll try to twist your words or even lie about what you say to him. Just tell him and the sheriff and whoever else asks that you want an attorney," he said.

"But won't that make us look guilty?" she reasoned.

"We can't worry about that now. I'll get us some help. I know Clayson, and if he thinks he can make a case against me, he will, no matter how much lying he has to do."

"Okay, if you think that's best," his mother said.

"I do. Call me if anything happens before I get home," he said, and then he had another thought. "Mom, who is the woman who was killed?"

"I don't know. I don't even know if Clayson knows."

"Okay, let me know if you hear who it is. Now I'd better get moving."

Sarah took Rhett seriously about calling him. She called him half a dozen times. Most of the calls were of inconsequential things, like Clayson angrily ordering her to get back in the house when she came out onto the back deck to watch what was happening at the barn. Another was about a coroner coming in and then leaving an hour later. She'd seen that from her bedroom window since Clayson had made such a fuss about her staying inside.

She also called when Clayson had come to the door an hour after the body had been removed and asked Sarah when Rhett was going to be home. When she told him she didn't know, he'd ordered her to call him the moment Rhett got home. Rhett told her she didn't have to do any such thing and reminded her not to tell Clayson anything else.

Susie Arnold, Rhett's older sister by two years, arrived two hours after Rhett first heard from his mother about the body in the barn. She had Sarah call Rhett and give him her father-in-law's phone number. Wilson

Arnold was a well-known and very successful defense attorney in Salt Lake. Rhett promised to call him when he learned anything of substance about the murder so he could talk to Mr. Arnold with at least a little knowledge of what he was up against.

But the most startling call came thirty minutes later. "Rhett, you'd better call Susie's father-in-law right now. Clayson came by just a few minutes ago. He was spitting nails," Sarah said. "He told me he was going to have a warrant to arrest you for murdering your old girlfriend and if Susie and I didn't call him as soon as you drove into the yard that he would arrest us for obstructing justice, whatever that means."

"My old girlfriend?" Rhett said, alarmed. "Mom, which old girlfriend did Clayson say was killed?"

"Charity Simmons—well, I guess it's Charity Gaffey now," Rhett's mother responded. "Didn't she marry that Gene Gaffey fellow?"

"She did, but they are divorced now," he said, distracted. He felt a pounding in his temples. Charity had called him three times in the past couple of months, basically seeking sympathy for the way Gene had treated her. She'd never said as much, but Rhett was pretty sure what she really wanted was for him to take her out again. He'd pretty much given her the cold shoulder each time. But if Clayson found out about those calls, he'd make them into something they were not.

"Okay," he said, knowing that under the circumstances it didn't matter that he had not killed Charity. It didn't even matter that he hadn't seen her since just before he'd left for his mission more than five years ago. Clayson Lebow would make sure the entire sheriff's department was fired up about it. "I'll give Mr. Arnold a call now. But, Mom, I haven't seen her since before my mission. I don't know what Clayson thinks he can prove."

"He said Charity called him about a month ago and told him you'd been trying to get her to go out with you and that you were angry when she turned you down," Rhett's mom revealed.

"That's a lie!" he thundered. "Maybe Clayson killed her for rejecting him and is trying to set me up."

"I would hope that's not true, Rhett, but Susie and I were just discussing that very thing."

CHAPTER TWO

SHERIFF CHANCY McCOY LOOKED UP from his desk and glared across it at Deputy Lebow.

"What do you need, Chancy?" Lebow asked.

"We need to talk, *Deputy* Lebow," the sheriff said, attempting to put the younger man in his place. "I just got a call from Wilson Arnold. Do you know who he is?"

"Can't say that I do," Lebow said, seemingly unmoved by the sheriff's stern look and voice.

"Do you know who Susie Arnold, formerly Susie Ketchum, is?" Sheriff McCoy asked.

"Of course I do. That's our suspect's sister. But her husband's name is Trae, not Wilson," the deputy snapped.

"That's right, Deputy Lebow. His father is Wilson Arnold, a top-notch defense attorney out of Salt Lake. Does his name ring a bell now?"

"Should it?" Lebow asked with a shrug.

"He's defended several cases here in Heber over the years, and he has a reputation for tearing cops apart on the stand unless they have all their ducks in a neat little row." The sheriff rubbed his short red hair and looked out his window for a moment. When he looked back, his deputy seemed unruffled. "Deputy, why do you think Mr. Arnold called me?"

"How would I know?" Clayson said flippantly.

"Well, perhaps it's because you've accused his client of murder, and he was curious to know what kind of evidence we have."

"Who is his client, Chancy?" Lebow asked innocently.

The sheriff slapped both hands on the desk and said angrily, "I'm Sheriff McCoy to you, Deputy. Mr. Arnold's client is Rhett Ketchum. And what do you think I could tell Mr. Arnold since you haven't bothered to do anything more than tell me you found a body in the barn at the Ketchums' ranch?"

"What else is there to tell?" the deputy asked. "You were in Provo for some kind of meeting, so you weren't at the scene."

The sheriff frowned. "Mr. Arnold feels like you have made accusations you can't back up. Since I hadn't discussed it with you, I couldn't tell him what you may or may not have said."

"How does he know anything? I haven't even had a chance to talk with the slime ball who killed Charity," the deputy said.

The sheriff shook his head. "Rhett Ketchum hired Wilson Arnold to defend him in the event that he gets charged with anything. Mr. Arnold says you told Rhett's mother and his sister you were going to arrest him for murder when he gets back from wherever he is," the sheriff said with a frown. "What possible evidence do you have that would lead you to tell them that?"

"Charity's body was in Shorty's barn, and I'm pretty sure his mother didn't kill her. So that leaves Shorty," Deputy Lebow said snidely.

"Shorty?"

"Yeah, that's what people call him."

"I see. Well, Deputy Lebow, didn't you learn anything in the police academy and in the years you've worked here? That isn't proof of anything. That kind of statement can get you and I both sued. You have no business jumping to such a conclusion. Now, I have detectives whose job it is to do the investigation. You do know that, don't you?"

"I have more evidence than where the dead girl was found," Deputy Lebow told him with a smirk.

"Is that so? Then, why don't you tell me about it."

"I know Charity really well. She is a former girlfriend of Shorty's. She married another guy, and that guy divorced her recently. They lived somewhere in the Salt Lake Valley," Lebow explained. "Charity called me a short while ago, and I guess I should have paid more attention when she did. She said Shorty's been calling her and trying to get her to come back to him, but she didn't want anything to do with him. She told me she was afraid of him. She felt like he might kill her."

The sheriff sat back and thought about what he'd been told, and then he said, his frown still very much in place, "You are to turn any evidence you have over to me. Write me a report about what you just told me. I want the report and all evidence you have within the next thirty minutes. I'll have a couple of detectives take it from here. And you are not to speak with Rhett Ketchum or any of his family from this point on. You are off the case as of this moment. Do I make myself clear?"

"Why? I can help. I know Shorty and the kind of guy he is," Lebow protested.

"And, according to Arnold Wilson, you also vied for the victim's attention," the sheriff said. "And don't deny it. You cannot be objective. Stay away from the case."

"All right, but if you don't get that worm in jail pretty quickly, he will find a way to get away with this. Shorty killed Charity, and he'd better be made to pay for doing it."

The sheriff looked at his deputy and hoped the man hadn't already created enough of a stir to get them sued. "The medical examiner has the body?" he finally asked, even though he already knew the answer.

"Yes, they took her there."

"Then he can tell us when she was murdered. And here's the big problem with your accusation, according to Ketchum's attorney. Rhett has been in Reno for three days, and the call I already put in to the medical examiner convinced me that she died within the past ten to twenty hours. Rigor mortis had already set in before you found her, and it has still not begun to relax. He will be more specific on the time of death later. Deputy," Sheriff McCoy continued. "You jumped the gun big-time. Rhett couldn't have murdered her when he wasn't even in the state. And you should have realized that."

"He could have hired someone," Lebow said stubbornly.

"And then put her body in his own barn? Come on, Deputy Lebow. That's stupid. If Ketchum was angry enough with her to kill her or have someone do it for him, her body wouldn't have ended up where it did."

"Of course it would. Shorty was going to move it later. He was gambling that no one would find Charity in there before he got back and probably planned to bury her somewhere where I could never find her," Deputy Lebow said. "That's just the kind of thing Shorty would do."

"That's farfetched, Deputy. He would have known his mother would have found her."

"Not so, Chancy."

"Sheriff!" he thundered.

"I can prove she wouldn't have found her," Clayson went on, undeterred. "His mother told me herself she hadn't been in the barn."

"Oh, did she now?" Chancy said doubtfully.

"Yeah, she did, so that's the proof we need."

"That's a long way from being proof of anything. But that's not your problem now, Deputy. Stay away from this case. Bring me whatever evidence you have, along with your written statement; then that's it," Chancy ordered, his face dark with anger.

The deputy slammed the sheriff's door on his way out. The sheriff shook his head and muttered to himself, "I think I have a loose cannon on my hands with that guy." He wondered why his predecessor ever hired him.

CHAPTER THREE

THE AIR-CONDITIONING IN RHETT'S GRAY Ford F350 felt good. It was a hot August day, and just walking from Wilson Arnold's office back to his truck had been uncomfortable. He was parked now in front of the offices of an agency Mr. Arnold had referred him to. After agreeing to assist Rhett against the accusations Clayton Lebow had made, Mr. Arnold had suggested Rhett might want to hire a good private investigator to assist him.

"I don't know any PIs," Rhett had said. "Who would you recommend?"

"I use Short Investigations. The owner and lead investigator is a man by the name of Max Fisher," he'd said with a smile that carried some kind of humor in it. "The man's a bulldog when he gets involved in an investigation. His daughter assists him with investigations, and they're both extremely bright. His wife handles his calendar, the agency's finances, and computer research."

Rhett had written down the address and thanked Wilson for his recommendation. "Has he handled situations like mine?" Rhett asked.

"He has, and again, I can assure you he's very good at what he does. But Rhett, don't let the appearance of his office throw you off. He works out of his home in Sugar House. There's a sign hanging from his front porch."

As Rhett sat in his truck, he watched the wooden sign swing slowly back and forth in the gentle breeze. It was a simple piece of pine with the letters burned into it. The yard at the front of the in-home business was well-kept. The lawn was mowed and trimmed. Flowers bloomed brightly in pots at either side of the steps leading up to the covered porch. Large trees shaded the entire front yard. The home was old but appeared to be well taken care of.

He reluctantly shut the truck off and stepped out into the oppressive heat. As he approached the porch, he looked closely at the house. It was a red-brick structure that had a second story. He could see a window above the porch. It was not a huge house, and he wondered how it worked as an office and home, but he supposed it must have worked well enough so far.

He climbed the steps into the shade of the porch. To his right was the swing he'd been watching, one of those he pictured young lovers holding hands in as it gently swung back and forth. To the left were a couple of comfortable-looking deck chairs. A welcome mat sat in front of the door. The design on the mat was of two figures dressed in karate attire, their feet high in the air as if they were kicking at each other. *That's strange,* he thought as he looked for and located the doorbell. The white button had a small sign beside it inviting him to press the doorbell and walk right in if the door was unlocked.

He pressed the button and heard the ringing of bells inside. He tried the door and, finding it unlocked, opened it and stepped through, welcoming the cool air of the interior. After shutting the door, he glanced around the room. There was a large desk to his right, with two hard-backed chairs in front of it. There was another desk, a smaller one, to the left. There were laptop computers on both of them, but the desks were clean. There were no papers or clutter, just a neat pen holder on each one. The large desk had a laser printer on the edge of it. Beyond the desks, the room appeared to be a compact living room with a TV, love seat, sofa, and small table. There was no one in the room.

He stepped toward the bigger desk, wondering if he should announce his presence or if he should step back outside and press the button again. He was spared making a decision when a deep, booming voice called from somewhere out of sight. "Have a seat, Mr. Ketchum. I'll be right with you."

As he took a seat, two thoughts raced through his mind. First, how did the investigator know who was there? And second, he felt slightly intimidated at the man's deep voice. Rhett was not a tall man. When he stretched, he could almost reach five-six-and-a-half. Officially he was five-six. He sang bass in the ward choir, but his bass was not nearly as deep as that of the giant who had yet to appear.

As he thought again about how the investigator knew he was Rhett Ketchum, he decided Wilson Arnold must have called and told him he was coming. But then Rhett thought about the little sign beside the doorbell button. Even if Mr. Fisher knew he was coming, how could he be sure it wasn't someone else who had followed the directions on the sign? He twisted in his chair and found the answer in the form of a small camera. In fact, he spotted three of them in the room. He then suspected that had he been observant, he might have seen one outside on the porch. Mr. Fisher, he decided, was very security conscious.

Rhett was turned toward the front door when the deep voice spoke again. "Ah, Mr. Ketchum. I see you found a chair."

Rhett turned as he came to his feet to greet the investigator. But instead of looking upward, he found that he had to look down. The man with the deep voice had a smile that covered his face and bright green eyes that twinkled. Rhett had always felt awkward about his short stature. Suddenly he didn't feel so short. As he stepped toward the detective, he judged himself to be around six inches taller. Mr. Fisher held out a hand and the two of them shook.

"I'm Max Fisher," the man said. "Some people call me Shorty." He grinned. "Kind of fitting, wouldn't you say?"

He was wearing a light-blue polo shirt and gray slacks, with shiny black oxfords on his feet. The muscles on his arms stretched the sleeves of the shirt.

"I'm Rhett Ketchum," Rhett said. "And people sometimes call me Shorty too."

Max pumped his hand and chuckled. "You can call me Max or Shorty, whichever you'd like. But since you're taller than me, I'll just call you Rhett." He chuckled again, a deep, throaty, pleasant sound. "Please, sit down again. My associate will join us momentarily." They both sat, and Max continued. "Wilson Arnold told us you were coming. He informed us you are being accused of a murder you could not possibly have committed. He says there are two reasons: One, you aren't a killer. And two, you were out of state when the murder occurred. So what would you like Patches and me to do?"

"Patches?" Rhett asked with a raised eyebrow.

Max grinned. "My associate," he said.

"I see. Well, I am from the Heber Valley. My father passed away about a year ago, so my mother and I run a small ranch there. I am also a professional bull rider. I've been in Reno the past three days. I was to ride again tonight, but, well, clearly I can't," he said. "But I did ride the past two nights."

"How did you do?" Max asked.

"I did okay. I won both nights. But by missing tonight, I'll forfeit the championship," he said as he thought angrily about why his plans had changed so abruptly.

"I'm sorry about that. I don't follow rodeos much, but Patches does. She may have heard of you. What kind of success have you had overall?"

"I've been a national champion the past two years. I was hoping for the same this year," he said, trying not to sound like he was bragging, just stating the facts.

"Excellent," Max said as his daughter entered the room. "Oh, here's Patches now."

Rhett was struck dumb. He didn't know what he'd expected, but the person strolling toward him now with an outstretched hand was a vision of beauty. She was about the same height as his mother. From the corner of his eyes, he caught a sly but proud smile from Max.

Rhett stood up and accepted her hand. It was slightly damp but soft and warm. He studied her face. It was oval in shape, with wide green eyes. Her bangs were cut to just above her eyebrows, and the rest of her blonde hair, long and wavy, hung down her back to well beyond her shoulders. She was slender but curvy and dressed in a red and yellow Western shirt and tight blue jeans. On her feet were a pair of red cowboy boots. "I'm Patches," she said.

"I'm . . . I'm ah, Rhett Ketchum," he mumbled.

She held his hand a little longer than custom would dictate. But Rhett didn't mind. She was studying his face intently. Finally, she smiled mischievously and let go of his hand. "Daddy, you didn't tell me our prospective client was a handsome cowboy. Can we keep him?"

"I didn't know," Max said as Patches sat down on the chair next to Rhett and then turned it slightly so she was at an angle to both him and her father. "And he will have to decide if he wants us to work for him or not."

"Daddy, if you would've told me it was Rhett Ketchum, I would have known. He's a champion bull rider. He's the best. What exactly can we do for you, Rhett?" she asked. "You don't mind if I call you Rhett, do you?"

"I've been accused of murder," he said.

Her mesmerizing green eyes instantly shed their sparkle, and Rhett was certain he saw a flash of anger shoot from them before they became steady and deadly serious. "That's ludicrous," she said. "That's not the kind of person you are."

He was humbled by that. "But you don't even know me," he said as he held her gaze.

"I know more than you think," she said. "Maybe Daddy didn't tell you, but I love the rodeo and I love horses, and I know a lot about some of the best rodeo cowboys." She smiled shyly then, and a touch of the sparkle returned to her eyes. "I've followed you on social media. I know you moved back with your mother when you lost your dad last year. I'm sorry about that, Rhett," she said sincerely. "I know you served a mission in England. And I also know you are single but used to have a girlfriend." Another shy smile.

"That's right. And it's a former high school girlfriend I've been accused of murdering and leaving her body in one of the horse stalls in my barn."

"Oh, Rhett, that's horrible!" the beautiful young detective said with the sort of horror on her face that Rhett was feeling inside. "Would you like us to find who killed her?"

"Yes, please, if you can," Rhett said.

"Tell us about the victim," Max suggested. "And that includes any recent contact you've had with her."

"I haven't seen Charity since I left on my mission when I was nineteen; it's been seven years. She had insisted she was going to wait for me—her idea, not mine. A short time into my mission I wrote her a letter and told her I didn't want her to wait," he explained. "I just didn't feel like she was right for me, and I didn't need the distractions she was causing with all her mushy letters."

"How did she take it?" Max asked even as Rhett could see in Patch's eyes that she wondered the same thing.

"She was unhappy and tried to talk me out of it in her next email. But I knew it was for the best." He chuckled mirthlessly. "I knew Deputy Lebow would be after her again. But I was pretty sure she'd reject him like she did before. When she and I dated in high school, he went out with her a few times, and then she told him to quit asking her. Anyway, she must not have been too broken up about my letter. She got married about a year later, but not to Lebow. He thinks I'm the reason she rejected him."

"And now he wants to blame you for her death," Patches said with a touch of fire in her pretty green eyes.

"It looks that way," he agreed. "She's called me maybe three times since she and Gene Gaffey got divorced a few months ago. She told me Lebow was calling her so much that it felt like he was stalking her. She kept telling him she was not interested. She told me it made him angry. I think Charity wanted me to take her out so she could tell Lebow to get over it. But I did not kill her. I would never hurt anyone."

"What about the deputy?" Patches asked.

"What about him?"

"If he hates you so badly and was rejected by her, maybe he's the one who killed her. It would make sense, in a warped sort of way," she said. "Leaving the body in your barn and all—seems quite suspect to me."

"That's what I need you guys to find out for me. Honestly, I don't think it was him. He seemed of the opinion that she was meant only for him. I suppose he thought he loved her. So I can't see him killing her, but it wasn't me. I desperately need your help," he said.

"Then let's talk fees," Max said. "And if you are still agreeable, then we'll have you sign a contract, and we will get to work on your problem."

Once the forms were signed and a retainer paid, Max said, "I'm sorry, but I need to go follow up on another investigation. I have an appointment in just a few minutes. Patches will get the information we need from you to get started." With that, he excused himself.

Rhett watched as Patches moved gracefully around the desk and sat where her father had been. She pulled a pen from the pen holder on the desk and a legal pad from a drawer and then said, "Okay, what I need first are names, addresses, and phone numbers of every person who can verify your activities of the past few days," she said.

"Gee, Patches, that's asking a lot. Names I can easily give you," Rhett said. "Phone numbers and addresses will be a little more difficult. But I can get you some. I can give you towns and states of a few folks as well."

"I understand completely," she said with a shy smile. "Just give me what you can, and we will take it from there. Our first objective is to prove you are innocent. People you were with at the time of the murder will help establish that."

"I'll do the best I can," he said. He pulled out his phone. "I have some numbers and even a few addresses in here. Should we start with those?"

"That would be great," she agreed. "And then we can go on to names of others who would remember seeing or speaking to you."

It took about fifteen minutes to compile the list. "I'm sorry I couldn't be more specific," Rhett said.

"Actually, this is a great list," Patches said. "Not all of us can be like my father."

Rhett cocked an eyebrow and said, "Meaning?"

Patches chuckled. "Dad has a photographic memory. When he hears, sees, smells, or reads something, he's got it. He doesn't need to take notes like I do. When he prepares to teach a Sunday School lesson, all he has to do is look at the lesson once, and it's there in his memory, scripture references and all."

"That's pretty amazing," Rhett said, duly impressed. "I've heard of that before, but I'd never actually met someone with a photographic memory."

"You have now. I try to write neatly, because when Dad gets back, he'll look at my notes and store them in that amazing brain of his, and I don't want him to have scribbles in there," she said with a grin. Then she grew somber. "If only his memory were the only thing we needed to put criminals in prison. The guys who put Dad in a coma and killed his cousin had no idea that when he woke up he'd be able to describe them like he did. He remembered their hair color, eye color, tattoos, what they were wearing, and so on. He told the cops everything, but despite that, the men who attacked him were never apprehended."

"Your dad was in a coma?" Rhett asked.

Patches nodded. "And Cousin Sammy died." She explained about how the two cousins were fishing and the other, larger, men tried to make them leave their fishing hole. "Dad and Sammy resisted and, well, it cost Sammy his life and put Dad in a coma."

"I'm sorry, Patches. That must have been awful."

She rubbed her eyes and then said, "It was worse than awful."

"Did the guys have anything to do with a case your dad was investigating?" he asked.

"He wasn't a private investigator then," she revealed. "After he recovered, he enrolled himself, Mom, and me in karate classes. He bought guns, and we learned to shoot really well. Then he started this agency."

"People you come up against in your type of work must find out pretty quickly they shouldn't mess with any of you," Rhett said with a chuckle.

"That's right," she said with a grin.

Rhett held both hands in the air, palms out, and said, "I get the message. I'm not going to lay a hand on you. I promise."

Patches laughed. "That's good, because I'd really hate to hurt you. It might mess up your bull-riding ability, and that would be tragic. Especially since you're my favorite rodeo cowboy." Rhett couldn't help but notice a light blush when she said that. But she let her smile fade along with the blush as she said, "Now, let's move on, Rhett. Next I need to know who all your family members are and as much about them as you can tell me."

When they'd finished that, she asked about neighbors and friends in the Heber area.

"Gee, Patches, by the time we get through here, you'll know more about me than I do," he said with a chuckle.

"A lot, anyway," she said.

For several more minutes, he talked and answered questions while she wrote on her legal pad. Then she said, "Now, I know this is personal, but I need to know as much about the victim as you can tell me. First, her name is Charity?"

"Charity Simmons. Well, Gaffey now."

"How old is she?"

"My age," Rhett said.

Patches grinned. "You want me to guess your age?" Before he could respond, she said, "Actually, I know. You're twenty-six. I've heard your age announced in rodeos. I may not have a photographic memory like Dad, but I do remember some things."

"That's right," he said. "I'm about three months older than Charity was. We went through school in the same grade."

"Describe her to me," Patches said. For a moment he studied the girl across the desk from him. "Not me," Patches said, making him blush now. "I know what I look like. Tell me about Charity."

"I was looking at you for comparison," Rhett said quite seriously. "She was about two inches taller than you and also very pretty."

Patches blushed again, deeper than before. "Thank you," she said, dropping her gaze for a moment. Then she looked him in the eye and asked, "What color hair did she have, and what color eyes?"

"Same as yours, in both cases, only her eyes weren't as bright. Her hair wasn't as wavy as yours, and she wore it differently."

Patches looked down with a smile on her face and wrote for a moment. Then with a very serious look on her face, she said, "Did you already forget my dad will read and memorize everything I write down?"

"No, I remember that," he said, cocking his eyebrows, not sure where this was going.

"Well, he's going to think you're flirting, and he's pretty protective of me," she said solemnly.

"Let me see what you've been writing," he said somewhat anxiously, leaning forward and reaching for her legal pad. "I wasn't flirting."

She snatched it out of his reach and said, "I've just been writing what you've told me."

"Please, don't get me into trouble with your dad. If you do, I'll tell him you flirted first," he said, trying not to smile.

Patches laughed and put the pad down as Rhett settled back in his chair, watching her face closely. "I did, didn't I?" she said. "Dad will be impressed—his daughter flirting with a celebrity. He says I should meet guys, not just hang around with my girlfriends. Does my flirting offend you?"

"Not in the least," he said. "You're quite a girl. Now, what else do you need to know about Charity?"

"I'm just teasing, by the way," she said as he sat thoughtfully for a moment. "Dad doesn't need to know *everything* we talked about. Just the parts that relate to your case."

"That's a relief," he said even as he wondered how much of their conversation she'd noted in writing. "So, anyway, Charity was a nice girl. She was fun to be with, but she wasn't someone I would have ever married. But, frankly, I was shocked when she married Gaffey. I think her parents must have been very disappointed because he had much different standards than her and her family."

Ten minutes later, Patches seemed satisfied with the information Rhett had given her about Charity. Then, with narrowed eyes, she asked him about his relationship with Deputy Clayson Lebow. After he'd described it the best he could, trying not to seem too negative about the guy, she said, "You guys really don't like one another, do you?"

"Honestly, Patches, I haven't concerned myself with worrying or even thinking much about him. I did worry about the way he was pursuing Charity, but I put that out of my mind and haven't thought about him until today," he said.

"He must hate you," Patches said.

"I suppose that's true. But I never meant to make an enemy of him," he said as he thought about all the times he'd simply ignored the barbs Clayson had thrown his way.

The next few minutes were spent discussing people Rhett knew who Charity may have been friends with.

"I need this," Patches said after finishing that line of inquiry, "so that we can talk to as many of them as we can find. We'll see if any of them remember things she may have said that could give any clues as to who her killer might be," she said. "And we'll find out if any of them might have had a motive to kill her and frame you. Now, tell me what you know about her ex-husband and his family and friends."

"Gene was older than us by six years. I barely even knew him," he said. "He wasn't a religious person. Rumor was, he was into drugs and alcohol, and he had a reputation as a ladies' man. That much I know. But I don't know his family very well. I suppose I would recognize his parents, but I'm not sure. I was told his best friend is a guy by the name of Bernardo Growfield and that he was best man at his wedding. I've heard he goes by Bernie. But I know nothing more about the guy. Sorry I can't help you more there."

"That's okay. We'll learn all about Mr. Gaffey and his family as well as his friends and associates. In my mind, Rhett, Gaffey is the prime suspect. Statistics tell us to always look at a spouse or ex-spouse first. That's what Deputy Lebow should be doing."

They were just finishing up when the front door opened and an attractive woman in her mid-forties came in. She was around five feet tall, slightly plump, and wore her blonde hair very short. But her green eyes shone just like Patches's. "Mom," Patches said, "this is a new client, Rhett Ketchum."

"Is he the bull rider you and your friends talk about so much?" her mother asked with a knowing smile.

Patches blushed again. "Yes," she admitted. "Rhett, this is my mother, Hallie."

Patches took a moment to fill her mother in on the basics of the case, and then she said, "I'll walk Rhett to his truck. I'll fill you in more in a minute."

"So you gossip about me?" Rhett asked, grinning, as they left the house.

She walked to his truck with him before responding. "It's good gossip," she finally said. "My friends are going to be so jealous." Rhett pulled his key fob out and unlocked the doors.

"Why is that?" he asked, suppressing a grin.

"Because I *met* you, that's why," she said. "We all think you're amazing."

"Not this week," he said, suddenly feeling despondent. "Deputy Lebow took care of that for me. I'd better get going."

Patches reached out and touched his arm. "We'll figure this out, Rhett," she said. "My parents and I are as good at what we do as you are at what you do. I don't mean to brag, but it's true. I'm still learning, but Dad's a good teacher. And Mom is a whiz with computers. At any rate, we have your back."

He looked into her eyes and forced a smile. "Thanks, Patches. I feel lucky meeting you guys. I feel a lot better now than I did when I first rang your bell. I was a nervous wreck."

They said goodbye, and Rhett got into his truck and drove off. When he pulled into the yard at the Diamond Bar ranch less than an hour later, there was no sign of any police vehicles. A bright-yellow Nissan that belonged to his sister, Susie, was parked beside his mother's truck. He pulled toward the house, parked, and headed inside to find his mother and sister sitting on the sofa in the living room. They were talking quietly, but they got up and hugged Rhett when he walked in. He knew they'd been crying, because both of them had swollen, red eyes.

"I'm so sorry about all of this," his mother said. "It doesn't seem real."

"That's what I've been thinking," he agreed.

"Somebody is out to get you, Rhett," Susie said. "It could be Clayson, or it could be someone else. You need to be really careful."

"I will," he said. "And we'll get through this. I didn't do it."

After explaining what he'd done in Salt Lake regarding hiring Susie's father-in-law and the Short Investigations agency, he asked if Deputy Lebow had been back.

"No, but Sheriff McCoy called a short while ago and told me he had assigned a pair of detectives to handle the case," Rhett's mother said. "I don't think he was very happy with Clayson."

"So if he isn't handling the case, who is?" he asked, relieved to hear that his old nemesis was not going to be involved.

"Detective Jay Ackerman will be the lead investigator," his mother said. "You may not know him. The sheriff said he came here from a large department in the Salt Lake area. He told me that Detective Ackerman is an experienced investigator even though he's only been working for Wasatch County for a few months."

"Thank goodness he's experienced," Susie snapped.

"The sheriff assured me Detective Ackerman will not be influenced by Clayson. He will be assisted by Kori Davis. She's a recently appointed detective, and Sheriff McCoy said she's intelligent and takes direction well. He thinks the two of them will make a good team," Rhett's mother explained.

"I just hope the sheriff is right and they don't listen to anything Clayson Lebow tells them. He's such a lowlife," Susie said. Then she grinned and said, "You know Kori, Rhett. Wasn't she a year behind you in school?"

"She was," he said.

"She was a cheerleader in high school," Susie explained to their mother. "She cheered with the squad as a sophomore when I was a senior. She's cute, Rhett. One of my friends has a sister your age—she says Kori had a crush on you in high school, but because of Charity, she didn't think she'd ever have a chance with you. This will be a good chance to get to know her," she said with a chuckle.

"She's probably married," Rhett said. "So don't you two get your hopes up. I'm doing just fine as a single man." Then, changing the subject, he said, "I wonder how long she's been in law enforcement."

"The sheriff said she'd worked for him for two years, and *she is still single,*" Susie told him. "He seems to have a lot of confidence in her. Anyway, Rhett, tell us what the investigators are going to do."

"Investigate," he said. Susie rolled her eyes. He ignored her and continued with, "Patches had a lot of questions for me. She wanted to learn everything she could about the people I've been with the past few days. She says the agency's first priority is clearing me. Then she had tons of questions about my family and friends and about Charity and her friends and ex-husband."

"Patches?" Susie asked, cocking an eyebrow. "Is that a nickname?"

"I'm pretty sure it's her real name. But Short Investigations is owned and operated by Max Fisher. Patches is his daughter and associate. His wife is also involved," Rhett said. "Your father-in-law recommended them. He says they are as good as they come, and I believe him. I was totally impressed. That reminds me, I need to call Patches and tell her about Detectives Ackerman and Davis."

But Susie was still hung up on Patches. "Tell us more about Patches," she said. "How old is she?"

Rhett took his phone from his pocket and looked for the number for the agency. "How old is she?" Susie pressed.

"Okay, Susie, I see where this is headed. So I'll save you asking more questions and tell you all about her. She's single. She's twenty-one. She's absolutely gorgeous. She dresses like a cowgirl and is a rodeo fan. She loves horses. And she says that yours truly is her favorite rodeo cowboy. What didn't I cover?"

Susie was grinning and clapped her hands. "That's probably enough. It sounds like she will be motivated to clear you and find the real killer. I just hope there isn't a conflict between her and Kori over you."

"Come on, Sis," Rhett said with a groan. "They are both detectives. Professionals. Anyway, I certainly have no interest in either of them," he fibbed. "And I hope you're right and they'll both be motivated to find the person who killed Charity."

"You know, I've always thought that you riding bulls was dangerous, insane even," Susie said. "But investigating murders is even more insane. Surely it must be a dangerous profession."

Rhett chuckled. "Don't tell Patches that," he said. "She and her parents are proficient martial artists and are experts in handling firearms. After I call her, I'll tell you a little more about them."

CHAPTER FOUR

PATCHES WAS SITTING ACROSS THE desk from her father as he scanned the notes she'd taken. She was sitting where Rhett had sat when she'd interviewed him. And she was thinking about him. She hadn't lied when she'd told him he was her favorite rodeo cowboy. But until she actually met him, saw him up close, she hadn't realized how cute he was. Just thinking about him now made her tingle.

"Patches," her father said, his voice deep and very serious. "Don't let your infatuation with our client keep you from doing your best to help me clear him of suspicion and find the person who killed his former girlfriend."

"What do you mean, my infatuation?" she asked innocently, even as she felt her face burning.

Max chuckled. "I think he likes you too," he said. "Reading between the lines of what you wrote down about your interview, I'd say you made an impression on the young man."

She shrugged her shoulders. "He only wanted me to get an idea about the victim and what she looked like. But I think you made a big impression, Dad," she countered.

Max gave her a knowing look. Then he said, "Maybe. But it's okay. I want you to notice guys. The right kind, at least. And I hope our investigation shows us that he is the right kind, not a cold-blooded killer."

"He's not a killer, Dad," she protested a little strongly.

He held up a finger and waggled it at her. "Hold on, Patches. Even though we work for Rhett and our main goal is to clear him, we'll still let the facts prove what kind of man he is as we uncover them," he said. "Remember, don't make unsubstantiated assumptions. We must keep open minds. So what have you learned so far?"

"I've made several phone calls," she said even as she shook her head with disgust. She felt like she knew Rhett's character, but she also had to admit that her father was right. She needed to keep an open mind. She promised herself she would try. "Every person I've talked to told me Rhett has been in Reno the past three days. I even called the hotel he was staying at, and they assured me he'd been staying there until he checked out today."

"That's a good start. And I'm impressed with the information you got from Rhett. You were thorough. Let's divide things up now so we won't be duplicating our efforts."

"I'll do whatever you ask me to," she said as her phone began to ring. She looked at the screen. "It's Rhett," she said. "I wonder what he wants."

As she stared at the screen, Max said, "Well, answer it, or we'll never know."

"Hi, Rhett, this is Patches. What can I help you with?" Patches said in her most professional voice.

"Hi, Patches. I just wanted to tell you that the sheriff has pulled Deputy Lebow off the case. So I'm not in jail yet," Rhett said.

"I'm glad to hear that," Patches responded, and she really was. The very idea of him being thrown into jail like a common criminal made her tremble. "Do you have the name of the officer who is going to be handling the investigation?" she asked him.

"Yep, that's why I called. There are actually two of them. The lead investigator is Detective Jay Ackerman. He's quite experienced, from what the sheriff told my mother. He's new to Wasatch County though. The officer assisting him is Detective Kori Davis. I went to school with her, but I don't know a lot about her anymore," Rhett said. "She's a year younger than I am."

"Is she pretty?" Patches asked teasingly.

"What does it matter?" Rhett asked a little sharply.

"I just wondered," she said, stung by his response.

"In that case, yes, she is pretty. And she's smart, too," he said. "And this is also in her favor—she likes horses and rides a lot."

Patches felt a stab of jealousy. But perhaps that was a good thing. She'd show Rhett who the best investigator was, and it wouldn't be the cute deputy.

"How tall is she?" Patches asked.

"Tall like me," he said with a chuckle in his voice. "In high school, she was popular with the guys. But for some reason, she's never married. Some guy is missing out."

"It sounds like it," Patches said sullenly. "So tell me about Mr. Ackerman."

"It's Detective Ackerman. He's fairly new to the department. He came to Wasatch County from the Unified Police Department in Salt Lake County. I'm told he's about forty. I'm hoping both he and Detective Davis will be fair and thorough."

They talked for a moment longer, and then the call ended.

"What was all that about?" her father asked after she hung up.

"Rhett called to tell us who would be handling the investigation for the sheriff. The lead officer is Detective Jay Ackerman, and assisting him will be Detective Kori Davis. It sounds like Deputy Lebow has been removed from the case," she explained.

"Good. Now, what was all that with Rhett? It sounded like you were flirting with him a little there at first," Max said without a trace of humor in his voice.

"I wasn't flirting. I was just teasing Rhett. I want him to have confidence in me, in us," she said with a red face. Her father gave her a stern look, his face impassive and his eyes unblinking. "What?" she asked.

"Patches, we have been hired to find the killer of Charity Gaffey. And unless you can be objective about this investigation, I will handle it by myself. If, and only if, we find that Rhett was not responsible, then I will feel good about you following your heart as far as he is concerned," he said. "I mean it, Patches. Get the stars out of your eyes and go to work."

"That's what I've been doing, Dad," she pouted.

"Then keep doing it, but focus on the facts, not on the handsome rodeo cowboy," he said. "And remember, this is not a competition between us and the sheriff's officers. We will work with them as much as we can."

Patches felt a surge of anger, but she tamped it down. Her father was right, and she knew it. "I'm sorry, Dad. I will do this the best way I can, just like you taught me."

Max smiled then. "Thanks, Patches. I really need you on this one. So there will be no more flirting with our client. Now, let's plan our strategy."

They made a list of people they needed to interview and the order in which their investigation would be done. The first thing would be to meet the deputies in Heber and try to develop a relationship with them that would make it easier to pursue the investigation. "I know Detective Ackerman. He's a good man and an excellent investigator. We are in luck. You and I will go to Heber together," Max said. As they headed for the door, Max's cell phone rang. He took the call and then, with a disappointed face, said, "It looks like you'll need to do this alone. I thought I nearly had the Harmon matter wrapped up, but apparently I'm needed once again. Sorry, Patches."

"That's okay, Dad. I'll do the best I can."

An hour later, Patches pulled up to the sheriff's office in Heber. She went inside and asked for Detective Ackerman or Detective Davis. She explained who she was and why she was interested in speaking with one of them.

A couple of minutes later, two officers in plainclothes came into the waiting area. The male said, "Are you Patches?"

"I am," she said with a smile. "And you must be Detectives Ackerman and Davis." The smile was a little forced. Kori Davis was very attractive. Her black hair was cut short, and her dark-brown eyes smiled right along with her lips. Patches had to work hard to quell the jealousy again. She forced herself to speak, but it was to Ackerman, not Davis, that she addressed her question. "Would you mind discussing the Charity Gaffey murder case with me?" She showed the officers her PI license and then added, "My father and I have been hired to look into the matter, and we were hoping we could coordinate with you."

Detective Ackerman's smile replaced the one Detective Davis had worn only seconds before. He was a nice-looking man and about six feet tall. He was a husky guy, with short brown hair and brown eyes that were several shades lighter than Kori's. "We'll do you one better, Detective Fisher, is it?" he asked.

"Yes, Patches Fisher. My father is Max Fisher," she said. "He was coming with me but had to go out on another case at the last minute."

"Yes, shorter fellow. I believe you call yourselves Short Investigations. I've met your father," he said. "I even worked a case with him in Salt Lake a couple of years ago. It was a pleasure working with him. Like I was saying, Detective Davis and I will do more than just talk with you. We were just going out to take a look at the barn where the body of Mrs. Gaffey was found. We'd be happy to have you come along. Rhett Ketchum will be meeting us there."

"Ah, Detective, do you think that's a good idea? Why don't we just let her know if we learn anything of significance," Kori said, her dark eyes shooting barbs in Patches's general direction.

"I want her along," Detective Ackerman said firmly. "If she's anything like her father, she may pick up on something we miss. I don't like some of the PIs out there, but Short Investigations is a class act."

"I won't be in your way, I promise," Patches said, smiling at the unhappy deputy.

"You'd better not be," Kori said sullenly. Then she turned sharply and said, "Let's go. Shorty is waiting for us."

Patches followed the detectives' black Explorer in her dark-blue Ford F250 pickup. They all parked in front of the large ranch house after passing through an entrance that had a sign high overhead that read, *Diamond Bar Ranch*. She had no sooner exited her truck and started toward the yard gate with the two deputies than the door opened and Rhett Ketchum came out and hurried to meet them. Despite herself, she was unable to slow the beating of her heart at the sight of the famous cowboy. She realized with a jolt that Kori Davis's dark eyes were shining and she had a big smile on her face. *She likes him,* Patches thought. *And there is nothing I can do about it unless I want Dad to kick me off the case.* Of course, it really wouldn't be right anyway. In all honesty, she couldn't blame Kori for liking Rhett.

***

Rhett was surprised to see Patches with the deputies. She had not said anything to him about coming here when he'd talked to her a couple of hours ago. She'd been in a fun mood then. She didn't look too happy now. Kori, on the other hand, was smiling broadly. He hadn't been kidding when he'd told Patches he couldn't imagine why she had never married. But she was a cop, and if she believed what Clayson was claiming, she could be throwing him in jail. His stomach churned uncomfortably at the thought.

"Detective Jay Ackerman," the sturdy officer said as he stepped through the gate ahead of the others and held out his hand. "I'll be leading the investigation from this point. Thanks for agreeing to meet with us. I think you already know the ladies, Detective Kori Davis and Detective Patches Fisher."

"Rhett Ketchum. It's nice to meet you, Detective," Rhett said. "I hope you can soon find whoever did this to Charity."

"Oh, we will, Shorty," Kori said as she also shook hands with him. "It's been a long time."

"I've been around," Rhett said as his brown eyes met Kori's darker ones. "I guess we just haven't bumped into each other for a while. How have you been?"

"I'm doing well, thank you," she said, smiling at him in a way that made his heart speed up. He remembered what his sister had said about her having a crush on him back in high school. But his time and attention had been on Charity then. Now it had to be on clearing his name.

"Let's begin at the barn, shall we?" Kori asked lightly.

"Sure," Rhett said as he caught Patches's eyes. "I didn't realize you were coming too."

"I stopped in to meet the officers, and they invited me to come with them. I hope that's okay," she said. "Dad wanted to come too, but he's finishing up another case." The cheeriness he'd felt in his conversation with her on the phone had turned to ice. He wasn't sure why. He hoped she hadn't already learned something that would make it more difficult for her and her father to prove his innocence. He was glad she was here though. He felt like at least she was more likely to view him with less suspicion than the officers. She should. After all, she worked for him.

"Of course it's okay," he said, smiling at her and getting a stony face in response. He turned to Detective Ackerman and said, "I'll lead the way."

When they reached the barn, Detective Ackerman said, "Okay, here's what I want to do. Mr. Ketchum, since you've already seen the place where the body was found, you just point out the stall, and then Detective Davis and I will have a look inside. I know there won't be much to see there now, but we need to get a feel for the location."

"That's fine," Rhett said and walked into the barn. He turned on the lights and walked to the front of the stall where someone had placed Charity's body. "Right in there," he said.

Patches stepped past him and followed the officers inside. But he noticed she didn't attempt to go more than one step beyond the gate to the stall. He turned and paced back and forth in the wide alleyway, thinking about what a terrible turn of events had occurred in his life. And he couldn't help but think about Charity. He'd never been in love with her, but they had enjoyed a lot of time together. He wondered how things would have turned out in her life if he hadn't written her off from his. He didn't kill her, but he found himself accepting some blame. After all, she probably would have waited for him and not married Gaffey.

He didn't know what was taking the detectives so long in there, but he finally quit pacing as he heard a phone ringing in the stall and then Detective Ackerman speaking softly when the ringing ended. He walked to the far end of the barn and looked outside. The sun was shining brightly, and there was a slight breeze blowing. He looked into the fields beyond.

The cows were grazing contentedly. His horses were frolicking in the pasture. His world appeared to be at peace, but it was far from it. Someone had killed a girl he had been fond of and had framed him for the crime. His world had lost its light; he felt dark and empty inside, and yes, even afraid. He shivered despite the heat.

He heard a step behind him and turned. "Shorty, we are finished in the stall," Kori Davis said. "I'm sorry all this has happened. But we will get to the bottom of it, I promise."

"You've got to," he said. "I didn't do anything to Charity."

"I know you loved her, but—" Kori began.

Rhett cut her off. "I didn't love her, Kori. I liked her, but that was all. She wasn't right for me. But she certainly didn't deserve what happened to her."

Kori laid her hand on his arm. "I'm sorry. Detective Ackerman and I need to interview you."

"That's fine. Let's go into the house. This whole thing is stressing Mom out terribly, so Susie got her out of the house. They went to town," he said as he noticed Patches standing in the middle of the barn, watching him. Kori finally removed her hand from his arm, and he smiled at Patches. She gave him another stony look, and then a shadow of a smile passed quickly across her face. Then she ducked her head. He didn't see where Detective Ackerman was. But as he and Kori headed toward Patches, Ackerman came out of the stall.

"It's time to talk, Rhett," Detective Ackerman said. "But let me remind you that anything you say can be used against you in a court of law."

"I know all that," Rhett said. "I have nothing to hide. Let's go in the house."

"Actually, I want to do this at my office. It will need to be recorded. You can follow us," he said.

The officer looked stressed. Rhett wondered if it had anything to do with the call Detective Ackerman had received while he was in the stall. His stomach clenched. Something had changed. He remembered the warning his attorney had given him about not giving any statements or even talking with the police unless Wilson was present. The subtle change in atmosphere now caused him to follow the counsel he'd been given. "I think I'll pass for now. My attorney instructed me to make sure he was with me in any interviews. I think I'll follow his advice."

"It's up to you, Rhett, but I am not accusing you of anything. You are not a suspect as far as I am concerned; at least, not at this point," Detective Ackerman said.

"So is that why you reminded me of my rights?" Rhett said, unable to keep the suspicion from his voice. "I have been accused by one of your fellow deputies. If you want to ask me anything, it will be with Mr. Arnold present."

"Then call him. We are going to talk," the detective said firmly. "Let's go to the office now."

"Am I under arrest for something?" Rhett asked, still not convinced Detective Ackerman believed him.

"No, you are not," Kori hastened to assure him.

Detective Ackerman smiled briefly as he said, "If I arrest you, you will know it. Right now I'm just trying to gather the facts. And for obvious reasons, we need to clear you of any involvement. This is in your best interest."

Rhett studied the officer's face for a moment. Then he glanced at Kori. She looked troubled. He turned toward Patches. She also looked troubled. He didn't like where this was going. He pulled his cell phone out and placed a call to Wilson Arnold. He was told to wait, that the attorney was in an interview at the moment.

He kept his phone to his ear. "Let's go," Detective Ackerman insisted. "We need to get this done for your sake."

"Not until I talk to Mr. Arnold," Rhett said decisively.

For the next couple of minutes, an uneasy silence prevailed. Detective Ackerman stood with his arms folded across his chest, a frown on his face. Kori appeared nervous, shifting from one foot to another and constantly brushing at her short black hair. Patches's face now displayed no emotion at all.

Finally Wilson Arnold's voice came on the phone. "Hello, Rhett. What can I do for you?"

Rhett walked toward the back of the barn again before he spoke. "The detective assigned to the case, Jay Ackerman, is insisting I go with him to the sheriff's office for questioning."

"Are you under arrest?" Wilson asked.

"He says not. He also says it's in my best interest to answer his questions. I told him I need you present before I talk with him."

"Good. If you are not under arrest, then you don't go with him. If you need me to come now, I will."

"I think you'd better. He wants to do the interview right away."

Rhett walked back to where the others waited, still holding the phone to his ear.

"How long will it be before he gets here?" Ackerman said. "You and I need to talk. And we need to do so as soon as possible."

"He says—" Rhett began.

"I could hear him," Wilson said, a touch of irritation in his voice. "I'm on my way."

"Thanks, Wilson. I appreciate it."

"That's what you hired me for. Tell him you will meet him there when I arrive," Wilson instructed him.

Rhett ended the call and looked at Detective Ackerman. "Follow us," the detective said.

"I'll be there by the time my attorney is," Rhett told him.

"Okay, I guess that will have to do," Detective Ackerman said and walked off. He did not look happy.

Kori Davis stepped close to Rhett and whispered, "He got a phone call. I don't know what it was about, but he was looking at something on his phone after that. He didn't tell me anything about it, but he's been really tense the past few minutes." She smiled at him. "I'll be there too, Shorty. Don't worry about him. He's a good guy, believe me." Then she followed the older detective.

"Would you like to talk to me?" Patches asked when only the two of them were left in the barn.

"What's there to talk about?"

"Hey, Rhett, I've got your back," she said, and for the first time since she'd arrived, she gave him a full-blown smile. "I'm on your side. I'm working for you," she said.

"Thanks," he said.

"Rhett, let's talk about Charity again and go over what we already discussed. When was the last time you saw her or spoke with her?" she asked.

"I haven't seen her since before my mission," he said. "But like I told you and your father, she called me several times in the past few months. All the calls were after her divorce. They were short calls," he said.

"Do you think there was any chance she expected to be here for you when you came home from your mission?" Patches asked.

"Not after my letter. I think I was pretty clear that we were through. She married Gene Gaffey a year after I broke it off. I'm certain she understood," he reasoned.

"Yeah, I'd think so," Patches said. "But other than those times you told me about that she called you, you have not talked to her in person or written to her or sent or received any texts or emails from her? Is that right?"

"There was no reason for me to contact her, and I wish she hadn't called me. I know Deputy Lebow is claiming I was trying to get her to date me, but that is a lie. I never even thought about her much. She has not been a part of my life for a very long time."

"Why would Deputy Lebow say something like that?" Patches asked.

"That's the question of the day," Rhett said bitterly as he began to pace. "He's out to get me. Maybe he had something to do with her death. At this point I wouldn't be too surprised, even though it sure seems like a stretch."

"Dad and I will look into it," she promised. "Tell me what kind of person Charity was."

"She was a good girl, fun to be around. I was shocked when I heard she was marrying Gene Gaffey," he said. "I mean, I had hoped she would move on and find someone else, but I never dreamed she'd marry out of the temple, and especially to someone with the kind of reputation Gaffey had. It never has made sense to me. Perhaps I'm to blame. Maybe when I broke off our relationship, it changed her."

"Don't blame yourself, Rhett. There must have been something about her that made you reconsider your interest in her."

"Patches, I liked Charity. We had fun together. But I did not love her in the romantic sense—ever. And I simply realized it was not fair for me to lead her on. I broke it off for her sake because I knew when I got home it wouldn't work out between us, that I didn't even want it to. She was wasting her time on me."

"All right. Perhaps we should head to the sheriff's office," Patches suggested.

"You go. I'll be along in a few minutes," he said.

"No, I'll wait for you," she countered.

***

"Hey, Kori," Clayson Lebow said as she walked into the sheriff's office. "Where ya been?" She didn't like the looks of the smile he gave her. Lately he'd been making her very uncomfortable.

"I've been out to the Ketchum's Diamond Bar Ranch with Detective Ackerman," she responded. "I've been assigned to work the Charity Gaffey murder with him."

"It should be you and me working that case," Clayson said with a frown. "I was the first officer there."

"That's not my call," she told him firmly.

"I understand that. But I would have enjoyed working with you." He flashed her a bright smile and even winked. "I guess we'll just have to spend some time together when we're off duty."

"Sure," she said, not knowing why she said it. She didn't dislike Clayson, but she also didn't care to be around him much. Surely he wouldn't ask her out. She hoped not. He'd been in love with Charity for forever, if what she'd heard was true. Why would he want to date her now?

As if reading her mind, he said, "You know, Kori, I've wanted to ask you out for a long, long time. But I never got up the courage. Until now. Maybe we could go to dinner tonight."

"I don't know if that's a good idea," she said and then wondered why she hadn't told him no in more certain terms.

"Well, I think it's a great idea. I'll pick you up at seven." He winked at her and walked rapidly off.

She stood there for a moment, wondering what had just occurred and how she had let it happen. She had no desire to go out with Clayson. The way he'd trapped her made her angry. Finally she shrugged her shoulders and headed back toward Detective Ackerman's office. His door was shut. He'd beat her back, so she hadn't had a chance to talk to him since he'd left the barn. She considered knocking but then decided not to. Instead she went into the squad room and began to go over her notes. Several minutes later Detective Ackerman poked his head in. "Hey, why don't you join me in my office. There's something we need to go over before Rhett and his attorney get here."

"Oh, sure. What was your phone call about?" Kori asked as she got to her feet.

"That's what we need to talk about," he said with a frown, making her stomach twist uncomfortably.

CHAPTER FIVE

PATCHES WATCHED RHETT'S FACE WITH concern. "Hey, it will be okay," she said after an uncomfortable moment.

Rhett took his cowboy hat off and ran his hand through his thick black hair. Then he looked again at Patches. "I don't know what's going on, Patches. But Kori told me that after the phone call he received, Detective Ackerman's whole attitude seemed to change," Rhett said. "She apparently doesn't know what's going on either. I sure hope you and your dad can figure this out. I thought after the sheriff took Lebow off the case things would be better, that they would look for the real killer and not just at me. It doesn't feel that way now."

"Lebow's probably poisoned the entire department," she said as she watched him put his black cowboy hat back on. It was so hard not to reach out and touch him, a simple act of reassurance. But she had to heed her father's warning. That was the kind of person she was. She respected and honored her parents.

"Kori seems okay," he said after a moment of thought. "I haven't seen much of her since I went on my mission. But she was always an honest person."

"She seems that way," Patches said as she fought back another wave of jealousy. He was just another client, and she needed to accept that fact. Just because she had idolized him from the first time she'd seen him ride didn't mean he would look at her differently. He had no interest in her other than as someone who could help him prove his innocence. That was just the way it was, she told herself. But regardless of how he felt, she was determined to find who killed Charity, and if that meant she had to fight against the investigating officers, then so be it.

"I'd offer you a seat," Rhett said with just the slightest of smiles. "But all I have is that bale of hay over there." He pointed to a bale that was beside one of the stalls, two stalls up from where Charity's body had been found.

"Then let's sit there," she said.

He waited for her to sit first, and then he sat beside her. The bale prevented the two of them from having a lot of space between them, and their arms touched as he sat and turned toward her. It was not cold, but she shivered. For a moment he looked at her, and she couldn't pull her eyes from his. They were full of worry and anguish. Patches folded her hands on her lap and waited for him to say something.

"Someone is trying to frame me for Charity's death," he finally said, his eyes unwavering on her face. "The very fact that her body was found in my barn is proof of that, don't you think?"

"Yes, I can see that," she said.

"So who knows what else that person might have done to make me look guilty?" he said sullenly and finally looked away from her.

"You were in Reno," she reminded him.

"Do you believe that?" he asked, surprising her.

"Of course I do, Rhett. I called the people you mentioned, and every one of them vouched for you. There was only one guy I could never reach."

"Who was that?" he asked.

"The guy you said is a fellow bull rider. It was—"

"Cal Thurley?" he asked before she could finish.

"Yeah, that's the name. I was told he wasn't having a very good rodeo and that he probably left early since it was clear he couldn't win," she said.

"He doesn't like me very much because I keep beating him. He's an okay rider, but he just doesn't ride as well as most of the rest of us."

"Yeah, that's what I was told by several people. They say you were in a good position to win with a decent ride tonight."

"Yeah, but I guess that won't happen."

"No, but there are a bunch of people who confirmed what you told me," she summed up.

"Thanks," he said, once again meeting her eyes and making chills come over her. "I wonder what the detective's phone call was about. Something sure changed his demeanor."

"I guess we'll know soon enough," she said. "Hey, is that your cat?" She pointed at a large gray tomcat some distance away from them.

"Yes, that's Magnum."

"He has something in his mouth. I can't tell what it is. He must have caught a mouse," she said. "He's taking it behind those feed barrels to eat it, it looks like." She wrinkled her mouth. "How nasty."

"I'm surprised he caught one. You'd think there wouldn't be any left in here he catches so many. Of course, this time of year the mice start to migrate from the fields back to the barn."

"Well, good for him. Mice are disgusting. Anyway, like I was saying, we'll soon know what has upset Jay."

"I'm betting another attempt has been made to make me look guilty," he said morosely. "And that the call was to inform Detective Ackerman of whatever it is. Apparently he believes it."

Patches stood up. She paced in front of Rhett as she spoke. "Whatever lies are told, Dad and I will work to disprove them. We might not look like much, but we are both good at what we do, especially Dad. For that matter, so is my mother. You can count on us."

"Thanks. My fate is in your hands, Patches," he said dejectedly as he too rose to his feet.

"That's a lot of trust you're putting in me," she said as she suddenly doubted her own ability.

He gave her a wan smile. "I also trust my Savior," he said.

"So do I," she responded. "With the Lord's help we can do this."

Rhett stepped a few feet from her. She watched him. His slumped shoulders suddenly became straight, and he spun toward her. "I can help too, you know. And I just thought of something."

"Tell me," Patches said softly.

"Okay. Follow me as I reason this out. Whoever put her body in this barn had to have either driven her or carried her here. Whether she was dead or alive at that point we have no way of knowing yet."

"That makes sense," she agreed. "There wasn't any blood on the floor of the stall as near as I could tell. So she might have been drugged and then killed there, or she was already dead when the killer dumped her there."

Rhett nodded his agreement. "Our dog sleeps on the front porch of the house. But you know how dogs are. They are light sleepers. Follow me," he said again as he suddenly became animated. He headed for the door of the barn. He stopped when he reached it. Patches stopped beside him. He raised his hand and pointed toward the ranch house. "The lane passes close to the house. If someone came down it, Scruffy would have known. And she would have announced it to the world. That's how she is. Not only that but if a vehicle drove down this lane, my mother would have heard it. Even at night. She's a light sleeper too."

"Where is Scruffy now?" Patches asked.

"Mom and Susie went to town to shop. Scruffy always goes with her. She rides in the back of the truck," he explained as he began walking again, leading the way out of the barn.

"What kind of dog is she?"

"She's a border collie, not too big, black and white. She's a cow dog," Rhett explained to her.

"Do you ever take her with you on your rodeo trips?" Patches asked.

Rhett shook his head. "No, she's a ranch dog. And anyway, Mom likes to have her around so she won't be alone when I'm gone."

"So even if someone was trying to walk quietly while carrying the body, Scruffy would know it?" she asked.

"She'd know all right. This driveway is gravel. It's impossible to be completely silent walking on it." He took a few steps, clearly trying to step lightly, but Patches could hear it easily. Then he stopped and faced her.

"Okay, so if they didn't come in past the house, how else could they have reached the barn?" she asked.

He pointed back to the barn and said, "From behind the barn. Come on, let's go back there, and you can see for yourself." She followed him around the barn. "From back here, if it was at night, Scruffy might not have heard anything."

"There is a road of sorts there," she said, pointing toward the lane that ran between two net wire fences with fields on both sides. "Where does it go from here?"

"It leads clear to the far end of the ranch." He pointed to an open-ended barn with large bales of hay beneath it. "We haul our hay on this lane, drive equipment to and from the fields, drive the four-wheeler to tend to the waterlines, that sort of thing. We drive trucks on it too. And there are more corrals back there quite a ways."

"Does the lane go clear through the ranch and to another road?"

"No, it goes as far as the last field, a pasture. There are fences there that separate our place from the neighbors to the south, east, and west," he explained.

"So someone would have to come through some fields to get to where we are now?" she asked. "And that would include a neighbor's fields?"

"There's no other way to get here."

She nodded her head. "So let's assume someone carried her body up this road from one of your neighbor's fields. Would they then have to enter the barn at the front, or could they open these doors at the back? And if they did, wouldn't that alert Scruffy?"

"There's a small door on the other side of the barn. It leads to the machine sheds over there." He pointed in the direction of the west side of the barn. "It could be opened silently. I'll show you." She walked beside him as they went around the barn. The door was near the south end of the barn, close to the big doors they had just been standing by. "Try it," he said.

She turned the nob and it opened silently to the inside. "Okay, so what we need to do is try to discover evidence of Charity's body being carried through this door."

"That's right," he said. "If we didn't have to go meet with Detectives Ackerman and Davis, we could look right now."

"Rhett, you go meet with them. They don't need me. You can tell me what they say," she said. "If it's okay with you, I'll have a look around."

"That's fine," he said. He glanced at his watch. "I guess I should be going."

"Let me ask something else before you go," she said.

"Go ahead," he said, looking at her with a new confidence that buoyed her up.

"Is your mother usually here all day?"

"Most of the time. Unless she has to go to town for something," he said.

"And she takes the dog?"

"Unless I'm here, and sometimes even then."

"So someone could have watched for your mother to leave and then drove right in during the daytime," she said.

The confidence fled from his eyes, and his shoulder slumped. "I never thought of that. So maybe it's a waste of time for you to go looking for evidence back there," he said, glancing across the fields.

"No, it's not a waste of time, Rhett. Charity's body probably hadn't been there that long when the anonymous informant called the sheriff's office and told them a body was in your barn. Would your mother be able to remember if she left anytime in the past couple of days?"

He brightened up. "Of course she would. I can call her right now."

"No, you go. You don't want to upset the deputies by being late. Give me your mother's number, and I'll call her myself," she said. He did that, and then she waved a hand in a shooing motion. "Go. I'm on it." Rhett had only made a few steps before she called his name. "Rhett, there is one more thing. The neighbors to the west—would they care if I walked in their fields or over to their yard?"

"No, the Whitneys are good people. I mentioned them to you when we were at your office. They are an older couple, and they live alone. Talk to them first if you want to. The neighbors to the south and the east would be okay too, but that would be a much longer distance from a road. I'd better hurry," he said and headed back around the barn.

Patches dialed Mrs. Ketchum's number, but it went to voicemail. So she left a message, explaining who she was and asking Mrs. Ketchum to call back as soon as she could. Then she hurried to her truck and drove back to the main road and the quarter mile to the Whitneys' home. Their house was set back just a short way from the road. An older blue Dodge pickup was parked in front of the house. She could see a two-car garage with the door open. It was near the house but separate from it. A small dark car was parked inside. She walked to the front door, watching for a dog. The one that wandered her way was old, had long gray hair, and was wagging its tail as she opened the gate and entered a small but nicely cared for yard.

She patted the dog's head and went on to the porch and knocked on the door. A woman with graying red hair who was about the same height as Patches came to the door. "May I help you?" she asked with a friendly smile.

"My name is Patches Fisher. I am a private investigator working for your neighbor Rhett Ketchum," she said, holding out her credentials.

The woman gave only a cursory glance and then said with flashing eyes, "We know what is going on. A deputy talked to us. He accused Rhett of murder!" She shuddered as she spoke. "Rhett wouldn't hurt a flea. The idea that he has been accused of killing that young lady is preposterous."

"I agree," Patches said, even as she remembered that she was supposed to be keeping an open mind. But this woman looked like she was a good judge of character, and it was hard to disagree with her appraisal of Rhett. "I'd like to speak with you and your husband for a moment if I could."

"Sure, come on in," the lady said as she opened the door wide and stepped back. "My name is Maggie Whitney. Evan is outside somewhere.

But he has his cell phone with him. I'll call and ask him to come in. We will be glad to help you if we can. That smarty of a deputy has it all wrong."

It sounded like Deputy Lebow had been doing his best to paint Rhett as a killer before his boss had pulled him from the case. "Thank you," Patches said as she followed Mrs. Whitney into a small but homey living room. She was a stout lady who moved with short, quick steps.

"Please, sit down, miss. Would you like a glass of water?"

"No thanks, I'm fine," Patches said.

"My phone is in the kitchen; I was just mixing up a batch of bread. I'll run in there and call Evan. I'll be right back," Maggie said and hurried out of the living room.

Patches looked around. There was a wall filled with pictures of the couple's family. She stepped over to it. There were a number of individual pictures and three family groups and some miscellaneous ones. Patches studied them for a moment, and then she noticed that one of the pictures was of Rhett as a teenager. He was standing beside a frail but pretty girl. He had his arm draped around her shoulders. The girl had bright-red hair and a big grin on her face. She was looking up at Rhett.

"That's our Nadia with Rhett," Maggie said as she entered the room. "She adored him. He was so good to her. He was two years older than her, but I believe that from the time Nadia was five or six years old she was in love with him. In her mind, they would both grow up and then she'd marry him one day."

"She's very pretty," Patches said as she quickly scanned the pictures of the three young families. Nadia's face was not in any of them.

"'Course, we knew that would never happen. She was born with a bad heart. She lived longer than the doctors ever figured she would. That picture was taken when she was thirteen. Rhett was fifteen, and he was so good to her, Miss Fisher. There is no way a young man like him could ever do what Clayson Lebow has accused him of doing. He doted on Nadia. When she passed just a year after this picture was taken, he was with us at her side. If she'd been healthy, I suspect she would have married him." She shrugged her shoulders. "He was a good boy, and he is a good man. The best."

Patches blinked back a tear. "You have a beautiful family," she said.

"Thank you. We had nothing but girls, all wonderful women."

A door opened and closed toward the back of the house. "That's Evan now," Mrs. Whitney said.

A few moments later Evan Whitney walked in. Patches stared at him, surprised. He was at least six feet tall and was what people must mean when they call someone a beanpole. He was slender with sinewy arms. He had a floppy felt hat on his head and was wearing heavy leather shoes. He towered over both Patches and Maggie.

The fellow smiled and asked, "Is this the young lady who is going to help Rhett?"

"This is Patches Fisher," Maggie said and then stepped beside the tall man and took his hand. "This is Evan, my husband. Now, tell us how we can help you prove Rhett's innocence."

"I hope to do that," Patches said. "I sure will do my best, and so will my parents."

Evan pulled his hat from his head and ran his hand through some thin gray hair. Just then, Patches's cell phone rang. "I need to take this. It's Mrs. Ketchum."

"We'll step out if you need privacy," Evan said.

"No, that's fine," she said as she accepted the call. "Mrs. Ketchum. Thanks for returning my call. As I explained in my message, I am a private investigator."

"Yes, Rhett told us about you. He said you and your father and mother are very good investigators. And his attorney agrees. What can I help you with?" she asked.

"Please, sit down," Maggie said again, pointing toward a soft chair.

Patches nodded and moved toward it and sat as she said into her cell phone, "Here's what I need to know, Mrs. Ketchum. Over the past day or so, the time when Charity's body had to have been placed in your barn, was there any time you were not at home?"

"You are wondering if someone could have driven to the barn, aren't you?" Mrs. Ketchum asked shrewdly.

"I am," she confirmed.

"I've been thinking about that. But there is just no way," Sarah Ketchum said with a touch of sadness in her voice. "I was home the entire time since the day Rhett headed for his rodeos in Nevada. I was either in the house, the corrals, the yard, or the vegetable garden the entire time. And no one could have come past without me and my dog knowing it. Did Rhett tell you about Scruffy?"

"He did," Patches said.

"Believe me, Miss Fisher, Scruffy is not a mean dog, but no one comes past our house without her alerting me. Susie and I were talking about this. Whoever did it had to have come in through the fields."

"That's what I needed to know, Mrs. Ketchum."

"You can call me Sarah," Rhett's mother responded.

"Thank you, Sarah. And please, call me Patches. I am with your neighbors right now, Evan and Maggie Whitney. I was about to ask for permission to take a look around their place and check the fence between their fields and yours."

"I'll help you," Evan said, rising from his seat.

She nodded gratefully, still holding the cell to her ear. "Rhett drove to the sheriff's office to speak with the investigating officers. His attorney is meeting him there. I'll let him know what we find out as soon as he gets back."

CHAPTER SIX

RHETT HAD WAITED SEVERAL MINUTES outside the sheriff's office for his attorney. As soon as Wilson arrived, the two of them spoke briefly.

"Do not say anything without me giving you the go ahead," Wilson cautioned him. "I'll nod if it's okay, but if I shake my head or tell you not to answer, then that's what you are to do. Is that clear?"

"It is. I'm glad you're here. I don't know what they think they've found, but there's something," Rhett said. He told Wilson about the mysterious phone call Detective Ackerman had received and his sudden change of demeanor following it.

"I'm glad you called me. I won't let them run over you, Rhett. Let's go in and see what kind of surprise awaits us. And don't worry so much. You are innocent. I believe it, and so do the Fishers. We have your back on this."

"Thank you. I wouldn't have any idea what to do or say without your help."

Wilson said, "That's what I'm here for. I'll take the lead." They walked into the reception area. Then he spoke to the receptionist. "Good morning, miss. I'm Wilson Arnold. I'm sure you know Rhett Ketchum. I am his counsel. We are here to see Detectives Ackerman and Davis."

She told them they were expected and allowed them to go back. The officers were waiting for them. Wilson introduced himself to them and said, "I don't have a lot of time, so let's get right to this."

"Sure," Detective Ackerman said, his face serious. "We'll use the squad room." He directed them to it. Once in the room with the door shut, he asked, "Where is Miss Fisher, Rhett? I thought she was going to be here with you."

"Change of plan," Rhett said sharply. "She's doing something else."

"Very well. Let's all sit down. I will need to record our conversation."

"Of course," Mr. Arnold said. They sat across a large table, the officers on one side and Rhett and his attorney on the other.

After the usual introduction for the recording, Detective Ackerman asked, "Rhett, do you use Facebook, Twitter, or other social media?"

"Just Facebook. I don't use it a lot. Why do you ask?" Rhett asked after getting a nod from Wilson.

"We got a call," the detective began.

"From whom?" Mr. Arnold asked, his eyes narrowed.

"We don't know, but it seems it was an accurate one," the detective said defensively. "We were directed to look at Charity Gaffey's Facebook page."

"Like you were directed to look for a body in my barn?" Rhett asked sarcastically.

"Let's hear what Detective Ackerman has to say," his attorney admonished him gently but firmly.

Rhett settled back in his chair. His eyes caught those of Detective Kori Davis across the table. She was slowly shaking her head. Rhett wondered what that was about. Detective Ackerman asked, "Have you been corresponding with Mrs. Gaffey on social media lately?"

Wilson nodded for Rhett to answer. "No, I haven't. She called me a few times in the past few weeks, but I haven't been on Facebook for quite a while," Rhett said. Kori nodded approvingly. It appeared that she believed him. He hoped so.

"Then how do you explain the series of exchanges with her over the past few weeks?" the detective asked with a glint in his eyes.

"There have been no exchanges," Rhett said, even as ice formed in his chest.

"That's not what we have learned from Facebook," the detective said, his eyes boring into Rhett's. "The anonymous caller was right again, just like with Mrs. Gaffey's dead body being in your barn."

Rhett started to deny the messaging again, but Wilson placed a hand on his knee and shook his head. Rhett understood the signal and kept his mouth shut. "When was the last time you were on Facebook?" the officer asked.

"I've read other people's posts sometimes. The last time I even opened Facebook was maybe a week ago. But that's all. I haven't posted anything on my page or commented on anyone's posts or even so much as liked something anyone posted," he said. "What am I accused of posting?"

The detective glanced at Detective Kori Davis. "Kori, will you get my laptop from my office please?" She left, and Detective Ackerman said, "I'll let you two read it. Maybe it will refresh your memory."

"It can't refresh something I know nothing about," Rhett retorted. "Can't you see that someone is setting me up?"

"Let's wait and see what it says," Wilson said smoothly. "I'm sure there's an explanation for it."

Rhett sat and seethed. Of course there was an explanation. The word was *framed*. He kept his thoughts to himself, and they sat in silence until Kori returned with the laptop and the detective booted it up. "Are you still in love with Charity?" he asked.

"I was never in love with her," he said after getting the nod from Mr. Arnold. "I dated her in high school and for a while after. We wrote back and forth for the first few weeks of my mission, and then I cut it off."

"Why did you cut it off?" Detective Ackerman asked.

"She had become a distraction. I was there to serve the Lord, and her letters were making it difficult for me. Her letters and emails were getting progressively more, ah, romantic and quite mushy. It was clear to me she felt differently than I did. I had no intention of dating her after my mission, so I wrote and told her I would not be writing to her anymore. She sent me a few more letters and emails after that, but when I ignored them she eventually quit sending them," he explained. "So are you going to let me see what your anonymous caller steered you to?"

"All in good time. First tell us what she said in those letters and emails she sent after you quit writing to her," the detective directed.

"I have no idea beyond the first one. In it she said she hoped I wasn't serious, that she was planning to wait for me," he said. "The rest of them I have no idea about."

"Why do you remember the first one and not the rest?" Detective Ackerman asked.

"Because I threw the letters away unopened, and I deleted the emails without reading them." Across the table, Kori smiled and nodded as if to say she approved of what he'd done. He was glad she was sympathetic. At least he hoped she was. She was certainly sending signals that indicated it.

"Is that a fact?" the detective said. Kori frowned at her partner. "Okay, why don't you read the Facebook correspondence between you and Mrs. Gaffey." He turned the computer so it faced Rhett and his attorney.

The computer showed Charity's profile. They both read for a moment. Rhett didn't touch the computer but followed along as Wilson scrolled down. It was a series of mushy exchanges about their love for each other and the desire to get back together. The last one, however, had a different tone. Charity's final post read: *Don't be angry, Rhett, but unless you make the effort to look me up and take me out, I will have to assume your love is not real. Please call me. I anxiously await your call. I love you, but I won't wait for you forever to act on our love.* She then left her cell phone number for him.

"None of this is real," Rhett said, shocked at what he'd read. "It never happened. Anyway, most people don't use Facebook to send personal messages. They either use Messenger or send texts."

"Were you angry because she wanted to move forward with the relationship, move from the Internet to the real world?" Detective Ackerman asked Rhett, ignoring what he'd just told him. "Did you kill her because of that?"

It was Wilson Arnold who responded, after signaling Rhett to remain silent. He said, "Your last question was out of order, Detective. Don't try anything like that again, or this interview will be over."

"How do you explain the Facebook messages on Charity's profile, Counselor?" the detective asked after scowling at Wilson. "You read them. They are right there. And they are obviously from Rhett."

"I didn't write that stuff," Rhett protested angrily.

"We are finished here, Detectives," Mr. Arnold said with a flash of anger. "I would suggest that you officers get busy and find out what really happened and who hacked into Charity's page and used it in an effort to incriminate my client. Let's go, Rhett."

Once they were outside, Wilson said, "Hallie Fisher, Patches's mother, is a computer genius. She can get to the bottom of this fiasco."

"I hope so. Did you notice the posts were all dated close together? Someone wrote them all the same day. Facebook records when a post is made. I can't believe the officers didn't see that. I was going to bring it up, but I decided to talk to you about it first."

"I'm glad you noticed that. Clearly they were not written by Charity. The anonymous caller, whoever that is, is most likely the author of those messages," Wilson said. "I'll call Mrs. Fisher and have her get to work on this. You go back and see how Patches is coming with her investigation at your ranch."

"Thanks for coming," Rhett said.

"That's what you're paying me for," the older man said with a smile. "Oh, and did you notice Detective Davis? I am pretty sure she believes you."

"I got that feeling too," he said. "I hope she can convince her partner."

***

"Jay, I didn't see those posts until Rhett and his attorney did. Can we look at them again?" Kori asked. She'd trailed the detective back to his office. "I noticed something fishy about them in addition to what Shorty explained about Facebook not being a place people would normally send romantic messages back and forth."

"These look pretty romantic to me, Kori. But what else would you like to point out? Did you see something I missed?" Detective Ackerman asked. He put down the laptop, opened it, and after a moment had the Facebook account of the dead girl opened before them.

Kori looked for a moment and then she asked, "Do you use Facebook much?"

"Only in investigations," he said. "I don't have time for that kind of trivial stuff in my life."

"I see. Well, let me show you something here." She pointed to the first post Charity had supposedly meant for Rhett to read. "There's a date here. Do you see that?"

"Yes, I saw that. It was today, about five hours ago. That would be when whoever called us discovered it, wouldn't it?" he asked as a flicker of doubt crossed his face.

Kori shook her head. "No, Jay, that's when it was posted. Most of these were dated this morning," she said. She pointed to more time notations as she scrolled down the page. "They were all in the past three days."

He shook his head. "Are you sure about that?" Jay asked. "Let me see another page. Yours, for example. You do have one, don't you?"

She grinned at him. "Of course." She opened her profile page and showed him several postings she'd made and others she'd received. She said nothing, just let him study them for a moment.

"Okay, I see your point," he said. "So is there some way to find out who did this if it wasn't Rhett?" he asked.

"I'm sure there is, but it would take someone with more experience than me," she said.

"I noticed who some of your Facebook friends are. Does everyone's account list their friends?" he asked.

"Yes."

"So you only have six, and one of them is Clayson Lebow," he said.

"No, I have more than three hundred," she revealed. "It just shows some of them, and you have to click to see the rest."

"So are you and Clayson pretty close?" he asked pointedly. "If you are, I don't think that would be helpful for our investigation."

Kori felt her face go red. "He keeps asking me to go out with him, but so far, I haven't. He was still hung up on Charity." She remembered then that she'd been tricked into a dinner date for that very evening. "Oh, except a little while ago he asked me to go to dinner with him tonight."

"And you accepted?" Jay asked.

"Not really. I told him I didn't think it was a good idea. He was really pushy. He told me he didn't see a problem with it and said he'd pick me up at seven. He walked off before I could tell him I didn't want to go with him. Jay, he makes me nervous, to be honest with you."

For a moment Detective Ackerman studied her face, and she felt herself squirming. "What?" she finally asked.

"I was just thinking, Kori. You should definitely go to dinner with him tonight. And if he asks you for another date, it might pay for you to accept," he said.

"Why would I do that?" she blurted. "I don't want to go tonight. I've been trying to think of a reason to call him and tell him I can't make it. Really, he's not my type. He's a friend, in a way, but that's all."

"He was awfully fast to blame Rhett for the murder, Kori. Maybe he knows more than he's saying. Maybe you can learn something that would help us in this investigation," he explained. "Even if it goes against your grain."

"I don't know," she said hesitantly. "Even with Charity dead, I think all he would do is talk about her."

"That's the idea," he said.

Suddenly Kori understood. "I see what you mean. Okay, I can try."

"That's a girl," the detective responded with a grin. "You will be undercover." But then he grew very serious. "Kori, be subtle, and be very, very careful."

"Careful? How?" she asked as she felt a chill descend on her. She had a feeling she knew what the detective was thinking.

"Be careful, as in, don't turn your back on him and be sure and carry your off-duty weapon all the time. This conversation doesn't go beyond the two of us. Don't even mention it to the sheriff. I will do that myself if I feel the time is right," the detective said. Kori stared at him and then nodded. "Let me be frank with you, Kori. I don't trust Lebow. If Rhett didn't kill Mrs. Gaffey, then I can't help but wonder if Lebow could be behind all of this."

Kori said what she had been thinking. "You mean like he's taking advantage of someone killing Charity and trying to make it look like Rhett did it because he doesn't like him?"

"I suppose that's possible," Detective Ackerman said. "But what I mean is that he might be the killer."

The chill in Kori's veins turned to ice. "Oh," she said, stumbling over her thoughts. "That's scary," she finally managed to say.

"That's why I said to be careful. Don't do or say anything that would tip him off to the fact that I suspect him. I may be wrong. I hope I am. But I can't help but wonder about his motivations. And the last thing I want is for you to be the next body in the barn."

"Now I'm really scared," she admitted as her palms began to sweat.

"You are a police officer, and I believe you are a good one. When the sheriff asked me to head up this investigation and to use you as my partner, he said it was because you were a rising star in the department. That's a big compliment coming from him," Jay told her.

"I don't feel like I'm that good. I just work hard," she said.

"You work hard, and you think smart. You noticing that detail on the Facebook thing that I completely missed proves it. But when you go out with Clayson, think of it as an undercover assignment from me. Do not take any chances," he stressed again.

"Okay," she replied, but she was feeling very shaky inside. She considered what her experienced and proven partner had just said. "Okay, I'll do what you ask. But I'm not going to enjoy it." She wiped her sweaty palms on her pants.

Jay smiled. "You'll do fine, Kori," he said. "We need to find Charity's killer. And, frankly, I'd like for us to do it before Patches Fisher and her father do. That girl seems pretty sharp. And I know Max Fisher and his wife are."

"That's what I was thinking about her," Kori said.

"Kori, I just thought of something else. Do you think Rhett or his attorney noticed that about the time-and-date problem when they were looking at Charity's page with us? Or were they so astonished at what was written there that they didn't notice it?"

Kori flipped a lock of her short black hair behind her ear and said, "Shorty's really a smart guy. I'll bet he noticed it. He knows he didn't kill Charity, so he'd be looking for little things like that," she reasoned.

"I suppose so, but Kori, keep one thing in mind," Jay cautioned, looking her in the eye very seriously. "Despite what I just said about Deputy Lebow, we can't rule Rhett out as a suspect just yet."

Kori felt ice form again in her chest. She didn't believe Rhett could have killed anyone, but even though she had been attracted to Rhett in high school, she knew she had to keep an open mind. And it hurt her to do so. Deep down, she still hoped, as she had for years, that Rhett would notice her. Maybe, if she could help prove his innocence, he would look closer. A girl could always dream.

"I have another question, Kori. Why do you call him Shorty?" Jay asked.

"That's what everyone called him in high school. It's what I've always called him. All his friends know him as Shorty," she explained.

"I just wondered," he said.

CHAPTER SEVEN

WHEN RHETT GOT BACK TO the ranch, Patches's truck was not there. He parked in front of the house and walked back to the barn. He wondered if she might have driven down the access road he'd shown her. He couldn't imagine she would have left without at least texting him.

Her truck wasn't back there, either. He climbed up on the fence and looked out over the fields. He didn't see her. He went back to his truck and drove to the Whitneys' farm. To his relief, her truck was parked in front of their house. He got out and went to the door. His stomach churned as he reached for the doorbell. This house held memories for him—both sweet and tragic ones.

His finger poised over the doorbell for a moment. Nadia Whitney had been as close to him as his sisters—maybe even closer. He knew she had loved him in her young-girl way, and he had tried to treat her the best he could. He'd truly come to adore her. He'd prayed often that her weak heart would not take her life. It still made him choke up as he recalled that last afternoon as he'd sat beside her bed in this very house, holding her thin hand as her gallant spirit slipped away.

He shook his head and pressed the button. Maggie Whitney answered the door, and her face lit up when she saw him standing there, the way it always had when he'd come to see Nadia. She held the door open wide, and as he stepped through, she let go of the door and took him in her arms and hugged him tightly. She always did that. And he knew it was because he had cared so deeply for her daughter. He suspected that if she had lived, Maggie would have wanted Nadia to marry him. And perhaps, he thought nostalgically, that might have happened. She was a beautiful girl with a sweet spirit who had been taken much too soon.

Maggie released him from the hug and said, "If you are looking for that cute detective, she's with Evan out looking for evidence. She seems determined to find out who killed Charity and to prove your innocence."

"That's why I hired her. She and her parents, that is. They came highly recommended to me by Susie's father-in-law, Wilson Arnold. Mr. Arnold is my attorney."

"They will prove you are not the kind of man who would do such a terrible thing," Maggie said confidently. "You're not capable of it. But I hear that rascal Clayson Lebow is out to have you arrested. I never did like that boy. And neither did my girls. But they all liked you, especially our little Nadia. She really loved you, Rhett."

He felt himself choke up again. "I know she did," he managed to say. "She was wonderful. I, ah, I guess I'd better go out and see if I can find Evan and Patches."

"That's such a funny name for a young woman." Maggie chuckled.

"I thought so too at first," Rhett said. "But getting to know her, any other name just wouldn't seem right. It fits her."

"Yes, I suppose it does," Maggie said, but the look in her eyes told Rhett that she had yet to be convinced. "Why don't you go out the back door, Rhett. You remember the way."

He found Evan and Patches sitting on a wooden bench beside the open door to a large shed that Evan used to work on his equipment. When Rhett approached, Patches smiled at him and stood up. "Hey, Rhett. Evan and I were just talking about what we learned. How did it go with the officers?"

"I'm not too sure. I think Detective Ackerman thinks I'm guilty. He got another anonymous call and—"

Patches interrupted him. "Do you mean like the call he got while we were in the barn?"

Rhett nodded and said, "It was another attempt to make me look guilty. But I'm hoping you guys can prove that what he learned is bogus."

"Rhett, that Lebow fellow is not to be trusted. I don't know this Detective Ackerman Patches was telling me about," Evan began as he rose to his feet, towering over the two of them. "But I hope he's more open-minded than Lebow."

"I do too," Rhett said.

"What was the call about?" Patches asked.

"The caller told Detective Ackerman to look at Charity's Facebook profile," he said.

Patches looked at him intently. "What was on there?" she asked.

Rhett told her, and she grimaced. "You didn't know anything about it, did you?"

"No, but Detective Ackerman apparently believes I wrote it. I don't think Detective Davis does."

"My mom is great with the computer. I do pretty well myself. We'll find out what's going on," Patches promised.

"Mr. Arnold said he would call her. All of the posts were entered very recently. I guess Ackerman doesn't understand that Facebook posts are timestamped," Rhett said. "I don't know if his partner noticed it or not."

Patches grinned. "Then I guess the officers will have to be educated."

Rhett's phone rang. He pulled it out and looked at the screen. "This is Detective Davis now. I wonder what she wants." He accepted the call and said, "Hi, Detective. What now?"

"I just wanted to tell you that you are right about the Facebook thing," she said.

"Of course I'm right. I'd know if I posted anything on Charity's profile, and I didn't," he said stiffly.

"Yeah, I know," Kori said. "I think Detective Ackerman doubts that the posts are actually genuine, but we need to figure out how and when someone made those posts on Charity's page. I just wanted you to know we're working on it."

"Thanks, Kori. We are working on it too," he said.

"We as in you and Miss Fisher?" Kori asked with a bit of a bite in her voice.

"Yes, but mostly her mother. Mrs. Fisher is a whiz with computers," Rhett said. "I appreciate you telling me this though. Hopefully you guys can see I'm being set up by someone."

"We will do our job, Shorty. I promise," Kori said with an emotional break in her voice. "You hang in there, won't you?"

"I'll try," he said, and a moment later the call ended. He stared at his phone, wondering about the emotion in Kori's voice. Unless he was reading things wrong, she was on his side. He sure hoped so.

"I take it they realize there is a problem with the Facebook stuff," Patches said, bringing him out of his reverie. "My laptop is in the truck. Let's take a look, shall we?"

Evan, who was still standing there towering over them said, "Why don't you two young'uns bring that computer in the house. And when you finish looking at whatever it is you're talking about, me and the little gal here can tell you what we discovered."

A few minutes later they were gathered at the Whitneys' kitchen table with Patches's laptop open in front of them. Maggie and Evan, though they didn't know anything about Facebook, were watching closely as Patches worked at the computer. She first opened Charity's profile. The series of messages there were just as Rhett had seen earlier. They studied them for a couple of minutes, and then Patches said, "There's no question that someone did this very recently. My mother will figure it out. I could take a stab at it, but she's better than I am. I'm still learning." She looked up at him and grinned. "But I'll get there."

"I have no doubt. Let's look at my page as long as Facebook is open," Rhett said. Patches did as requested, and Rhett gasped. "How did that happen?" he said, stabbing his finger at the screen where a picture of Charity's pretty face smiled at them with a caption below it that read: *She's not so pretty now. You are going down for killing her.* The name of the person who posted it was unfamiliar to Rhett, and he certainly didn't remember accepting any friend request from them. The profile picture was simply a black square.

"Wow!" Patches said. "Someone is really harassing you. Let me call Mom and have her start working on this, and then we'll talk about how Charity's body was taken to the barn. Or at least how Evan and I think it was."

Rhett's stomach was roiling. And his anger was building. While Patches spoke with her mother, Rhett once again opened Charity's Facebook page. To his amazement, there was another post there—from him. He threw his hands to his head and rubbed for a moment. Then he again focused on the screen. The same picture of Charity that had been on his page was smiling at him now on hers. Beneath it the same unfamiliar person had written: *This pretty face is not so pretty anymore. You should have paid attention to me, Charity. I meant what I said.*

It didn't specify what he had said that he meant, but the meaning was pretty clear. "Patches," he called out. "Come look at this."

She walked in from the kitchen with the phone still to her ear. She leaned down and looked for a moment, and then she said, "The hacker's still at it, Mom. There is a new posting on Charity's page." She listened for a moment, and then she said, "Thanks, Mom," and closed her phone as Rhett's again began to ring.

"What now, Kori?" he asked a moment later.

"Someone is using your account right now," she said.

"Well, it's not me, and I have three witnesses who can prove it," he said sharply.

"I'm not accusing you, Shorty. I know you are better than that. You didn't kill Charity. Detective Ackerman is sitting right here with me, and he says to tell you he agrees with me. We are both watching the computer screen. Someone is up to no good. Rest assured that we will get to the bottom of this."

"Thanks, Kori," he said. "And thank Detective Ackerman for me."

After that call was over, he said, "I think the cops are seeing the light. So what did you and Evan find outside? I'd like to see."

***

"Thanks for doing that, Kori," Jay said. "I know you didn't want to, but I think it's for the best. If Ketchum believes he is no longer a suspect and he really is the killer, he'll relax his defenses now and maybe slip up somewhere."

Kori got up and said as she turned toward the door, "You're right. I don't like it. I hate lying, and I hate misleading people." She stomped out of his office.

His voice followed her. "You didn't lie. You told him I said to tell you I believed him. So your conscience should be clear. And Kori, he may be innocent, but we have to be sure. Don't be angry."

Kori had stopped just a few steps beyond his door. She looked back. "I have a date to get ready for," but she made no statement regarding what he'd just said. She knew someone was setting Rhett up for Charity's murder, and she did not like it one bit. She promised herself as she left the building and headed for her patrol vehicle that she would do everything in her power to find the real killer and give Rhett back the peace of mind he deserved.

She cared for him. She had hoped ever since he had broken off his relationship with Charity all those years ago that someday he would feel for Kori the way she felt for him. Even though she was pretty sure he hadn't noticed her the day he reported his mission in his ward, she had been there. But then, so had a lot of others. Kori shuddered. If the sheriff knew the feelings she secretly held for Rhett, he would pull her off the case as fast as he had Clayson. She had to hide her feelings—for now, at least.

As for Clayson, she couldn't believe she was having dinner in a little while with him. She felt a chill at the very thought of it. If it were a perfect world, she'd be having dinner with Rhett. But sadly, she thought, it was not a perfect world.

***

"You were right, Rhett. Whoever killed Charity carried her through Evan's field. There were tracks of only one person, a shoe that looked to me to be about a size eleven. It was some kind of hiking shoe," Patches said. "Would you like to go see? We were careful not to disturb the tracks."

Rhett jumped up from his seat and said, "Let's go. And I want some pictures of the tracks. I have much smaller feet, and the only footgear I wear are cowboy boots. Well, I have some moccasins and irrigating boots, but other than that, nothing. I even wear my boots to church."

Patches smiled at his back as she followed him to the door. "I believe you, Rhett, but I already took pictures."

"Thanks, I should have known you would." He looked down at her feet and grinned. "You probably don't wear those pink boots of yours to church, do you?"

She grinned back at him. "I have other colors." She paused for a moment and then added, "But I don't wear them to church."

"I'll stay here," Evan said with a smile on his face as he followed them outside. "You young people go ahead. But I can testify to what I saw if you need me to, Rhett. There has been no one authorized to be in that field except for you and Patches, and those tracks certainly aren't mine."

"Thanks, Evan," Rhett said. "We'll try not to do any damage to your corn."

"Do what you have to, my boy. I just want the truth to come out. I'd give the whole doggone crop up to save you. You are like a son to Maggie and me," he said with a catch in his voice.

Rhett felt his eyes fill with moisture. He turned back and said, "And you are like family to me." Then before his emotions got the best of him, he headed toward the corn field, but he walked slowly until Patches was beside him. "Okay, show me what you found, Patches."

"The tracks leave the lane just beyond that bunch of cottonwood trees up there." She pointed ahead about a hundred yards. "Evan figured the murderer must have parked his car behind the trees so it wouldn't be visible from the house. But we couldn't identify any clear tire tracks, as it is grassy around the trees. We could tell a vehicle had been there because of the grass being bent down, but that's all."

Rhett spotted the tracks leading into the cornfield before they reached the trees where the vehicle had parked. It was easy to follow the tracks in the relatively soft dirt of the corn field, even though the corn was over their heads. It was mid-August, and there had been quite a bit of rain the past few days but none since the tracks had been made. At one point in the field, several corn stalks had been broken and the ground was smoothed out. It appeared that something had been placed there for a while.

"He took a break here," Patches said as she pointed to the spot Rhett had just noticed. "He dropped the body right there." She pointed. "There will be dirt on the clothes Charity was wearing. We need to let the medical examiner know; it's important that it be matched with this soil here."

"We should take a sample," Rhett said.

"I already did," Patches noted.

"I'm glad you are on my side," he said with a smile. "We need to call Detective Ackerman and Detective Davis. They need to see this too."

"Let's wait until we've followed the trail all the way to your barn," Patches suggested. She looked at the sky. "It doesn't look like there will be any rain today, so a small delay won't hurt anything." She looked down again at the spot where they believed Charity's body had lain for a short time. "The killer dropped the body again beside the fence between Evan's farm and yours. I'm sure we'll find where he carried her again on the other side. Evan and I didn't cross the fence, and I want to see what evidence we can find on your side of it before we tell the officers what we've found."

Rhett nodded in agreement, and they again began to move along slowly. The sun was lying low on the western horizon. When they neared the fence, Patches looked toward the sinking sun. "Call the officers. I didn't realize it was getting so late. We don't want them here after it's already dark and they can't see the tracks clearly."

Rhett tried Detective Ackerman first, but the call went to voicemail. After several rings, he was thinking about ending the call to Kori but decided to wait and see if it went to voicemail too. Rhett and Patches reached the fence that separated Evan's farm from the Ketchum ranch, and there was still no answer.

***

Kori was trying to ignore her phone as it rang in her purse, but Clayson said, "Aren't you going to answer that? It could be about Charity's murder."

Kori had then pulled her ringing phone from the purse and opened it. As soon as she saw that the call was from Rhett, she hit end before Clayson could stop her. "Hey, you shouldn't have done that," he said.

"It was a friend. I'll call back later. It's no big deal."

"You just don't want whoever was calling to know you are on a date with me," Clayson said with a touch of anger in his voice.

"If I didn't want anyone to know we're having dinner together, why would I have let you bring me to a restaurant right here in Heber? We aren't exactly hiding," she said, trying to keep her voice light even as she wondered what Rhett wanted and hoped people didn't think she and Clayson were an item.

They had ordered and were waiting for their meals to be served. Clayson wanted to talk about the murder, so she let him, hoping he would say something that would give her a hint of what he knew about the case and what, if anything, he might be hiding. But mostly all he could do was talk about what a terrible man Rhett was. It was making her ill to listen to him. Finally, between his ranting and her wondering about the call she'd missed, she pushed her chair back. "I need to go to the restroom before our meal comes. I won't be long."

She couldn't miss the dark look that crossed Clayson's face, but she tried to pretend she didn't notice, smiled a sweet albeit forced smile at him and, grabbing her purse, headed for the restroom. As soon as she was behind the closed door, she opened her phone and redialed Rhett. A moment later his voice came on the line. "Hi, Kori. I'm glad you called back. There is something you and Detective Ackerman need to see before it gets dark."

"Oh, gee, Shorty, I'm sort of tied up right now and will be for at least an hour, maybe more," she said. She wished she could think of a way to get out of completing the dinner, but that just wasn't going to happen. "I've only got a minute to talk, so why don't you tell me what it is that you want us to see."

"It's evidence that proves whoever killed Charity brought her through my neighbor's field. Patches and I have some photos of the tracks, but we were hoping one of you guys could come see it today just in case there is more rain tomorrow and they get messed up," Rhett said, sounding urgent.

"I'll have Jay call you," she said.

"He isn't answering his phone," Rhett told her.

"I'll find him and have him call you," she promised, hoping she could do so.

A minute later, after ending the call to Rhett, Kori tried Jay's cell phone. But she couldn't reach him either, so she left a message telling him that it was urgent he call her back. Then she called the dispatcher and asked her to see if she could locate Jay, stressing that it was extremely important. Then she told her that if she contacted Jay to have him call Rhett Ketchum on his cell and gave her the number. She asked the dispatcher to let her know as soon as she had delivered the message to Jay. Then she fussed for a moment with her hair and her makeup, hoping the dispatcher would call. But finally she couldn't wait any longer and rejoined Clayson at the table.

"Took you long enough," he grumbled.

"Sorry, but that's how it is with us girls," she said lightly. "Look, there comes the waitress with our dinner now."

They were about halfway through eating their meals when her phone began to ring again. She pulled it from her purse. As she hoped, it was the dispatcher. "Hello," she said into her phone.

The dispatcher told her she'd reached Detective Ackerman and that he was going to call Rhett. "Thanks," she said and ended the call.

"Who was that?" Clayson asked.

"The dispatcher. She had a call, but it's nothing that can't wait until we're through. I didn't realize when the sheriff asked me to be a detective that my free time wouldn't be mine anymore." She forced a chuckle. "I'm glad it wasn't urgent; this food is good, and I would have hated to cut our date short." She felt guilty about lying but reminded herself that this was an undercover assignment from Jay. She was acting a part.

"That's good, because I am enjoying your company," he said in a seductive voice that chilled her.

They were almost finished when her phone rang again. She dug it out and when she saw that it was Jay, she knew she had to take it. She answered by saying simply, "Hello."

"Are you still with Deputy Lebow?" he asked, his voice low.

"Yes," she said.

"I was afraid of that," he said, continuing to talk softly. "There is no doubt our victim's body was brought all the way through the neighbor's cornfield and then through Ketchum's pasture. I was hoping you were finished and could come out here and look at it too, but that's okay."

"All right," she replied. "I'll follow up in the morning."

"Call me after Lebow takes you home," Jay instructed.

"I can do that," she said. "Sorry I can't help you now."

"Have you been able to learn anything from him that might help?"

"No," she said.

"All right. Talk to you later, Kori," Jay said and abruptly ended the call.

"What was that about?" Clayson asked. "Was that Jay Ackerman?"

Kori didn't want to lie, so she said, "He wanted me to help him, but it can wait until later."

"Is it about the murder of my girlfriend?" he asked.

"It was," she confirmed hesitantly.

"What did he want? What's going on?" Clayson pressed.

"Clayson, I can't talk to you about that," she said. "Sorry."

"Bull," he said so loudly a couple at the next table looked their way. "I'm a deputy too."

"Clayson, I was told by the sheriff not to discuss it with you. I can't go against what he told me," she said, keeping her voice soft.

Anger flashed in his eyes. "I think we're finished here," he said abruptly. "I thought we were friends." He dug in his pocket and pulled out some cash and slapped it onto the table. "That ought to cover the tab," he said. "Let's get out of here. I can't believe you would help cover up Rhett's guilt, but I'm not stupid. I know that's what's going on here."

Kori protested, but he was apparently convinced. As they passed the cash register, he paused long enough to get a toothpick, which he put in his mouth and began to chew. There was no conversation all the way to her house, and that was okay with her. She was anxious to get out to Rhett's ranch and see what he and Patches had found. And despite Jay's wishes that she try to go out with Clayson again, she had no intention of doing so. He was such a jerk, and she wondered with a touch of fear if he was *more* than a jerk—if he could possibly be a killer.

He stopped his light-blue Charger and didn't even offer to get out and open her door for her. As she got out, he rolled down his window and tossed the badly chewed toothpick out. A moment later he drove off, squealing his tires. She stood and watched him. His simple act of throwing out the toothpick made her angry. He knew it was against the law to litter. She picked up the toothpick and dropped it into her purse. Not that anyone would have likely noticed it there, but it bothered her. Clayson was such a jerk.

CHAPTER EIGHT

It was dusk by the time Detective Davis arrived at the ranch. Rhett, Patches, and Detective Ackerman met her in front of the house and led the way to the barn. "We will need to hurry," Patches said to Kori. "Detective Ackerman has already seen what I found, but I would like you to see it as well."

"Are we going into your pasture?" Kori asked Rhett.

Before Rhett could respond, Patches answered. "We are, but what you mostly need to see is across the fence in Evan Whitney's cornfield." Patches led the way. "You can see a few partial tracks by the small barn door and a few spots in Rhett's pasture though."

"Kori, maybe we need to start looking for someone larger than Rhett," Detective Ackerman said as they exited the Whitneys' cornfield a few minutes later. He turned to Rhett. "But first I would like to see your footwear. I will need to get a search warrant."

"You don't need to do that," Rhett said. "I will give you permission. I'll even put it in writing. In fact, you can look at anything I have, including in my truck, my iPhone, and my laptop. I have nothing to hide."

"That will work for the footwear," the detective responded. Then he said, "I will be getting a warrant for your laptop and cell phone."

"I already told you that you could look in them," Rhett said, leading them to his room.

"It would be best to show that you did not exchange messages with the deceased woman via text, Messenger, or email. You understand, I'm sure."

"Yes, but I need my cell phone," Rhett protested, trying to keep his anger in check.

"You can get a cheap one tomorrow. But I won't take yours until I get the warrant."

"Aren't you afraid I'll delete stuff?" Rhett said, his anger beginning to boil over.

"It wouldn't matter if you did. It can all be retrieved."

Rhett didn't respond but opened his closet, standing aside, his fist clenched, as the officers conducted their search. A short while later, after completing the search, Kori said, "Wow, Shorty. You sure do have a lot of boots."

Rhett heard the front door open and close, and the sound of his mother's and sister's voices as they returned home from their trip to town. "Six pairs," he said to Kori. "That's all. And only two of them are dress boots. I'll bet you have a lot more shoes than that in your place."

Kori grinned. "You're right about that."

After entering the room with Susie, Rhett's mother asked, "What's that about boots?" She turned to Kori. "All this son of mine wears is cowboy boots. He didn't even keep his mission shoes after he came home. Of course, they were worn-out, but he didn't replace them. That's why I'm so puzzled about the dirty hiking boots Susie and I found in the back of my truck this afternoon. I've never seen you wear hiking boots, Rhett. Do you have any idea where they came from?"

Rhett's stomach took a tumble. "From whoever hacked my email," he said glumly. "What size are they?"

Detective Ackerman was all business again. "I'll need to take them," he said. "Are they still in your truck?"

"I didn't take them out, did you, Susie?"

"No," Susie responded. "Would you like me to get them?"

"Don't touch them," Detective Ackerman said firmly. "With your permission, Mrs. Ketchum, I think I should get them myself."

She shrugged her shoulders. "Whatever you think, Detective."

A minute later they were all gathered around Sarah Ketchum's white Chevy Silverado. There was a silver toolbox right behind the cab that was fastened down. "My husband put that toolbox in the day we bought this truck four years ago. The boots are in the empty space beneath it."

"Did either of you touch the boots?" Ackerman asked.

"No, we just noticed they were there when we were loading those two sacks of chicken feed," she said, pointing to the sacks near the tailgate.

"Good. I'll remove them," Ackerman said, pulling on a pair of latex gloves.

Rhett was standing a few feet from the truck, flanked by the two female detectives. He glanced first at Patches, who smiled reassuringly, then at Kori, whose smile was strained. She spoke up. "Shorty, don't look so worried. I know you wouldn't be caught dead in a pair of hiking boots." Then her hand flew to her mouth. "I'm sorry, poor choice of words. The point is, I've known you pretty much all my life, and even in school all you wore were cowboy boots."

Rhett said nothing. He watched as the officer retrieved first one and then another of the boots and set them on the tailgate of the Silverado. "Don't anyone touch these but me," Detective Ackerman said as he opened one up and looked inside. "If these were the ones worn by the killer in the field, you were wrong about the size, Detective Fisher," he said, with a smile teasing the corners of his mouth. "These are size twelve."

"Rhett wears nines," his sister was quick to point out.

The detective ignored her comment and said to Kori, "Detective Davis, we will need to send these to the lab for processing right away. And we will have the soil fragments on them compared to the soil you collected in the field. We'll need to bag these. I have a large evidence bag in my Explorer. Watch these boots while I get it."

Rhett could see that his sister was getting angry when she snorted. He tried to catch her eye, but he didn't before she said haughtily, "What's the matter, Officer? Are you afraid one of us will hide them?"

"Susie, he's only doing his job," Sarah said calmly. "We all know they aren't Rhett's."

"Well, someone sure wants the cops to think they are," she retorted.

"It's okay, Susie," Rhett said as he stepped over to her. "It's pretty clear someone is heaping one thing on top of another in an attempt to frame me. It isn't going to work." *But what if I'm wrong?* he wondered. The thought made him shudder.

"That's right," Kori spoke up. "We'll find out who is doing this."

"Not if I find out first," Patches said. Rhett glanced at her. There was fire in her eyes, and she had her little digital camera in her hands.

She stepped over to the truck and took some pictures of the boots. When Detective Ackerman came back a minute later, she asked him to lay them down so that she could take pictures of the soles.

"That's a good idea. Why don't you do the same," he instructed Kori. "I should have had you take one before they were moved. But since I neglected to do that, why don't you go ahead and take one of where they were as well as a couple of Mrs. Ketchum's truck."

A few minutes later the boots were bagged and in Ackerman's Explorer. He turned to Rhett. "There is one more thing," he said. "I will need a sample of your DNA."

"What for?" Rhett asked suspiciously.

"To test against the boots," the officer said calmly.

"I've never seen those boots in my life," Rhett argued. "Why do you need to check them for my DNA? They're way too big for me."

Ackerman stared at him for a moment, his face unreadable. Then he asked, "When you were you a kid, did you ever wear your father's boots or his slippers or shoes?"

Rhett's eyes narrowed. "Of course I did, but I did not wear these big things."

"The test will prove you've never touched them, if nothing else," the detective said.

"You've got that right," Rhett said, perturbed at the detective's apparent skepticism. "How do you want to get the DNA?"

"I have some Q-tips in my vehicle. I'll just need to swab your mouth."

"Then let's get it done," Rhett said irritably.

Kori was standing there with a red face. She shook her head when Rhett caught her eye, but she didn't say a thing. Patches, however, spoke up. "I'd like a copy of the lab result as soon as you get it back, Detective."

"Not a problem," Ackerman agreed.

A minute later he'd swabbed Rhett's mouth and enclosed the Q-tip in an evidence bag and marked it. "That will be all for now. We can go, Detective Davis. I think we have everything we need."

Everyone was tense when the officers left. And everyone, including Patches, was incensed at the injustice being carried out against Rhett. She said, "I thought he was convinced. But those boots, even as big as they are, seem to have given him an excuse to suspect you again." She balled her fists. "It makes me so angry."

Rhett, trying to lighten the mood, including his own, said, "I wonder how the detective would have twisted it if I had big feet and the shoes we found were tiny ones."

None of them laughed.

***

Back at the office a few minutes later, Kori accompanied Jay to his office, carrying the items of evidence they had gathered. Kori had been seething all the way from Rhett's ranch. She was struggling to control her anger because she knew that if she blew up at Jay, it would almost certainly get her pulled off the case, and that was the last thing she wanted. She needed to be there to balance out the injustices that kept coming along. But she needed to do it quietly.

So, in a controlled voice, she said to Jay once they reached his office, "How long will it take the lab to get the results back on the boots?"

He looked up at her. "I don't know, but one of us needs to deliver everything we have in the morning. I'm not going to mail anything. I don't want something to get lost."

"I can do that if you need me to," Kori responded. "I could also swing by the medical examiner's office and get the victim's clothes so they can be compared with our soil samples."

"There is no hurry on that," Jay said. "We know the body was taken through the field. What we don't know is who carried it there."

"Okay, in that case I'll take them directly to Salt Lake to the lab," she said.

"No, I think I'll do it myself. And then I can try to locate Gene Gaffey and talk to him," he said. "I'll leave first thing in the morning."

"I can go with you," Kori said. "Wouldn't it be best to have both of us interview him? He might be a suspect."

Jay rubbed his chin for a moment. Then he said, "I suppose he could be, but no, I need you to follow up on some things here."

"What exactly?" she asked. She got the feeling he didn't fully trust her.

"Get a search warrant for Rhett's cell phone and laptop and for the companies that support them: AT&T, Comcast, or whoever. We want all of his communications over the past two months. And once you get the warrant signed, go and seize the items," he said.

Now Kori was certain he didn't trust her, because he'd given her an assignment she couldn't duck without openly defying him. She bit back an acidic response and said, "Sure, I'll do that. Anything else?"

"Talk to all of the people who live within a couple miles of the Diamond Bar Ranch and see if any of them saw or heard anything last night or yesterday. By the time you have all of that done, I should be back."

"Got it," she said, still seething. In order to keep her response from showing, she turned and walked from his office. "I'll get it done," she called back over her shoulder. It was ridiculous. All she could ask Rhett's neighbors was if they saw anyone suspicious and if so to describe them or their vehicles. If she and Jay had descriptions of a vehicle or a person of interest, it would make sense to ask, but as it was, it would be a total waste of time.

"Kori," Jay called from his office.

She stopped and turned as an idea struck her. She would ask people if they had seen Rhett or his truck during that time period. That would be worth her time. "Did you need something else?" she called as she started toward Jay's office.

"Yes, come back in, and let's talk," he said.

She wondered what he had on his mind. But she simply smiled and reentered his office. He shut the door. "We can't be too careful about what we say when someone might overhear us. I forgot to ask you earlier: How did the date with Clayson Lebow go?"

She had forgotten about that. Not that it was a memorable experience. Far from it. But she had gotten so wrapped up with what had happened at Rhett's ranch that it hadn't been on her mind. It was now. And she told Jay exactly what she thought. "It was horrible, Jay. I can't do that again."

"That bad, huh?" he asked as the sternness of his face cracked with a hint of a smile. "What happened exactly?"

"All he wanted to do was pump me for information," she answered. "And when Shorty called me, I told Clayson I had to go to the restroom. I didn't tell him it was so I could talk to Shorty. But Clayson knew something was up when I came back to our table. When I talked to you, even though I was careful what I said, he wanted to know exactly what was going on. He specifically asked me if it was about Charity's murder."

"I was afraid of that," Jay said as he moved back behind his desk, sat down, and motioned for her to sit as well. "How did you respond?"

"I admitted your call was about the murder but that I wasn't supposed to discuss it with him. He got really angry. We didn't talk all the way to my place, and frankly, that was okay with me."

Jay sat there thumping his desk with one finger, deep in thought. Finally he spoke again. "Kori, I'm sorry. I won't ask you to go out with him again. But please watch your back. I don't trust him."

"That makes two of us," she said. She was tempted to make a remark about how he also didn't trust Rhett, but she refrained. She said nothing more as he again thumped the desk.

He spoke again. "When you talk to Rhett's neighbors, I want you to expand the query. You clearly know what Clayson Lebow drives, since you rode in it." He grinned sheepishly. "Without mentioning him by name, describe his pickup to them, and see if anyone saw it."

That rocked her. "Actually he was driving a car, a flashy light-blue Dodge Charger. But I know what his pickup looks like. It's a fairly new red Dodge Ram," she said.

"Good, ask about both of them. And include Rhett's and his mother's trucks. We need to cover all the bases." He held up a hand. He read the protest on her face, she guessed. "I know," he said. "You think I'm pushing too hard on your friend Shorty, as you call him. But Kori, I'm simply doing my job, and you need to do yours too. Any questions?"

She shook her head, not mentioning that she'd already decided to ask about Rhett's truck. "Then you can go. And remember to be cautious. And, Kori, I'll call you when I get back from the city so we can compare notes on our day's work."

She stood. "Okay," she said as she turned to the door.

He pointed a finger at her and had that shadow of a smile on his face. "Kori, do you have any idea what size shoe Clayson wears?"

"Probably an eleven or twelve," she said.

"That's what I was thinking. I wish I had some way of obtaining some of Clayson's DNA too," he said.

For the first time since she'd reentered Detective Ackerman's office, she smiled. She reached into her purse and pulled out the toothpick Clayson had discarded on the sidewalk in front of her apartment. "Would this do?" she asked and then described how she'd come to have it in her purse.

"Good job, Kori," he said enthusiastically.

"I didn't think about it in terms of DNA—I just didn't like him littering," she admitted.

"Well, Detective, I'll put it to good use," Jay promised.

A moment later she was again walking down the hall, but her anger at Jay had dissolved. Maybe they would get to the truth of who killed Charity Gaffey after all.

CHAPTER NINE

PATCHES WALKED INTO THE HOUSE to find her mother busy at the computer. Her father was sitting at the other desk watching his wife. "Hi, Patches," they said in unison.

"Are you finding anything?" she asked.

"We can prove our client did not make those entries on the murder victim's Facebook page. And I can also show that his page was hacked," her mother, Hallie, said, looking up from the monitor.

"That's great. Any idea who did it?" Patches asked.

"Now that's a much more difficult thing to figure out," Hallie responded.

"If I told you some names of people to consider, would it help?" she asked.

"It might. Who did you have in mind?"

"Deputy Clayson Lebow and Mr. Gene Gaffey," she said without hesitation.

Her father smiled but said nothing. His wife said, "I don't know if I can figure out if it was either one of them, but I'll try." She began to type and work the mouse again.

"So, Patches," her father began. "Why don't you tell me everything you've learned today."

For the next half hour, even though it was getting late, she summarized her day. Max listened carefully, storing all the information in that amazing brain of his. He inserted an occasional question to clarify some point she had made. When they were done he said, "Your mother has dinner staying warm. Why don't we all take a break and eat. Then, Hallie, you can work at the Facebook mystery for a little while longer. And Patches and I will make plans for tomorrow."

*****

Kori was back in the office by seven the next morning. Jay arrived shortly after her. She accompanied him as he gathered the evidence that needed testing. They discussed their plans for the day, and then he left. She began working on the search warrant for Rhett's electronics, and by ten she had finished. A half hour later they were approved by a judge. Then she drove to Rhett's house. Her stomach was a nest of squirming worms. She hated what she had to do. She parked in front of the house, beside his sister's car, and got out.

She didn't even get as far as the front gate before Rhett came out of the house and approached her. "What's up?" he asked when they both reached the gate.

"I'm sorry, Shorty, but I guess I have to collect your cell phone and laptop," she said as the worms threatened to bring up the small bowl of cereal she'd eaten for breakfast nearly four hours earlier.

He nodded, his face sober. "Come on in. I bought a new phone today, a cheap one. I'll give you the number. I already called Short Investigations and gave it to them."

She followed him into the house. Right at that moment, she hated her job. He put his devices in a box and handed them to her. "I suppose you'd like my passwords for them," he said.

"That would help," she agreed. That bowl of cereal was still giving her trouble. She prayed she wouldn't throw up right there in Shorty's living room.

He gave her the information on a slip of paper. "I hope that's all you need," he said, his voice carrying a touch of anger.

"I'm sorry, Shorty," she said, her voice breaking. "I hate doing this."

"I'm sure you do, and I hate having you do it, so I guess we're even."

"I hope so," she said.

His face softened. And when he spoke his voice was kinder. "Hey, Kori, I'm not mad at you. I'm sorry if I sound like it. It's just that . . . well, you know, while I'm being treated like a suspect, the real killer is getting away with killing Charity."

"We'll get whoever it is," she said, praying she could and would be able to keep her promise.

"You do that," he said as he walked her to the door and then followed her out to her department SUV.

They spoke for a few more minutes to each other, their conversation friendly. The remnants of the bowl of cereal had settled now. She soon got in her vehicle and drove off. She was almost back to the office when she got a call from dispatch, instructing her to go to an address out in the country. She asked what it was about. The dispatcher didn't know. All she could say was that a man had called and said he needed to see Detective Kori Davis, that it was very important, and that he hoped she could come soon. The caller did not give his name to the dispatcher, but he'd told her Kori would know him when she got there.

"I'll head there now," Kori said and was told by the dispatcher to be careful. "I always am," was her reply.

Ten minutes later, as she approached the address she'd entered into her GPS, a shot rang out and glass filled the back of her vehicle. Then another shot came, and another. She felt a tire go down and heard a bullet come through the metal of her vehicle. Something plucked at her shoulder as the passenger window blew out. She knew she'd been shot. Another bullet blew out the windshield, and when she instinctively ducked her head due to the glass that was pelting her and in attempt to dodge further bullets, she flew off the road and rammed a tree. She did not lose consciousness, but the airbag exploded and she could barely move.

Kori was afraid the shooter would come and finish her off. She struggled for her service weapon and managed to pull it out of the holster and hold it in her shaky right hand. Pain increased in her shoulder. She wasn't sure she could lift the gun and fire it if she had to. To make matters worse, blood streamed down her face from numerous cuts, and some of it filled her eyes. Her entire body was in pain. Fear stabbed her heart. She was aware of a vehicle pulling up on the road she had just left. She struggled to get her door open, but it was jammed. She reached for her mic but couldn't get it.

She heard a door open on the road. She rubbed at her eyes, trying to clear them. She managed to clear one of them just enough to enable her to see a shadowy figure approach the passenger side of her vehicle. She raised her pistol, but just then another car approached, and the figure turned. A moment later she heard a door slam and a vehicle drive off, screeching its tires.

Kori could hear the dispatcher calling her. The call was coming in on her handheld radio. There was no sound from the radio in her car. She assumed it had been disabled in the accident. She tried to reach the handheld. She remembered laying it on the seat beside her when she'd left Rhett's place. When Kori didn't answer, she heard the dispatcher calling all other cars, asking anyone who was in the general area to check on her, giving them the address she was headed to, and explaining that she was concerned about her well-being.

Kori struggled to reach her portable unit. She couldn't see, but she used her right hand, the one that held her service revolver, in an attempt to feel for it. She had no success. She finally simply relaxed the best she could and prayed.

Someone approached the car. "Officer, are you okay?" a woman's frightened voice asked.

"I'm shot," she stammered.

"I'll call for help. The guy that drove off—was it him?" the woman asked as she stuck her head in the window of the passenger side.

Kori nodded.

Kori had no idea how much time passed before she was aware of more cars stopping on the road. She tensed, but then she relaxed when she heard Sheriff McCoy's voice call out her name. "Kori, can you hear me?" he asked from somewhere near the car.

"Y . . . yes," she stammered. "Please . . . help . . . me."

"An ambulance is on the way," he said in a reassuring voice. "Mrs. Weeks called 911. She says the man who did this jumped in his vehicle and drove off when she came up the road."

Kori couldn't answer. And knowing now that she was safe, she allowed blackness to envelop her.

***

Max and Patches were sitting on a sofa in a house in Murray. Gene Gaffey was not smiling. A big man, he sat slouched in an easy chair across the room from them. He was staring at his feet. Max had asked him a question, but so far he hadn't answered. The investigators waited patiently. Finally he looked up, and his hazel eyes met Max's. "We just fell out of love, I guess," he said.

"My question was who decided to divorce: you or Charity?" Max said.

Gene's eyes narrowed. "I heard your question," he said. "And I answered it."

Max felt heat rise in his neck. But he controlled his anger. Calmly he said, "That was not an answer; that was a statement of the cause. Did you say to her one day, 'Charity, I want a divorce; I don't love you anymore'? Or did she—"

Gene cut him off. "Okay, okay! I know what you want me to say. You want me to blame her. Well, then, that's what I'll say. She was continually getting on my nerves by harping about the way I lived. We fought about our differences. She kept reminding me she could have married that guy Shorty. Although I do say he was a giant compared to you."

Max bristled. Patches laid a calming hand on his arm. He caught her eyes for a moment, and she smiled. He nodded at her and looked back at Gene. "Mr. Gaffey, did she demand a divorce?"

"Yeah, that's right. She told me one day that she was going to leave me and go get Shorty back," he said, fire in his eyes.

"Oh yeah?" Max said.

"She thought I cared, but like I said, we'd fallen out of love. I told her to go for it," he said.

"Just like that?" Max pressed. "Or did you remind her she was married to you and you weren't going to let her just walk away?"

Gene was getting angrier by the minute. "I didn't care if she left, but I told her she wasn't going to go back to Shorty. No way."

"Why did you tell her that?" Max asked calmly.

"Because I knew he wouldn't want her after being married to me. Maybe you didn't know this, but he told her he didn't want her to wait for him. I told her that since she now smoked a little and drank some he wouldn't look twice at her."

"How did she take that?" Max probed.

"She slapped me," Gene said flatly.

"And then what did you do?" Max asked.

"What any man with self-respect would do. I knocked some sense into her."

Once again Max felt heat under his collar, and the calming presence of his daughter kept him focused. "Did you hurt her badly?" Max asked.

"Not any worse than usual. She knew better than to back talk me," he said. "I had to remind her from time to time who was boss."

"I thought marriage was a two-way street," Max said.

"Marriage is for a woman to obey her husband. And she didn't do that very well. And then, get this, after I'd provided for her for years, she told me the next day she had talked to a lawyer and that she was going to take the house and the car I bought for her. When I asked what she thought she'd leave me, she said, and this is a quote, 'You get your truck and the privilege of paying alimony.'"

"And you put her in her place again, didn't you?"

"Of course I did. And guess what? She left after that. She was a slow learner. And yes, I had to pay alimony, but I ended up with the house," he said.

"But only when you paid her half its value, or I miss my guess."

"Yeah, but I didn't have to put up with her whining in the house."

"So you still live here?" Max asked.

"Not this house, mister." Gene sneered. "I ended up having to sell it to pay her half. I rent this dump."

"You fell out of love," Max said flatly. "But you also fell into hate, didn't you? And you were probably behind on your alimony payments." Of course, Max already knew that. His wife had done some research and discovered that Gene owed Charity more than ten thousand dollars. Max waited for Gene to answer.

He didn't have to wait long. "That's right. She threatened to take me back to court. Stupid woman."

"Did she?"

"She tried, but someone took care of the problem for me. Court was to be next week," he said with a haughty laugh.

"So you killed her over ten thousand dollars," Max said calmly.

Gene jumped to his feet and charged across the room. Max and Patches were on their feet to meet him. Gene stopped abruptly but jabbed a finger in Max's face. "Don't you dare go accusing me of killing her, you stupid man. Now get out, both of you, or I'll throw you out. And I'll take pleasure in doing it."

"We'll go," Max said. "But I intend to keep digging. I have a feeling you may have killed your wife and tried to frame Rhett Ketchum, whom you were jealous of."

Gene made a serious mistake at that point. He threw a punch at Max. It caught Max off guard, and he fell onto his backside. But he was up in a flash, dodged the next blow, and delivered one of his own. Gene moved in on him and again succeeded in hitting Max, but it was only a glancing blow. Max had had enough. The floor shook when Max Fisher took the man down so fast that if anyone had been watching, they would have missed it if they blinked. Max stood over him and said, as Gene gasped for breath, "Don't you ever hit me again."

He turned to his daughter, who had been watching, ready to launch herself into the fight if she'd needed to. "Let's go, Patches, before this man makes me hurt him."

Max ushered Patches out ahead of him. Before he got the door shut, Gene choked out a threat. "I'll . . . kill . . . you . . . for . . . this."

"It won't be as easy to kill me as it was to kill Charity," Max said, and before Gene could get another word out, he slammed the door so hard the windows shook. "Let's get out of here before he can get up and go for a gun."

They piled into his old green Chevy pickup and left. "That went well," Patches said with a chuckle.

"Yes, it did. Gene Gaffey needs to be looked at a whole lot closer. He hated his ex, and she was coming after him for money he owed her but almost certainly didn't have. Motive reeks in that man's breath," Max said with an exaggerated shudder.

"So we found the killer—now what?" Patches asked.

"We found a suspect, but that's all at this point," Max corrected mildly, looking over at her as he waited at a red light.

"His shoe size looked about right," Patches observed. "We need something with his DNA on it."

Max grinned at her. "I need to teach you a little more about sleight of hand."

"Don't tell me, Daddy. You already got something."

"A couple of cigarette butts," he said.

"I saw them on that end table beside where you were sitting," Patches said.

"But you didn't see me take them, did you?"

"No."

"Neither did Mr. Gaffey. I'll teach you how it's done, Patches," he said with a grin. The light changed, and Max started through the intersection.

"You're pretty slick, Daddy," Patches said with admiration.

"But I made us an enemy," Max said. "Probably shouldn't have done that, but I did what I had to do to establish motive. We need to watch out for him. He seems to enjoy violence. Did you get the description of the vehicles he had in the driveway?"

"A silver Corvette, quite old, I'd say, and a newer silver Dodge pickup," she said. Then she recited the license numbers of both of them.

"That's my girl," Max said proudly. "You keep working at it, and your memory will be as good as mine."

"I wish," Patches said.

"At any rate, watch for Gaffey and his vehicles."

"Why did you take more than one cigarette butt?" Patches asked a moment later.

"One is for us to take to a lab, and one for Detectives Davis and Ackerman," he said. "When you want cooperation from law enforcement, you go the extra mile helping them. Always remember that. It reaps great rewards. Let's go home and have some lunch. And perhaps you might call one of the detectives and tell them you'll bring the cigarette butt to them this afternoon. And then it would be a good idea if you brought them up to date on what we learned from Gene Gaffey."

***

Detective Jay Ackerman was passing Park City when Sheriff McCoy called him on his cell phone. "Jay, someone tried to kill Kori. She's been shot."

"What?" Jay responded in a loud voice, his heart suddenly pounding hard. "How is she?"

"She's in the hospital. If it weren't for Polly Weeks coming along when she did and spooking the shooter off, Kori would probably be dead," the sheriff said. "Polly said the guy had a pistol in his hand. She thought for a minute he was going to shoot her when she slowed down. But instead he jumped in his vehicle and took off."

"Did she see what he was driving?" Jay asked.

"It was gray. That's all she remembers."

"But it was a man?" Jay asked.

"She thinks so. He had something over his face. She was so rattled when she thought he was going to shoot at her that she didn't remember much."

"So all we have is a gray car and possibly a man?" Jay asked.

"She didn't say a car. She said it could have been a pickup," Sheriff McCoy responded.

"Rhett Ketchum drives a gray pickup," Jay said darkly.

"We'll need to find out where he was, that's for sure," the sheriff agreed.

"I'll work on it," Jay promised.

"Come to the hospital first," the sheriff said. "I'm hoping we can talk to Kori soon and that she can give us further details."

"I'm on my way," Jay said. "I'll meet you there."

CHAPTER TEN

PATCHES'S MOTHER DIDN'T QUITE HAVE lunch ready when she and her father got home, so she dialed Detective Davis's number. After a moment it went to voicemail, so she tried Detective Ackerman's. His phone also went to voicemail. She waited for a couple of minutes and then tried them again in the same order. She didn't reach Davis, but Ackerman answered his phone.

"Detective Ackerman," he said. "Is this Patches?"

"It is," she responded. "I have something for you and Detective Davis. I'd like to bring it to you this afternoon. Would that be okay?"

For a moment the officer didn't answer, and when he did, it was with a growl in his voice. "I guess, but I've kind of got my hands full."

"I could meet with Kori," she suggested.

"Don't we wish," he said. "She's in the hospital. Someone ambushed her and pumped a bullet into her. And I intend to catch him."

Patches gasped in shock. "How bad is it?" she asked.

"I don't know yet. The sheriff and I are waiting for her to come out of surgery."

"Do you have any idea who did it?" she asked, not believing he would know.

"You bet I do!" he thundered so loud she pulled the phone a few inches from her ear. "He was driving a gray pickup. I'll be looking for Rhett Ketchum as soon as I can get free from here."

Patches felt sick. "You think it was Rhett? I can't believe it."

"Well, you'd better believe it. He'll be in jail as quick as I can get my hands on him, and don't you even think of interfering."

"How do you know it was him?" Patches asked defensively.

"Gray pickup," he snapped.

"How do you know that?"

"There was a witness. She couldn't identify the shooter for sure, but she did the vehicle. Kori's lucky she's still alive," Jay said.

"Who was the witness?" Patches asked.

"Polly Weeks," he answered. "The sheriff knows her quite well, and he tells me she is as reliable as they come."

"I see," Patches said. "I'll head for Heber in a minute. I do have something you need," she said and hung up before he could argue with her.

"What was that all about?" her father asked, a scowl on his face.

"Someone shot Detective Davis," she said. "Detective Ackerman thinks it was our client."

"Then we'd better find out where he is and where he has been," Max said. "Let's eat and then get on it."

"I'm not hungry," Patches said. "I think I'll head for Heber. I want to give Ackerman the cigarette butt. Maybe when I tell him what we've learned he won't be so quick to blame Rhett."

"You eat something," her father said. "Then you can go. I'll take the other cigarette butt to the lab and then make some phone calls and see if I can find out where Rhett is and what he's been up to. Don't you try to contact him until I give you the word, all right, Patches?"

Patches really had lost her appetite, but to appease her parents, she choked down half a sandwich and then headed for her truck. She went straight to the hospital in Heber, hoping Ackerman was still there. She found him with the sheriff. They were talking to a doctor in a waiting room. "How is she?" she asked.

"She's going to live," Jay said. "But she won't be able to work for a while. So I guess I'll have to go it alone."

"I'll assign someone to help you," Sheriff McCoy told him. "There's too much to do to go it alone."

"I'll help if I can," Patches said. Jay scowled at her, but he said nothing. So she pulled the little evidence bag from her pocket and handed it to Jay.

"What's this?" he asked.

"Dad marked the bag. It's a cigarette butt my father got from Gene Gaffey. It has his DNA on it," she said.

"Thanks, but I don't know that it will make any difference now. I'm afraid Rhett Ketchum could be our killer," he said.

Sheriff McCoy spoke up before Patches could respond to his accusation. "Jay, go slow here. I don't want any mistakes in this case, either for the girl from the barn or Kori Davis, especially Kori."

"I know what I'm doing," Jay said sharply.

"I know you do," the sheriff agreed. "But I think we should listen to Miss Fisher. I want to know how her father got this piece of evidence. So let's make sure you keep the evidence chain intact, and then let's sit down over there in the corner where we can have a quiet conversation."

Twenty minutes later, Patches left the hospital. She believed the sheriff and the detective both realized now that Gene Gaffey was a viable suspect. The sheriff had asked if her father had kept another butt from Gene's house. She'd confirmed that he had, and then the sheriff said, "We'll hang on to this one for now if you'll let us know what he finds out."

She had assured him that they only wanted to cooperate and help in any way they could. She called her father as soon as she was back in her truck. "Did you find Rhett?" she asked as soon as he answered his phone.

"I sure did," Max responded. "I talked with him on the phone. He's at home. He says he's been working on the farm all morning. He was really upset when I told him about Detective Davis."

"Was his mother with him?" she asked anxiously.

"She was home. I spoke on the phone with her as well, and she says his truck has not left the place all day. He's been out working with the cattle."

"That's good," Patches said, "because Detective Ackerman thinks he may have shot Kori."

"Why don't you go out to his ranch right now. I asked them both to make written statements and I'd like you to pick them up. And I think, from what they said, that his sister is still there. If she is, get one from her as well," Max instructed.

When Patches pulled up in front of the Ketchum house, Susie's car was there, but Rhett's truck was not. She hurried to the house.

"Patches, this is so horrible," Sarah Ketchum said when she answered the door. Her eyes were red from fresh tears. Susie was sitting in the living room with a laptop on her lap. "Come in, please."

"Thank you. Is Rhett gone?"

"Oh, yes, he headed for the hospital as soon as he learned from your father that Kori had been shot," Sarah said.

Susie put her computer aside and stood up. "He was right here on the ranch all morning and until after he spoke to your father," she said. "Your father indicated that the officers think Rhett may have shot Kori."

"I'm afraid that's true," she said. After being invited to sit down, she told the women about her visit to the hospital and her conversation with the officers. Finally she said, "I'll need the statements my dad asked you both to write. And I'd like one from you, Susie, as well. Your statements will confirm that Rhett was at home when the detective was shot."

"We are glad to help in any way we can," Sarah said. "Rhett's been staying busy to keep his mind off this mess. It's eating him up with worry."

As they were writing, Patches asked them if they knew Polly Weeks. They did; they explained that she was a good, honest woman. Before leaving with the statements in hand, Patches also had a phone number and an address for Mrs. Weeks. She intended to speak with her as soon as she could.

***

When Rhett reached the hospital, he'd watched as the sheriff and Detective Ackerman left. Having been warned by Max that Ackerman had threatened to arrest him, Rhett had parked as far from the detective's SUV as he could and then waited until both of them left before heading inside.

Kori was awake when he stepped into her room. She managed a small smile for him. He stepped quickly to her bedside. "I'm sorry about this," he said softly.

She gave him another feeble smile. "Thanks," she said weakly. "I'll be all right pretty soon. Sit down." One arm was hooked to an IV, but she waved the other one toward a chair. He pulled it close and sat down. She reached to him, and he let her take his hand. For a moment neither of them said anything.

Finally he spoke. "Kori, whoever did this will get caught, I promise."

"But I won't be able to help in the investigation for a while," she said. "The sheriff is going to assign someone else to help Jay."

"That's okay. Whoever he assigns will be able to help. You just need to rest and concentrate on getting well," he said.

Kori squeezed his hand. For a moment she kept her eyes closed. When she opened them, a tear ran down her face. Rhett reached up and brushed it away. "It'll be okay, Kori," he said, hoping he was right.

She shook her head very slowly. "Jay thinks you shot me. I know you didn't. But whoever he gets assigned to work with him will believe him. I need to be there to make sure they don't focus only on you and let whoever shot me and whoever killed Charity get away with it."

"I didn't do it. I would never hurt you, Kori."

"I know that," she said with that same weak smile. "And I also know you would never have hurt Charity."

Rhett shook his head. "Whoever did this is intent on getting me blamed. But I didn't do it."

Kori squeezed his hand again. "I know that. Will you stay here with me for a little while?" she asked.

"Sure, if you want me to," he said.

"I do. You are a great guy, Rhett," she said. "I feel better just having you here."

This time Rhett squeezed her hand. Then he touched her forehead with his other hand and gently brushed her matted hair.

"I look awful, don't I?" she said.

"No, you just look hurt," Rhett said. Kori really was a pretty girl. He didn't mind spending a little time with her if it made her feel better. As long as her partner didn't come back while he was with her and arrest him.

***

Patches was invited into Polly Weeks's house by a stocky woman with short gray hair. She appeared to be in her sixties. "Are you Polly Weeks?" Patches asked.

"I am, and you are?" the woman replied.

"My name is Patches Fisher. I am a private investigator. I'd like to speak with you about the shooting of Detective Kori Davis," she said.

"I'm afraid I'm not a very good witness," the lady said. "But please be seated. Would you like a glass of water or milk?"

"I'm fine," Patches said as she took the proffered seat. Polly sat near her. "I know you've already spoken to the sheriff, but if you don't mind, I'd like to speak with you as well."

"How are you involved in this, Miss Fisher?" Polly asked.

"I have been hired to try to help Rhett Ketchum establish his innocence in the murder of a young woman by the name of Charity Gaffey," she said.

"Oh, yes, I heard about that," she said. "It is a terrible shock. What did you need to ask me?"

"I would like to know exactly what you saw and heard when you drove up on the shooting of Detective Davis," Patches said. "Did you see the actual shooting?"

Polly shook her head. "I don't think so, but I might have. I've been thinking about it since it happened. I think I'm still a little bit in shock."

"I can imagine," Patches said sympathetically. "What do you mean by you might have?"

"Well, I saw the deputy's car suddenly swerve and run off the road and into a tree. I had my air-conditioning on, and my radio was playing. So I didn't hear a shot, or shots, I should say. I'm pretty sure there was more than just the shot that hit the poor dear girl."

"Why do you say that?" Patches pressed.

"Well, it's just that when I slowed down at the accident scene, some guy was running away. He jumped in his car and left. I'm pretty sure he had a pistol in his hand," she said. "I'm lucky he didn't shoot me too. I had no idea what I was getting into. I didn't realize then that shots had been fired. I just thought the deputy lost control of her vehicle and wrecked. But now, after thinking about it for several hours, I remember seeing glass shattering *before* the wreck. And afterward, when I was looking at the car, there were bullet holes in it."

"So that's when you realized you may have witnessed a shooting?" Patches asked.

"That's right. I hurried to the car and could see the girl was badly hurt, so I ran back to my car and grabbed my phone and called 911. Then I went back and spoke to the girl, just trying to calm her."

"I see. Now, Mrs. Weeks, you say you saw—"

"Please, Miss Fisher, don't call me that," Polly interrupted. "Just call me Polly."

Patches smiled at her. "Of course, if you will call me Patches."

"That would be nice. Now, you were asking . . ." Polly said.

"Yes, you mentioned you saw a man with a gun and a vehicle. Can you describe them to me?"

"I will try. I couldn't tell the sheriff very much at the time. I was so shook up my mind was a mess. But after thinking about it, I can tell you a little more," she said.

"Okay, let's start with the gun. What did it look like?"

"It was a pistol. I think it was some kind of automatic. I'm pretty sure it wasn't a revolver. My late husband had a revolver, and he told me about automatics. He didn't like them."

"Okay, and how was the shooter dressed?" Patches asked.

"He was wearing a cowboy hat and had something covering his face. I don't really remember much other than that because I was focused on the gun in his hand, and my heart was thudding so hard it hurt. I was afraid I was about to get shot."

"What color was the hat?" Patches asked as she pictured Rhett and his black hat.

"Gray, I think, like most cowboy hats are." She squeezed her eyes shut and kept them that way for a moment. When she opened them again, she said, "Yes, it was gray. I'm sure of that."

"Okay, describe his truck if you can."

"Did I say it was a truck?"

"That's what Detective Ackerman thinks, a pickup," Patches said. "But you tell me."

Slowly Polly shook her head. "It was gray, but it was a car, not a pickup. I'm sure of that now. But I can't tell you the make. And I don't think it had Utah plates, but again, I'm not sure. I'm just remembering a little at a time."

"Do you remember anything else about the car?" she asked.

Polly thought for a moment. Then she said, "It was quite new and sporty-looking," she said. "And when he took off, it was real fast. It left smoke from its tires."

Patches had passed the scene of the shooting and accident on her way to Polly's. She decided to stop and look the area over as soon as she finished here. She spoke with Polly a little longer, but when it appeared she was not going to be able to remember anything else, Patches thanked her and left.

When she stopped to look at the area where the wreck had occurred, she examined the marks that had been left when the car had peeled out. She wondered if anything could be determined about the tread by an expert. She would ask her father about that as well. She looked around for several minutes, and finally she left. Next stop, the hospital. If Rhett was still there, she'd get a statement from him. If not, she'd speak to Kori and then try to catch Rhett back at his home.

She entered the hospital after driving around the parking area and spotting Rhett's truck. Then she went in. She approached the door to Kori's room and peered in. Her heart stuck in her throat when she saw Rhett sitting beside the bed, Kori's hand in his. She quietly backed away. That was the last thing she'd wanted to see. A silly wave of jealousy passed through her as she hurried out of the hospital.

CHAPTER ELEVEN

PATCHES FOUGHT THE URGE TO cry. She had no right to expect the secret feelings she had for Rhett to be returned in kind by him. After all, she barely even knew him. And he hardly knew her at all. She was almost to her truck, rubbing her eyes, when all thought of crying fled at the sight of Detective Ackerman parking his SUV near hers.

She watched as he got out of his vehicle, a dark look on his face. He didn't seem to notice her and strode quickly toward the front doors of the hospital. Patches, suspecting he was here to arrest Rhett, followed him. She was determined to stop him from making that mistake, for his own sake as well as for Rhett's.

She caught the elevator after he did but managed to catch up with him at the door to Kori's hospital room. "Well, hi, Detective. It looks like we're both coming to see how your partner is doing," Patches said, hoping to deflect any idea that she had followed him into the hospital.

Jay stopped short of entering the room. He turned to Patches and said with a frown on his face, "She will recover, no thanks to your client. I'm told he is in there with Detective Davis now. That's pretty cold. No, Miss Fisher, I am here to arrest him for the attempted murder of Kori."

He reached to open the door, but Patches stepped in front of him. "Isn't this a little hasty?" she asked. "You need to speak with Polly Weeks before you embarrass yourself."

Jay folded his arms across his chest and scowled down at Patches. "The sheriff already did that, as I told you before. She identified the killer as a man driving a gray pickup. So if you don't mind—"

Patches interrupted him as she stood her ground. "I just spoke with Polly. She told me in no uncertain terms that the killer drove a gray sedan, a sporty one, not a pickup, and that it had out-of-state plates," she said. "You should check with her again before you go in there and get egg on your face."

"As if you care if I get egg on my face," he said with a grunt. But he unfolded his arms. "Are you sure of what you just said?"

"Call her, Detective. She's remembered several details she didn't right after. For example, the shooter was wearing a gray cowboy hat. I don't think Rhett even owns one. He wears only black. You've been in his house. Did you see any gray hats in there?"

Jay backed away from Patches. "I could call Polly, but, well, I know your father, and you wouldn't be working for him if you lied about things like this. I guess I owe you an apology—and a thanks." He shook his head. "I need to get this right. Seeing Kori like this has really upset me. I guess it's made me act in haste. I'm sorry. I owe you one. Kori is a great person and was a great help to me, Patches. But now I need a partner."

"I'm so sorry about her, I really am," Patches said. "I guess I'll be going."

"I thought you were coming to check on her."

Patches shook her head. "I already did," she confessed. "But she doesn't know it. Rhett is in there with her. I left without them knowing I peeked in."

Jay cocked his head to one side. "Why would you do that?" he asked. Then his eyes grew wide. "Oh, I see. You kind of fancy the guy, don't you? And you think Kori does too."

She didn't respond. All she said as she stepped past him was, "Thanks for listening to me. You're a good officer. You'll get this right." And with that she hurried toward the elevator without looking back.

**

Rhett stood up quickly and stepped away from Kori's bed when the door swung open and Jay Ackerman strode in. He picked up his black hat from an adjacent chair and said, "Hello, Detective. I was just leaving, or did you need to see me?"

"Actually I do have one question. Do you have any gray cowboy hats?" Jay asked.

"No. I only wear black ones. Why?" Rhett asked with a puzzled look.

"Just curious," he said. He paused, seeming to think. Rhett glanced at Kori and then back at Jay, who said, "Do you know anyone who would want to hurt Kori who wears a gray cowboy hat?"

Rhett shook his head. "I can't imagine why anyone would want to do this to her." He glanced her way, and Kori gave him a fairly bright smile. Then she spoke up. "Jay, Clayson Lebow wears a gray hat."

Jay's face went dark. "He does, doesn't he?"

Rhett was anxious to get away. He'd enjoyed sitting there with Kori. He'd enjoyed it more than he had imagined he would. But he was not comfortable with Jay Ackerman. So he said, "I gotta go," and left the room.

He left the hospital quickly and strode to his truck. He was surprised to see Patches leaning against his front fender. She had a somber face. Even when he said, "Hi, Patches. It's good to see you," and smiled at her, the somber look remained. He wondered what was going on with her. Awkwardly he asked, "Did you need to see me?"

She pushed away from his fender and said, "I don't know if this is as important now as it was a few minutes ago, but I should ask anyway. Where were you when Kori was shot this morning?"

"What?" he asked, taken aback. "Surely you don't think I would hurt her, do you?"

"No, I'm pretty sure you wouldn't. I didn't realize you two had a thing going. But knowing you do, I'm sure you wouldn't hurt her," she said.

Rhett was almost certain she had a catch in her voice, and she ducked her eyes as she spoke. "Wait a minute, Patches. I don't know what gave you that idea. We don't have a thing going, but she is a friend, and she's hurting. I came here to console her and ask her if there was anything I could do to help her. I didn't see you in there." Suddenly he remembered that someone had opened the door and then let it close again a few minutes ago. "Did you come to see her too?" he asked. "Someone started to come in and then left. Was that you?"

"I came to talk to you," she said, her face still very somber. "But I decided it could wait."

Rhett shook his head. "Okay, so here I am. And I can tell you I was at home when she was shot," he said a little sharply.

"I believe you," she said. "But Jay Ackerman didn't. He came here to arrest you just now."

Rhett felt the blood drain from his face. "But he changed his mind?" he asked.

"He did, with a little help from me," Patches said. Now her somber look was replaced with a smirk. "I kept him from embarrassing himself."

Rhett was really confused now. "Patches, why don't you tell me what in the world you're talking about. I'm missing something."

"There was a witness to the shooting. Her name is Polly Weeks."

"I know Polly. She's a good lady."

"Yes, she is, but she was pretty shaken. She told Sheriff McCoy someone in a gray vehicle shot Kori. He asked her if it could have been a pickup, and she said it could have been. Based on that, Jay assumed it might be you."

"Did Polly also say the shooter wore a gray cowboy hat?" he asked, thinking about the question Jay had asked him.

"Yes, but she didn't remember that until later, when I spoke with her a little while ago," Patches said, that cute little smirk still on her face. "And by then she'd had time to settle down and think things over. She told me the shooter not only wore a gray hat but that he drove away in a sporty gray car with out-of-state plates. Now, before I go, I should get a written statement from you about where you were when the guy in the gray hat shot Detective Davis."

He said, "Sure. Do you have some paper I can write on?"

"In my vehicle, over there," she said and pointed across the parking lot.

She started toward her truck without another word. He wondered why she'd seemed angry. Surely it couldn't be because of her seeing him with Kori. But maybe that was exactly what it was. That made him smile. She was a really cute girl, and he was getting to really like her. Of course, he also liked Kori. But that's all it was. They were both nice girls, ones he could easily call his friends.

Patches broke up his thoughts when she said, "Here you go." She handed him a clipboard with a legal pad on it.

"Thanks. This will only take a second," he said. It actually took closer to two minutes. When he was done he handed it back to her. "Will that do?"

"Perfect," she said after reading through it.

"Is there anything else?" he asked.

She was thoughtful for a moment, and then she said, "Rhett, do you know anyone who drives a car matching Polly's description, who might want to harm Kori or Charity?"

He took off his black hat and ran a hand through his longish dark hair. There was a thought niggling at the edges of his mind, but he couldn't quite reach it. He finally said, "I don't think so."

"Okay, if you think of something, you have my number," Patches said as she grabbed the door latch to her truck. "I'd better get going."

"Patches," he said, and she hesitated.

He grinned. He couldn't believe what he was about to say, but he did it anyway. "Please don't tell your father this, but I think you're cute." He watched her as she blushed, and then, without another word, he turned and headed for his truck.

He was a good twenty feet away before she called his name. "Rhett, I might tell him," she said. He turned and looked back at her. She was grinning. And she certainly did look cute.

***

The sheriff was working in his office with the door shut. He was studying the names of the officers in his department, trying to decide who to assign to help Detective Ackerman. He was considering assigning another detective, but he couldn't really do that without cutting himself short on other investigations. He was leaning toward assigning one of the road deputies for just this one case.

There was a knock on his door. "Come on in," he called out without looking up from the list of names.

"Sheriff, do you have a minute?"

He looked up to see Deputy Clayson Lebow standing there. "What do you need, Deputy Lebow?" he asked sharply.

"I, ah, I was just wondering who was going to help Detective Ackerman, Sheriff. I know you think I am biased, but believe me, I have an open mind, and I would like to help him. I won't let anything stand in my way or cloud my judgment," he said. The sheriff didn't respond right away, so Clayson went on. "I already know a lot about the case, and it wouldn't take Detective Ackerman long to bring me up to speed."

Sheriff McCoy continued to study the young deputy. He considered him a loose cannon, but he did make a good point. If he could just be sure Lebow would be unbiased. The sheriff frankly doubted it, but in all fairness, he thought he'd give Jay a call and get his feelings on it. He said, "I'll consider it, Deputy. Thanks for coming in."

"How soon will you let me know?"

"I will make a decision within the hour," he said. "I'll call you if I decide to let you work on the case."

"Thanks, Sheriff. I will do a good job, I promise," Lebow said.

"Sure. You may be excused now," the sheriff said.

After the deputy was gone, he studied the list again. There were reasons both for and against each of the other deputies. He didn't care for Lebow, but perhaps Jay could keep him on a short leash—use him to run errands, make calls, that kind of thing. He picked up the phone.

***

Jay only stayed with Kori for a few minutes. She couldn't add to what he already knew, and she was tiring fast. "I'll check back," he told her with a smile. "You get feeling better now."

He was crossing the parking lot to his truck when he got a call on his cell. "Jay, Sheriff McCoy here. I need to run something by you."

"Sure thing, Sheriff. What is it?"

"You need a partner to replace Kori. I'm hoping you have both her shooting and the murder of Charity cleared up before she is well enough to go back to work," he said.

"I can handle it if I have to," Jay said, knowing even as he said it that it would be best to have some help, even if it was just to run errands for him.

"No, you need help," the sheriff insisted. "And I have someone in mind. But I wanted your thoughts on it before I make the assignment."

"Who?" Jay asked.

"Clayson Lebow. He volunteered. He said he would be unbiased and only do what you ask him to," Sheriff McCoy said.

For a moment, Jay was too stunned to respond. But, finally, he said, "Only if you insist, Sheriff. I don't trust him, and frankly, I haven't mentioned it to you before now, but I'm not sure he isn't involved in some way."

"Woah, Detective. That sounds a little extreme," the sheriff reacted.

"Maybe so, but Kori and I feel the same. He hates Rhett Ketchum, and he's jealous of him. And he also now has a thing for Kori. Clayson's been asking her out," Jay reported. "He's angry with her because she has made it clear to him that she doesn't care for him. I may be way off base here, but I think Kori has feelings for Rhett."

"I'm glad you told me all this. It sounds like it's best that Kori is off the case. I had no idea she had feelings for Rhett. But I agree that to assign Lebow might not be such a good idea," the sheriff said. "I'll see who else I can come up with."

"Wait a minute, Sheriff. Maybe it wouldn't be such a bad idea to let me work with Lebow. It could be better having him close than to have him working out there on his own, and I think he would be," Jay said as he considered it. It would give him a chance to feel Lebow out and to keep a close eye on him.

"Maybe I should give it some thought before I make up my mind," the sheriff said. "You may be right."

"No, it's okay. Just go ahead and assign him, Sheriff. If it becomes a problem, I'll let you know right away. There is no way I'm going to let him mess up this investigation," Detective Ackerman said. "And he might just slip up and give me information he doesn't intend to."

"And you could check into his own motives at the same time?" the sheriff asked. "Maybe that is a good idea. Okay, I'll give him a call and have him meet you here in thirty minutes. Will that work for you?"

"Sure, I'm headed into the office now."

***

Deputy Lebow was ecstatic when he left Sheriff McCoy's office. He was back on the case. The sheriff believed him when he said he was unbiased. He chuckled to himself. He'd get Rhett Ketchum now, and the man would either get the death penalty or die in prison. The thought made him giddy.

He was sober-faced when he was called into Detective Ackerman's office a few minutes later. "I guess we're partners, huh, pal?" he said to Jay.

"Temporarily, that's right. But let's get one thing straight right now: I'm the lead investigator. You will do what I tell you to. Do you understand that?" Jay asked with a frown.

"Sure do. Whatever you need, I'm your man," Clayson said. "We'll get this case solved. You can count on me."

"Good. Now, we are actually working two cases. As I'm sure you've heard, someone tried to kill Detective Davis," Jay said.

"Probably the same jerk," Clayson said. "We'll get him."

"Yes, we will," Jay agreed. "Now, here's your first assignment: I want you to check any video cameras you can find around town that might have filmed a gray sports car driven by someone wearing a gray cowboy hat. It will have out-of-state plates."

"What's that got to do with Charity's murder?" Clayson asked with a scowl.

"We don't know. But whoever was driving that car may have shot Kori. I want to find anything I can about it. If anyone—a grocery store, a convenience store, the Department of Transportation, or any other place with cameras—did happen to get a picture of it, I want anything you can get me. A license number and the state of the plate would be especially helpful, as would a front shot of the driver. So get on it," Jay instructed him.

"The guy who shot Kori was driving a gray pickup like the one Rhett—"

"I don't know where you heard that, but it's wrong. Rhett had nothing to do with what happened to Kori. I know that for a fact. We are looking for a gray sports car. Go see what you can find," Jay said. "Oh, and while you're at it, look for that car in every hotel and business parking lot in town. And if and when you find anything, get back with me immediately."

"But what if you're wrong about the car?" Clayson asked stubbornly.

"Deputy, I told you the ground rules. You do as I say. Now get to it," Jay said with a touch of anger in his voice.

"Yes, sir," Clayson said and walked out.

He was fuming when he got to his truck. He wasn't some flunky. He was being sent on a wild goose chase, and it made him angry. But he knew he needed to at least make a cursory effort to follow Jay's instructions. He would find the evidence against Rhett on his own, though, *or make some up if he had to*. He was back on the case.

***

Jay didn't think for one minute that Deputy Lebow would do as he asked, but he would know if he followed his instructions or not. He'd already called several businesses and told them to give Lebow whatever video they had that might help. He'd call them back if the deputy came back without any evidence.

A half hour later he was on his way to Polly Weeks's house to confirm what she had told Patches. And maybe by now she would have recalled a little more.

CHAPTER TWELVE

"You must have impressed Detective Ackerman," Max Fisher said to Patches when she came home late that afternoon.

"Why do you say that?" Patches asked.

"He just called and gave us some information. Not many officers do that for us," he said.

She smiled but said, "He likes you. He told me so. That's why he took what I told him seriously. What did he have for us?"

"A couple of things. First, the autopsy on Charity Gaffey showed that she died by strangulation."

"Ooh, Dad, that's awful."

"Yes, it is. Unfortunately, that means she could have been killed either at the scene or somewhere else shortly before being taken to the barn. The time of death could only be determined within a few hours."

"I think she was dead first," Patches said as she put a stray strand of blonde hair back in its place behind her ear. "Otherwise, how could she have been carried there? She would have put up a fight, and we would have been able to tell that."

"Ackerman told me there was quite a lot of alcohol in her system. So she could have been too drunk to resist or may have even been passed out," Max revealed.

"Was there any sign of drugs in her body?" Patches asked.

"Just the alcohol."

"Did he tell you anything else?" Patches asked.

Max frowned. "He said it seems both you and Deputy Davis seem to be a bit enamored of Rhett. Don't forget what I told you. Your feelings, if you have any, could taint your objectivity."

"Don't worry, Dad. It's Kori's objectivity that matters. She likes him a lot, and I think it goes both ways," Patches said as her mother joined them in the living room. "But it doesn't matter now, because she can't work the case until she gets better, and it should be solved before that happens."

"Okay, my girl, just stay objective," Max said, and then his frown turned upside down, and he chuckled. "Ackerman said you kept him from getting egg on his face, and he sincerely appreciated it. So tell me about what Polly Weeks saw when Kori was shot."

After Patches filled her father and mother in on what she had learned that day, Max said, "I have an appointment to meet with Bernie Growfield after dinner."

"Who is that?" Patches asked.

"He is Gene Gaffey's best friend. I met him at a Ford dealership where he works as a car salesman," Max said. "He said he didn't have time to talk to me then, but he has agreed to meet with me tonight. I was going to take your mother with me, but since you're here, I'd like you to go with me."

"That would be great if you would, Patches," her mother said. "I have some things I really need to do on the computer."

"Okay, I'd like that," Patches agreed.

"I don't like the guy," Max said with a frown. "That's why I need someone there with me. I need an unbiased person to help interview him."

"Why don't you like him?" Patches asked. "That's not like you to decide that the first time you meet someone."

Max shook his head. "I shouldn't hold it against him, but he bears a resemblance to one of the men who killed Sammy."

Patches felt her heart jump. "Dad, would he be—" Patches began, but her father cut her off.

"No, he is not one of the guys—he's far too young. But the resemblance disturbed me. I tried not to let it influence my attitude, but I must admit it did."

Patches's mother spoke up then. "We can't blame your father. That was a terrible day for him and for all of us." No one spoke for a moment, and then Hallie broke the silence. "Dinner is ready. Let's eat."

An hour later Max and Patches stepped out of Max's old green Chevy pickup in front of a newer house with rock facing and a large attached garage in Taylorsville. Parked on the driveway in front of the garage was a silver Dodge Charger. As they walked up to the door, Patches looked into the car as she passed it. There was a green ball cap on the front passenger seat.

The door was answered by a man in his early thirties. He was more than six feet tall with messy black hair hanging over his ears and the collar of his blue sport shirt. Brown eyes met hers briefly before they shifted to her father. The guy was quite good-looking, but she didn't like the dark gleam in his eyes or the frown on his face. "Mr. Fisher, come in. And who is the pretty girl?"

"This is my daughter, Patches," Max said. "She helps me in my business. Patches, meet Bernardo Growfield. May we come in?"

Patches took note of the man's muscular physique as he held the door open and beckoned for them to enter. "Sorry about the mess," he said as he led them into a small and cluttered living room. The TV was on. A baseball game was in progress on the large screen. Bernardo muted the sound and said, "I prefer Bernie," he said with an ugly smirk on his face.

Patches took a strong disliking to the guy just from the way he looked at the two of them and the sound of his voice. She wondered if he'd acted like this earlier when her father had met him at the dealership. If he did, her father's dislike could have come from his attitude rather than from any resemblance he had to the man who had killed his cousin.

"Okay, what do you need to talk to me about?" Bernie asked after they were all seated.

"We have been hired to look into the death of Mrs. Charity Gaffey," Max said.

"What about it?" he asked even as a strange look crossed his face. "I understand her old boyfriend Rhett Ketchum killed her and left her body in his barn."

"Actually it may not have been him," Max said.

"Sure it was," Bernie argued. "He hated my buddy Gene for marrying her. And when they got divorced, Ketchum wanted her back. But she wouldn't give him the time of day. So he killed her."

"Just like that?" Patches asked.

"Just like that," Bernie said. "So what else can I tell you? He was jealous and killed her."

"My understanding is that Rhett didn't want her back," Max said.

"You understand wrong," Bernie said.

"How do you know that?" Patches asked.

"It's simple. When she left my buddy Gene, she talked to me from time to time. She worked at a business next to the dealership, so it was only natural we would see each other sometimes in the café where we both ate lunch quite frequently," he said. "My buddy was rough on her at times. I used to tell him to cut it out or she'd leave him one day. He didn't believe me. Too bad, 'cause she was a looker, that girl was. Anyway, she mentioned to me several times that she had a friend, maybe she said old *boyfriend*, who was trying to get her to come back to him, and she wouldn't. She even told me she was getting to be afraid of him. She said he had a nasty temper."

"I see," Max said at that point. "Did she say if he ever threatened her?"

"Probably, but I don't remember everything she said," Bernie told them. "I kept telling her she should give Gene another chance, but she wouldn't hear of it. So I just tried to give her a friendly ear to vent to when she needed it. It's too bad. I hope that Ketchum guy fries for what he did."

Max told him the approximate time Charity was killed and then asked, "Where were you then?"

"Probably at work," he said. "I work all sorts of shifts. When I'm not at work I'm either here or at the bar."

"Which bar?" Max asked.

"Well, there are a few of them I like to hang out at," Bernie said. After some prodding, he gave them the names and approximate addresses of four places. "Check with them," he said. "Somebody will remember seeing me." Then his face grew dark, and his eyes burned with anger. "Hey, Mister, you aren't trying to accuse me of something, are you?"

"Not at all," Max said. "An officer was shot over in Wasatch County." Max told him when Kori was shot. "Where were you then?"

Bernie came up off his chair and balled his fists. "Hey, short stuff, I didn't have nothing to do with none of this stuff. I think you two can leave before I knock you through my window."

Max and Patches had come to their feet the moment Bernie did. "I didn't mean to upset you," Max said. "And by the way, since you seem to have a short memory, let me remind you that my name is Max, but you can call me Mr. Fisher."

Bernie's face flushed. "Get out, you idiot," he said.

"It's Mr. Fisher," Max reminded him, but he was already heading for the door, keeping Patches in front of him.

"Don't come back, or I'll make short work of you," Bernie said as they stepped through the door.

Patches slammed the door shut behind them. "Ooh, that guy makes me so mad," she said.

"Yeah, me too," Max said.

They had not yet reached their pickup when the door opened and Bernie stepped outside. "Hey, I just thought of something," he said. "Why don't you come here for a moment. It might be important to you."

Max and Patches looked at each other, and then Max started back toward him. Patches caught up with him and kept pace as they approached Bernie. She didn't have a good feeling about it. Bernie also kept walking until they were only a yard apart. And then he stopped. Max and Patches did the same. Max asked, "What is it you thought of?" he asked, no emotion in his voice.

"I don't like people to slam my door," he said.

"Is that all?" Max asked.

"Did I shut it too hard?" Patches asked innocently.

"Yeah, but I blame it on your old man," he said derisively. "He should have taught you better."

As he spoke he stepped toward them, and without any warning, he threw a hard punch down at Max's face with his right hand. The punch never landed. Max didn't need a lot of warning. He caught Bernie's fist with his left hand and then stepped to the inside of Bernie's reach and threw a karate chop with his right hand that left Bernie gasping for air. Max let go of the fist and said, "Don't you ever try that again."

Apparently Bernie was not too bright. He tried to throw another punch, but this time it was Patches he aimed it at. She dodged, but the blow glanced her and knocked her to the ground. Max's legs moved like lightning, and Patches, who was slightly stunned, heard something crack. She didn't need to be told what it was. Bernie collapsed onto the sidewalk grabbing at his left knee. She was pretty sure her father had cracked if not shattered Bernie's left kneecap with two fast but powerful kicks.

They left Bernie howling in pain and threatening to kill the two of them. After they had driven away, Max called 911 and reported an injured man and gave the address. Then he said, "Are you okay, Patches?"

"Yeah, he didn't get me full-on. I should have been ready," she said. "Sorry."

"You don't have to apologize. But you do have a red spot on the side of your forehead. Do you have a headache?"

"No, I'm fine, Dad."

"Okay, but we both need to be more alert after this. It's one thing to be trained and to practice but quite another to have to react to an actual attack. Honestly, dear, I wish I hadn't had to do that to him. We may need to talk to him again."

"I agree," Patches said. "You saw his car, a silver Dodge Charger. I don't suppose Polly Weeks could have mistaken silver for gray."

"I wondered that too. But did you see a gray hat in his house?"

"No, but it could've been in another room," Patches said.

"Or in the trunk of his car. The only hat in the car I could see was a green cap. The car did have Utah plates, but I suppose those could have been changed. We'll come back here later. I want to talk to the neighbors," Max said. "But I'd rather do it when Bernie isn't home."

***

The sun was hanging low in the eastern sky when Rhett and his mother walked with his sister to her car in front of the house. Susie was leaving for home, but she seemed a little reluctant to go. "I hate to go until I know you are going to be okay, Mom," Susie said.

"Don't worry about me. Your little ones need you more than I do," Sarah said.

"Trae's mother doesn't mind watching them while he's at work. I could stay another day," she said.

"No, there's no need for that. I'm fine, and Rhett is here. But call when you get home," Sarah suggested.

"I will, Mom. And if you need me, I'll come back. I could bring the kids with me tomorrow."

"I don't know if it would be wise to bring the children here unless it is really necessary. I'll be fine," Sarah argued as Susie opened the door of her bright-yellow Nissan. "But I sure appreciate you coming so quickly when I called. I was pretty shaken up."

"Who wouldn't be?" Susie said. She let go of the car door and gave her mother a quick hug. She also hugged Rhett. "Wilson will make sure the cops don't take advantage of you, Rhett. He's a good man and a very able attorney."

"I'm sure he is," Rhett agreed.

The three of them talked for a moment longer, and then Susie got into the car and drove off. They watched her until the little yellow car was out of sight. Then Sarah said, "Let's walk out past the barn and watch the sunset for a few minutes. I'd like to look at something beautiful, wouldn't you?"

"Sure, Mom," Rhett agreed. Any kind of a diversion would be nice. He was more worried than he cared to let on. But despite his worries about this attempt to frame him for murder, he was more worried about his mother. He knew this was tough on her.

They stood in back of the barn as the sun sank below the mountains to the east. There was a smattering of clouds in the sky. Within minutes they turned first to orange, then to pink, and finally to a fiery red. "This is a wonderful place to live," Sarah said after a few minutes of silence. "It has always been so peaceful." She looked up at her son. "Until now. Son, I'm frightened. What's happening? If I didn't have my faith in God, I think I'd fall to pieces."

"Ah, Mom, you are strong. We'll be through this before long. I think Detective Ackerman is committed to finding the person who killed Charity and that his focus is turned away from me."

"I hope so. And that girl Patches—she seems very bright. She and her father will probably figure things out before the police do," Sarah said.

"At least she seems to believe me," Rhett said as his eyes fell on Magnum as he came out of the open barn door.

"Does he have a mouse in his mouth?" Sarah asked. Then she said, "No, that's not a mouse. I wonder what it is."

Magnum came right up to them and dropped the object on the ground in front of Rhett. He leaned down to pick it up, but the cat slapped at it, knocking it away, then chased after it. Mother and son watched as the cat played with the small tubular object. "I think that's some kind of lip balm—ChapStick or something like that."

Rhett watched without comment as the cat batted it around. Then, finally, he seemed to tire of the game and came back to Rhett and dropped it at his feet. This time, when Rhett bent to pick it up, Magnum allowed him to and began to rub against his blue jeans, purring softly, his back hunched.

"It is ChapStick," Rhett said. He stared at it as his mother stepped closer. "It's green tea mint flavor, I think. It's a little scratched, so it's not terribly clear." He handed it to his mother.

She looked closely at it and then said, "I think you're right, but I've never heard of that flavor before. I like plain-old cherry."

"I use ultra, with the sunscreen in it," Rhett said as he took the tube back from his mother. I wonder where this came from."

He tossed it from hand to hand for a moment, and then he suddenly tightened his right fist on it. "I wonder . . ." he began.

"What?" his mother asked.

"Could it possibly have belonged to the killer?"

"Or Charity?" Sarah said.

"Surely the cops would have picked it up if it had been in the pen where Charity's body was left," he mused. "Or even if it was anywhere on the floor, they would have probably picked it up. I didn't see it. I don't think Patches and the officers did either. So where could it have come from?"

"Maybe Magnum found it first and hid it somewhere. It's been chewed on. Perhaps he's played with it before he brought it to us just now," Sarah suggested.

"Shoot, I bet any fingerprints would be destroyed by now. But I think I should call the Fishers just in case they want to see it." Rhett dropped it into his pocket, and they headed back to the house as he hit the speed dial for Patches. "Maybe this is what Magnum had when Patches and I saw him after the officers left yesterday, Mom. We thought it was a mouse."

CHAPTER THIRTEEN

PATCHES'S PHONE BEGAN TO RING, but she ignored it and let it go to voicemail. She was busy at the moment trying to reason with a couple of police officers. They had come to the house just minutes ago, saying they'd received a complaint from Bernardo Growfield, who'd had his kneecap broken, and that someone had called 911. Bernardo had been treated at an emergency room and released. He'd called the police from there, claiming he'd been assaulted by Max Fisher, who had hit him in the knee with an iron rod.

"It wasn't an iron rod," Patches said hotly. "Bernie hit me, which knocked me down. And when he did, Dad kicked him in the knee."

The cops weren't having any part of it. First they argued that a man no larger than Max could never break a big man's kneecap with his foot. And furthermore, they argued, the complainant had said that Max and Patches started the fight. When Max asked where the iron bar was, the officers said they wanted to look in Max's truck because Bernie had told them Max had thrown it in the back of his pickup.

Max invited them to have a look. Of course, there was no iron bar to be found. But the officers said he could have thrown it away after leaving Growfield's home. They finally said they would need to arrest him and take him in for assault with a deadly weapon.

Patches stepped between her father and the two officers and said fiercely, "Why don't you do your job and check with his neighbors. I would guess someone saw something. Bernie was shouting when he came out of his house and attempted to assault us. And look right here." She tapped the red spot on her forehead. "This is where he hit me. Dad was only trying to protect me."

When asked what they were doing at Bernie's house in the first place, it was Patches who explained that they were investigating a murder and that the victim was the former wife of Bernardo Growfield's best friend.

The officers looked closely at her bruise and then finally backed down and agreed to go talk to some neighbors. An hour later they returned and apologized to Max after explaining that the attack had in fact been witnessed by not just one but three different neighbors. Then they wondered if Growfield should be arrested. "For what?" Max asked. "My daughter is not hurt badly. He wanted to assault both of us but failed. I'd just as soon let it lay."

"And so would I," Patches said when one of the officers sought her opinion.

It was only after the officers left again that Patches remembered the call she'd had from Rhett, which she had not taken. It was almost eleven now, and she feared Rhett might have already gone to bed. But her father said, "Call him. It could be important."

So she called, and Rhett answered right away. "I'm sorry it took me so long to get back with you, Rhett," she said. "There were a couple of officers here threatening to arrest Dad."

"Why would they want to do that?" he asked incredulously.

"Dad and I had just interviewed a man by the name of Bernie Growfield. Does that name mean anything to you?"

"No, should it?" Rhett asked.

"Just wondered," she said and quickly summarized what had happened. "It's all settled now because there were witnesses," she concluded. "But Dad and I want to go back and talk to the neighbors about Bernie. He drives a silver Charger, a very sporty one."

"Silver, not gray?" he asked.

"Yes, but I can't help but wonder if Polly Weeks could have mixed up silver and gray," she said. "The guy strikes me all wrong, and he certainly has a bad temper. Anyway, enough of that. What did you call about? Is there a problem of some kind?"

"Not really. But do you remember my cat, Magnum?"

"Yes, big gray thing. He caught a mouse while we were in the barn."

"It may not have been a mouse," he said.

"What do you mean? Could it have been a bird? I didn't see it that well," Patches said.

"No, it may have been a tube of ChapStick, green tea mint flavor."

Patches was puzzled. She brushed at her hair. Finally she said, "ChapStick? What makes you think that?"

He explained, and she said, "Are you saying it couldn't have been yours or your mother's?"

"That's exactly what I'm saying," he said. "But it probably doesn't help. There probably wouldn't be any fingerprints left. Magnum had mauled it pretty badly. I had a hard time reading the flavor."

"Wait. It may not have fingerprints, but whoever used it would have left DNA on it when they spread it on their lips. Put it in a safe place, and I'll pick it up from you. Well, maybe Detective Ackerman will. I think I should tell him," she said a little morosely. But she didn't want to hamper the relatively good working relationship they seemed to have going right now with the detective.

"Should I call him?" Rhett asked. "I wouldn't like to get him out of bed and stir his ire at me again."

"No, I'll call him," Patches said. She chuckled. "But I'll call him in the morning."

"All right. So tell me more about Bernie Growfield," he said.

"I think we should at least consider him a person of interest, although I can't imagine a motive. But he sure has a temper."

She recounted the rest of the interview with Bernie, and then she said, "I guess we should get some rest. I'll talk to you tomorrow as soon as I figure out what to do about the ChapStick." She suddenly remembered the autopsy report Jay had shared with her father. "There is one more thing, Rhett. Charity died from strangulation. Detective Ackerman called dad and told him. So now we know why we didn't find any blood in the barn."

She explained that Charity had likely been very drunk, and they talked about the strangulation for another moment and whether it might have been done right there in the barn. Finally Patches ended the call.

***

Rhett was in a corral behind the barn working with a colt when Jay Ackerman sauntered around the barn and approached him. "Looks like a nice filly," Jay commented as Rhett led the weanling to the corral fence.

"She is, for sure," Rhett said. "Are you here for the ChapStick?"

"I am, if you're sure it couldn't be yours or your mother's or sister's," he said.

"I'm sure. It's in the house. I locked it in my small safe. Let me turn this colt out, and then we'll go get it," Rhett said.

"You are right, Rhett," Jay said a few minutes later as he examined the small tube. "It's an unusual flavor. I'll take it to the lab and have it tested for DNA."

"I suppose Patches told you about her father's confrontation with Bernie Growfield," Rhett said.

"She did. I knew Max was pretty good at self-defense, but it amazed me that he could so easily defeat someone so much bigger than him. Of course, anyone would fight hard if someone assaulted their daughter. But Patches tells me she is okay."

"Yes, she only got a glancing blow from the guy's fist," Rhett said.

"I will do a little nosing around," Jay told him. "By the way, it looks like they are going to let Kori go home today. She'd probably be glad if you stopped by her apartment later."

That surprised Rhett, but he said, "Thanks. Maybe I will."

"She'd appreciate it," Jay said. "She's pretty down over not being able to work for a while."

***

Kori got up from her sofa and limped to her apartment door. Her knee had been wrenched when her vehicle slammed into the tree and it hurt quite a bit, so she was moving slowly. The bell had already rung twice. She glanced at her watch as she walked over. It was a little after three. She wondered who it might be. She opened the door, and there stood Clayson Lebow with a bouquet of roses in his hand. "Peace offering," he said awkwardly as he held the roses out to her.

"Thanks, Clayson," Kori said, surprised. "Why don't you come in for a minute."

He sat on a hard-backed chair while she found a vase and put the roses in it. Then she put them on her coffee table before settling down on the pillows she'd stacked on her sofa. "They're nice," she said, referring to the flowers.

"I'm sorry you got hurt. But I promise that Jay and I will find who did it to you," he said. "I have my suspicions, but we need to find proof."

"You and Detective Ackerman?" Kori asked.

"Yes, didn't anyone tell you? I've taken your place on the investigation."

"Oh," Kori said as she about choked.

"We'll make a good team. I checked all the cameras around town yesterday and found several that had caught a small gray sports car on them. Actually several small gray sports cars. They weren't all the same one. I had hoped to get one that showed the license plate but came up empty there."

Kori was still stunned to hear that Clayson was on the case again. She knew he hated Rhett. She wondered about the sheriff's and Jay's reasoning behind using him. "I'll bet one of them was it, but I don't know what more you could do," she said.

"Yep, that's about the end of that line of inquiry," Clayson said. "Listen, can I get you anything? You know, something to eat or drink. I'm sure you aren't up to cooking right now."

"Thanks, Clayson. But I'm fine. I'm really not very hungry. My stomach is a little upset."

"Do you have some Sprite or 7UP? That helps nausea."

"No, I wish I did, but I'll be okay."

Clayson rose to his feet. "I'll be back with some for you in a few minutes."

"You don't have to do that. I can call my mother, and she'll—"

Clayson cut her off with a wave of his hand. "Hey, no need to bother her. I'll get some for you. And you take it easy."

With that, he was out the door. Good to his word, he was back ten minutes later with a six-pack of 7UP cans. "I'll put it in your fridge so it will get cold. You lie back down," Clayson said solicitously.

"Thanks. You can put two cans in there. Leave the others on my counter," she said.

He did as she asked, and then, uninvited, he seated himself again. "I'm so sorry about this, Kori," he said, sounding sincere. "And I'm sorry for being so rude the other night. What I said and how I acted was uncalled for. I hope you'll forgive me."

"Forget it," she said. "It was partly my fault." She didn't really believe that, but she felt that Clayson might divulge more if she didn't alienate him.

"No, it was not," he said firmly. "I promise it won't happen again."

They visited for a few minutes about nothing important. Kori was anxious for him to leave. He seemed too solicitous. And it bothered her. She wondered why. And she needed to rest. Finally he stood up. "I'd better get going," he said. "I'm going out to talk to Polly Weeks."

"What do you need from her?" Kori asked.

"She seems to be a little confused. First it's a gray pickup truck the shooter was in, and then it's a gray car. Nothing about out-of-state plates the first time, and then she says the plates weren't from Utah," he said. "I'm going to give her a chance to clarify. Frankly I think she was right the first time."

Kori felt her temper rise, but she asked as calmly as she could, "You still think it was Shorty, don't you?"

"Oh, no, not at all. Rhett's in the clear, but we need to be sure what the guy was driving, that's all. I'd better get going then."

"Thanks, Clayson, for the flowers and the 7UP. It was very thoughtful of you," Kori said even as she forced herself not to disagree with him. She knew good and well that he would like nothing more than to stick the murder and the shooting on Shorty.

After Clayson was gone, Kori picked up her cell phone from the end table next to her sofa and called Jay's number. She was almost ready to give up when he finally answered. "Kori, what's up? You should be resting. Frankly I think the doctor was a bit hasty letting you go home so quickly."

"I wanted to," Kori said. "I can heal just as well here as there. In fact, better."

"Well, you take it easy. What can I do for you?" Jay asked.

"I just had a visitor bringing roses," Kori said.

"That's nice. Was it Rhett Ketchum?"

"I wish," she said. "No, it was your *partner*, Clayson Lebow. Why didn't you tell me he was working with you? I think that's a big fat mistake."

"Okay, Kori. Don't get worked up. The sheriff asked me to use him. And I agreed on the condition that he do only the tasks I assign him. And it also gives me a chance to watch him closely. I'm still not at all sure he isn't somehow complicit in all of this," the detective said.

"Okay, that makes me feel better, but only marginally. He's a jerk, roses or not. What do you have him doing?"

"He spent yesterday checking cameras around town."

"Looking for the gray car Mrs. Weeks saw?" she asked.

"That's right," Jay confirmed. "But he didn't come up with much. He found several gray cars, but he says he couldn't make out any license plates on any of the videos he located."

"Is he being straight with you?" Kori asked doubtfully.

"I hope so, but I can't be sure. He did visit some places. I know, because I called a couple of them. I wish I had time to look at the one video he brought me," he said. "But I'm way too busy, Kori."

"I'm not," she replied.

"Are you saying you'd like to look at it?" he asked, surprise in his voice.

"Sure. There's not much I can do, but I can sit here and watch a video. I just can't go out and collect more myself," she said. "Or did Lebow get copies of all the ones with a gray car in it?"

"No, and that concerns me. But he says he looked at everything very carefully," Jay said. "I hope he did, but I have my doubts."

"I wish I had the video," Kori said.

"Hey, I have an idea. Hang on a minute, and I'll call you back. Don't go anywhere," he said with a forced chuckle.

"Don't worry. I'm stuck here."

Detective Ackerman called back in less than five minutes. "Okay, here's the plan, Kori. I'm here at the state lab, and I met Patches Fisher here."

"Why?" Kori asked.

"She had some evidence that needs to be tested for DNA, but don't worry about that right now," he said. "She's agreed to help me. She is going to Heber to collect copies of the videos Lebow didn't get and bring them to you. Then you can look at them when you feel like it. And maybe she can catch you up on what she has been doing."

"That's great, Jay. I appreciate that," Kori said. "Tell her I'll rest now and be ready to watch the footage when she gets it here. I suppose it will take her a few hours."

"It will. So you just rest and sit tight," Jay said.

"Okay, I'll do that," she said. "But I do have a question. What do you have Lebow doing now? You said he was going to do whatever you need him to."

"That's right," Jay said. "And I'm just giving him some busy work for today."

"Busy work, as in interviewing Polly Weeks again and trying to make sure she saw a car, not a pickup?" she asked with a snip to her voice that she couldn't suppress.

"What are you talking about? He shouldn't be talking to her at all."

"He denies it, but I know he is going to try to convince Polly she saw a pickup and not a car. Jay, he is intent on proving Shorty is the one who killed Charity and who shot me," she said, trying her best to keep the bitterness out of her voice.

Jay said a couple of things that he quickly apologized for. But he went on, "That guy is a loose cannon. I guess I should talk to the sheriff again."

Kori was thinking about it, and she said, "No, don't do that yet. I think he will mess up and lead you right back to himself. In my opinion he's involved, whether he is the killer or not. Either that or he hates Shorty Ketchum so bad he won't let himself think anyone else might be the guilty party regardless of where the evidence leads."

There was a moment of silence on the line, and then Jay said, "All right. We'll see how this thing works out. Hopefully he'll stumble and show his true colors. Now, you get some rest."

Just then there was a loud bang, and Kori screamed. "Somebody's shooting!" she cried out.

"Get on the floor, Kori!" Jay ordered. "I'll get someone out there. I should have realized whoever shot you would not quit. Are your doors locked?"

"Yes," she said.

"Get your gun, and stay on the floor," he ordered. The line went dead.

CHAPTER FOURTEEN

KORI CRAWLED AWKWARDLY TO HER bedroom, where she'd left her service pistol, her injured shoulder searing and her knee aching. Her heart was thudding in her chest, and she was having a hard time breathing. The killer was after her again! She couldn't imagine what she had done to make herself a target of Charity's killer.

She sat on the floor with her pistol in her hand, leaning against her dresser, hoping to hear a siren soon. Her apartment was a duplex with a small yard out back. Her neighbors, a young couple, were probably both at work. They commuted together each day to their jobs in Salt Lake City. So she was sure no one else was in danger. She kept expecting to hear another shot. But she didn't. Her heart still pounded, but she gradually got her breathing back to normal.

Suddenly her doorbell rang. Was it someone coming to help her? She hadn't heard any sirens. The doorbell rang again. Then someone knocked hard. She sat huddled on the floor trying to ignore the door. Then she heard someone tap on her bedroom window. She just about jumped clear out of her skin. She pointed her pistol at the window. Then she heard a voice calling.

"Kori, it's me, Shorty. Are you okay in there?"

Never in her life had Kori felt so much relief. "Yes, I'm on the floor. Someone shot at me again."

"Can you make it to your front door and let me in?" he called out.

"Yes, but it will take me a minute," she said.

She could feel blood seeping under the bandage. Ignoring the pain she got to her feet, stood wobbling for a moment, and then was finally able to limp to the door. She unlocked it, and Rhett stepped in, shutting it behind him. Kori fell into his arms, and he held her tight. She was not crying, but she certainly felt tears threaten. She held them back. She was a cop. She was supposed to be strong. And she was going to do her best to be just that.

"Let's get you to your sofa," Rhett said as she finally heard sirens approaching.

He helped her settle into the pillows she'd laid on one end of the couch. It was only then she noticed blood on his neck and on the collar of his blue western shirt. "I'm sorry," she said. "I'm bleeding again. I must have torn the stiches out. And I got blood on you."

"We need to get you back to the hospital right away," Rhett said, avoiding any comment about the blood. "I can't believe they released you from the hospital so soon."

"I insisted," she said as there came another knock on the door, followed by the door opening. Sheriff McCoy stepped inside.

"Kori, are you okay?" he asked, looking from the blood on her shoulder to her face.

"It's just my stitches," she said. "I think I tore them loose crawling on the floor. I got blood on Shorty."

The sheriff looked sharply at Rhett. Then he said, "Is that a bullet wound on your neck?"

"I'm afraid so. It wasn't Kori who was getting shot at this time. But the guy only got one shot off before I managed to get my rifle in my hands and tumble out of the truck. He drove off."

"Shorty, you're shot? Why didn't you say so?" Kori asked anxiously.

"It's nothing. Sheriff, she needs to be in the hospital again," Rhett said.

"You're right," Sheriff McCoy said sternly.

A moment later a city police officer and another deputy arrived. Kori left for the hospital with another deputy, worrying about why Rhett had been shot.

***

Rhett listened as the sheriff explained to the city officer what had occurred. "It's in your jurisdiction, but I believe it's all part of our ongoing murder investigation."

The officer said he would take a statement from Rhett so he could make a report but that he would leave any further investigating up to the sheriff and his deputies.

After recording Rhett's statement, the officer left. The sheriff said, "Is there damage to your truck?"

"I don't think so. My windows were down, and I believe the bullet came in one window, nicked me, and went out the other one," Rhett explained.

"Whoever this is must be after you. And you said to the police officer you saw a gray car take off but didn't get a good look at it before he shot at you. Could it have been either silver or gray?"

"I suppose it could have been either one. But I'm not positive he was after me or if I just happened to get to Kori's place at the wrong time. He could have shot at me anywhere. You need to get her some protection, Sheriff," Rhett said.

"I'll do that. Now, you need to go have that looked at. I think you need some stitches, and it needs to be disinfected. When that's done, I'd like you to come in and meet with Detective Ackerman. He'll be back in town in a little while."

Rhett agreed. He went to the emergency room, and as soon as they had stitched him up, he went looking for Kori's room. She had just had new stitches put in her shoulder. She was a bit groggy, but she managed to smile. She was a smart lady, Rhett decided. She said, "I have a feeling if you hadn't come along when you did he would have killed me this time."

"I think you may be right," Rhett said. "The sheriff said he was going to get you some protection; there's a deputy outside your room right now."

She nodded. "So were you coming to see me before the gunfire?" she asked almost timidly.

"Yes. I brought some flowers to the hospital, but when they told me you had been released, I decided to take them to your apartment. And then, well, they are in my truck. Is it okay if I bring them in here?" he asked.

"That would be nice, Shorty," she said.

Rhett left to get the flowers, and when he got back, Kori's mother had joined her in the room. She was visibly shaken. Rhett said a few comforting words to both of them, left the flowers, and beat a hasty retreat.

There wasn't much to tell Detective Ackerman. But Rhett told him all he knew. Then Jay told him the ChapStick had been delivered to the lab. "Once I get some results, I can compare them to other DNA samples we have collected. I have DNA from Charity's ex-husband and from his buddy Bernie Growfield. Max Fisher obtained cigarette butts from both men by sleight of hand. We'll see what shakes out."

Rhett hurried home after leaving the sheriff's office. He was afraid his mother would hear about the incident and be worried sick. Fortunately she hadn't heard a word about it, but shock covered her face. She fussed about his wound and asked him how he was going to keep himself safe now that someone was out to kill him.

"Mom, I think I just got in the shooter's way," he said and explained his reasoning. She wasn't convinced, but she calmed down. She had called Susie, and Susie and her kids showed up thirty minutes after Rhett got home. It worried Rhett to have the children there, but Susie's mother-in-law had gone out of town and she didn't have anyone else to leave them with. It worried his mother as well, and yet she seemed relieved to have Susie there. Rhett told them he was going to go try to get some work done on the ranch. His mother and Susie asked if it was wise for him to go outside, knowing someone was after him. Again he told them that he was pretty sure it was Kori they were after, and he left the house.

***

Patches was making the rounds collecting the videos Clayson Lebow had neglected to get. She was getting angrier with each stop. The deputy had only visited a small number of the locations where there were cameras operating. He'd lied to Detective Ackerman. It appeared he'd checked just enough locations to keep Jay from questioning him about his work. And she supposed it was simply by chance that the places Jay called had actually been visited by Lebow. By the time Patches had located cameras from all the locations she could think of, she had a thumb drive with several hours of footage. She had only recorded the portions in which a gray or silver car appeared. She knew Kori had planned to watch it all, but since she was back in the hospital, Patches wasn't sure what to do. Finally she called Detective Ackerman, who asked her if she would mind examining them in more detail herself.

That was exactly what she had hoped for. "There is something else you need to know," Patches said. "Deputy Lebow did not check all of the locations with cameras. Many of the people I talked to hadn't seen or heard from him."

"Oh boy," Jay said. "I had a feeling that was the case. I only called three of them. I won't even have you bother with the footage Lebow gave me, because it's probably worthless. I'm going to have to deal with the guy. I'll talk to the sheriff about it. Thanks for your help."

Patches suddenly chuckled.

"What?" Jay asked.

"I was just thinking about the pink vehicle I saw on one of the videos. It's not on any of the footage I obtained, but it sure looked out of place."

"Yeah, who would want a pink car?" Jay asked.

Before Patches headed for Salt Lake late that afternoon, she stopped by the hospital to check on Kori. Until she spoke with the injured deputy, she had no idea Rhett had been shot. "I thought the bullet had been aimed at your place," Patches said.

"It probably was, but I think Shorty came along at a bad time. He'd heard I was out of the hospital and had come to make sure I was okay," Kori said. "I thought you knew about his injury. I was talking to Jay when I heard the shot, and I know you were there with him."

"I was, but he didn't know anything about Rhett at the time. And he took off for your place in a hurry," Patches explained. "Nice flowers," she added as she noticed the bouquet.

"Rhett brought them," she said, and Patches felt her heart thump uncomfortably. Kori went on. "I also have roses at home. Deputy Lebow brought them. I don't want them. I don't know about you, Patches, but I don't trust that guy."

That was exactly how Patches felt. After her visit with Kori, her next stop was Rhett's house. He and his mother, his sister, and his sister's young children were just sitting down for dinner when she arrived. She attempted to excuse herself, but Sarah Ketchum insisted Patches eat with them. Patches argued, but then Rhett looked in her eyes and said, "Please, Patches. We'd love to have you."

That was all it took. She settled down with them for dinner. They made her feel right at home. Several times during the meal she caught Rhett gazing at her, a little smile on his face.

***

Max Fisher had spent the day interviewing as many of the late Charity Gaffey's friends as he could locate. A general theme had emerged. She'd been trapped in an abusive marriage and had wanted out for months. No one spoke highly of Gene Gaffey, and although none had previously pictured him as a killer, they all felt that with his history of violence toward his wife, it was a possibility.

It was suppertime now, but he'd asked Hallie to hold dinner for him. He'd just had a text from Patches telling him she was eating with the

Ketchums. She had planned to help him with the day's interviews until Jay Ackerman had asked her to help him with the cameras in Heber. So Max had proceeded on his own and wasn't quite finished yet.

He had a list of Charity's friends stored in his head. And it seemed like on each visit, he would add another name or two. This kind of work was tedious, but Max had learned it was necessary. One never knew when there would be a break from someone.

He headed to the home of a divorcee who had been friends with Charity for three years. She lived in a nice house in Cottonwood Heights. Max guessed she must have gotten the house in her divorce. He rang the bell and waited. A tall, willowy woman with blonde hair that hung to her waist answered the door. She looked down at Max with eyes the color of the sky. "Can I help you, sir?" she asked.

"Are you Maddie Rollinson?" he asked.

"I am. And you are?"

"My name is Max Fisher. I am a private investigator. I am looking into the death of a woman I am told was a friend of yours," he began.

Her eyes narrowed, and her voice, when she spoke again, was filled with ice. "Charity Gaffey," she said. "I hope you catch who killed her. Whoever did it is a piece of trash. She was a very good friend of mine. Please, come in."

She opened the door wide, and Max entered. She showed him to a clean, neat living room with white furniture. She waved him to a chair that was so soft it almost swallowed him when he plopped down into it. She sat on a sofa just a few feet from him. "Now, Mr. Fisher, what do you want to know? I will help in any way I can. I want the killer caught."

Max, even though he could recall every word of an interview, always used a small recorder so that he could play the interviews back to his wife and daughter and to the police if it became necessary. Maddie did not object, so he set the recorder near her. "First please tell me how close you and Mrs. Gaffey were."

"Very close, and don't call her Gaffey. She was going to take her maiden name back. She grew to detest Gene. And so did I, although, I'll tell you, I got there much quicker than she did," Maddie said. "He is a cruel, unfeeling, jealous man."

"Do you think he was capable of killing his ex-wife?" Max asked.

"Absolutely. He was livid when she finally left him. I had encouraged her to get away from him for the past year. My own ex-husband was controlling, but he wasn't nearly as bad as Gene. I told her over and over again how glad I was to be single again and that she should do what I did. I even offered to let her live here with me. I have plenty of room, and we got along like sisters. We were best friends."

"Did she take you up on that?" Max asked.

"Yes, eventually. She was living here when she was murdered," Maddie answered.

"Tell me about Gene. Did he know she was here?"

"Oh yes, but he only came here once. I threatened to have him arrested if he ever came back. He never did," she said.

"Do you have a reputation as someone not to meddle with?" Max asked with a grin.

"As a matter of fact, I do," she said. "When I told my husband to leave, he did. And when his attorney told me he was going to have the judge give this house to him, I set him straight. I heard he told my ex he was lucky to get away from me and giving up the house was well worth it." She grinned. "Now, Mr. Fisher—"

"Max, please," he requested.

"Of course. Max, I am not a mean woman. I only get terribly angry if I'm crossed. My ex crossed me. Gene Gaffey quickly learned it was best not to come around here. So he didn't after that one time," she said. "But he did manage to contact Charity when she wasn't here. He tried to get her to go back to him, but she wasn't about to." Maddie laughed. "She knew she would have to answer to me if she even thought about it."

"What would you have done if she had?" Max asked.

"I would have dragged her back here," Maddie said. "There was no way I was going to let that scum mistreat her again. Charity was a sweet person. She deserved someone better than Gene. And she thought she knew who that might be."

Max leaned forward. "Really? Who?"

"She dated a kid in high school she really liked. He went on a mission, and after a few months, he wrote her a Dear Jane letter. I think it broke her heart. She told me she married Gene on the rebound. He and Rhett were as different as two men could be. Rhett Ketchum, that's the guy she liked. He's a champion bull rider these days. I've never met him, but she dragged me to a rodeo so she could point him out to me. She didn't attempt to contact him that night, but I could see even from a distance that I would tower over him. He's not very tall, and I am, but he's a handsome guy, I can tell you that. I can't blame her for wanting him back. Although, frankly, I'm not a religious person, and she would have had to make some big changes to ever get him to look at her again. She told me she would do that and do so gladly."

Max knew Charity had contacted Rhett by phone, but nevertheless, he asked Maddie, "Did she ever speak with the cowboy? Did she call him or go to see him or anything?"

"She did," Maddie said. "She called him on the phone several times, but he let her know he wasn't interested. Of course, he told her nicely. I think he's a real gentleman. I encouraged her to go see him in person, let him see she was changed. I thought maybe if he actually laid eyes on her again, the old spark might return. Charity is . . . was . . . a beautiful girl. But she didn't dare go see him."

"Did she see other men?" Max asked.

"Oh yeah, she dated a little. One guy from Heber, a cop by the name of Clayson, I don't remember his last name, called her all the time."

"Clayson Lebow," Max said.

"Yeah, that's the name. Charity said the guy was crazy about her. She'd gone out with him a time or two in high school, but then she and Rhett had begun to go steady, and he got squeezed out." Maddie was silent for a moment, and Max waited. She drummed her long fingers on her leg for a moment. Finally she spoke again. "He was in love with Charity. But she didn't want anything to do with him. She felt like Lebow was part of the reason Rhett didn't want to date her. Lebow told her Rhett was a creep and that he wasn't someone she should go out with. Charity didn't appreciate him saying that, and she told him so."

"Did Lebow ever come here to see her?" Max asked.

"He came twice, and both times, against her better judgment, she went to dinner with him. They even went to a movie after dinner on the second date. But she finally told him not to come back, that she wasn't interested."

"Did he?" Max asked.

"Come back, you mean?"

"Yes."

"Not that I knew of, but he kept calling her. She was thinking about getting her cell number changed. Tell me something, Max. Is it true her body was found in the cowboy's barn?"

"It was," Max said. "But she was brought in through the fields from the back."

"I'm sorry to ask this, but I do want to know, if you can tell me. How was she killed?" Maddie asked.

"She was strangled," he said, watching her face as the color drained away. She shuddered and wiped her eyes with a long index finger. "We don't know if she was brought there before or after she was strangled," Max continued. "If she was killed there, she didn't fight whoever brought her there. She was carried there. At this point we just don't know."

"I can help you with that," Maddie said. "She wasn't killed in the barn. No one could have carried her through any fields if she'd been alive. She would have fought every inch of the way."

"She had a great deal of alcohol in her system," Max said. "She could have been so drunk she passed out."

Maddie's long blonde hair began to sway as she shook her head back and forth. "No way. She'd quit drinking a few months before she left Gene. I know for a fact she didn't touch alcohol. She did when I first met her, but she hasn't drunk for a long time. I quit drinking myself about the same time. And in case you wonder, she wouldn't have been high on drugs either. She never used drugs. Even when she was married to Gene she didn't touch the stuff. He did, but she said she would never use with him, and I believe her. That was one of the things they fought about."

"Maddie, the autopsy showed a lot of alcohol in her system," Max said. "That is indisputable."

"She didn't drink it, I can promise you that. She had even started going to church again. I didn't go with her, but she went every Sunday," Maddie said. "She wanted to somehow get Rhett to notice her again. Seriously, she loved the guy. If she had alcohol in her, someone forced it down her throat."

"Would Gene do that?" Max asked.

"He would, I suppose. And if he couldn't do it alone, he could have gotten his best friend to help him," she said.

"His best friend?"

"Yeah, a creep by the name of Bernardo Growfield. He goes by Bernie. He's as big a creep as Gene. He hit on me one time, but I put him in his place. So he turned his attention to Charity," she said with a shudder.

"Maddie, did she ever date this Bernie fellow?"

"Good grief no, not that he wasn't trying to get her to. He practically stalked her," she said. "She worked at an office near the dealership where he sold cars. She said he used to walk by and look in the window where her desk was."

"And Gene was okay with that?" Max asked.

"Are you kidding me? Gene wanted her back. Bernie never let on he was interested in Charity. That would have made Gene angrier than ever."

"Angry enough to kill?"

"Yeah, I think he would have killed Bernie if he'd known what Bernie was up to, but I don't think he had any idea. Charity threatened to tell Gene if Bernie didn't leave her alone. He kind of backed off after that. The creepy guy."

"Maddie, someone wanted it to look like Rhett killed Charity. Would either Gene or Bernie be capable of that?"

"Without a doubt. I know they were both extremely jealous of Rhett, even though he wasn't interested in Charity. Although I think in time he would have been. She was a changed woman."

"Can you think of anyone else who might have been angry with either Charity or Rhett?" Max asked.

She pressed on her eyes. And for a long moment she seemed to be deep in thought. Finally she said, "I don't know, but there is this one cowboy who hated Rhett."

"A cowboy?" Max asked.

"Yes, a fellow bull rider."

"Do you know his name?" Max asked, his interest piqued.

"Only his first name. Cal was all I heard," Maddie answered.

"Tell me about him. How do you know he hated Rhett?"

Once again Maddie's long hair swayed gently as she slowly shook her head. "When I tell you Charity had it bad for Rhett Ketchum, I mean it. She wanted him so badly sometimes he was all she talked about. When the rodeos were close enough, she even went to watch him ride," Maddie said. "But she would not go see him face to face. Go figure, huh?"

"What about Cal?" Max pressed gently.

"Well, you know that rodeo I went to with her in July?"

Max nodded.

"We ran into this guy named Cal in the parking lot. We had walked past Rhett's truck. I think Charity hoped she would accidentally run into him, although she wouldn't admit it to me. But it was this other guy we saw instead. There was a woman with him, although she never approached us. The guy asked what we were doing looking in Rhett's windows. Charity really did do that. I'm not sure what she expected to see. Anyway, the guy asked her about it. She just said she was a friend of Rhett's. That she was proud of what a good rider he was."

"How did the guy react to that?" Max asked.

"He spit a stream of tobacco right onto Rhett's windshield, right where it would block Rhett's view from the driver seat," she said. "Charity was stunned. But I asked the guy what he did that for, and he said that if Rhett didn't cheat, he would beat him every time they rode.

"I made him mad when I said I didn't see how a guy could cheat riding bulls. I told him that either you had what it took or you didn't."

"Did he have a response to that?"

"Oh yeah. He said he knew for a fact that Rhett bribed the judges. I asked him how he knew it, and all he did then was spit again—right on my shoe. Then he grinned a dreadful grin and said, 'You just tell Rhett that Cal is onto him and I'll make him wish he wasn't so crooked.' Then he said something about how he was the best bull rider there ever was and walked off."

"I need to figure out who Cal is," Max said.

"I'm sure Rhett will know," Maddie said. "You can ask him."

"One more thing about Cal," Max said. "Did either of you tell him your name?"

Maddie tilted her head back for a moment and looked at the ceiling in thought. Finally she lowered her head. "Not intentionally, but as I think back to that night, I remember saying to Charity, before we knew Cal was watching us, 'Charity, why don't you wait right here until he shows up,' and she told me she was too chicken."

"I guess he might have been able to figure it out from there if he'd wanted to badly enough," Max suggested.

The color again drained from Maddie's pretty face. "Oh, Max. What if he killed her? It's my fault if he did."

"Maddie, you are not to blame, even if this guy is the killer. But let me ask you a couple more things about him."

"Okay," she said, blinking furiously.

Max could tell Maddie still felt guilty. "About how tall was Cal?"

"I am five-eleven. I would say Cal was about three inches shorter than me. Of course, that's hard to judge. He had a cowboy hat on."

"What color was the hat?" Max asked.

"Gray, why?"

"I just wondered," he said. "Did you happen to look at his feet? If so, could you guess what size boots he might wear?"

Maddie finally allowed herself to smile again. "Bigger than Rhett's. I know Rhett has small feet, because Charity mentioned that to me several times."

"And what about the woman who was with Cal?" Max asked.

"She was even taller than me, and big. Not fat, just really big."

Then Max thought of something else. "One more question about Cal. Do you have any idea what he was driving?" Max asked.

"Not a clue," Maddie said.

"Can you think of anyone else who might not have liked Charity or Rhett?"

She slowly shook her head. "No, I don't think so." Her hair flowed gently, and she frowned in thought. "Wait, there is someone else. How could I forget? There is a lady that used to work where Charity did. Charity talked about her a lot. The woman was a real witch. She was always trying to undercut Charity in one way or another. It all came to a head when Charity got a promotion and a raise. This woman was really angry. She said the only reason Charity got it and not her was that she was constantly flirting with the boss," Maddie said.

"Do you know what she looks like?" Max asked.

"Only from what Charity told me. She is—how do I say this—a big woman, I guess. Not fat, just big-boned. Her hands and feet are large. She's way bigger than their boss and rather plain. I know that's not very nice, but it's true, I'm afraid. She has long, stringy hair—I don't know how often she washes it. And her eyes are, well, I guess you could call them muddy brown. She never wore makeup of any kind, and she smelled bad. I don't think she had a clue what deodorant was for. She didn't wear lipstick, but Charity told me she was always putting ChapStick on. She was very jealous of Charity. And I just thought of something else. I wonder if that was who was with Cal that night. She was back in the shadows, so I didn't get a good look at her, but her size and build were the same. Anyway, this woman made such a fuss about Charity getting the promotion that she got herself fired. Yeah, I would say she hated Charity, and she's big enough she could have carried Charity across a bunch of fields."

"Do you know her name?" Max pressed as he let the ChapStick comment take root in his fertile brain.

"Oh yeah, sorry. Her name is Angel Affut. And I'm not kidding about *Angel*. She must have had parents who didn't have a clue, because she's no angel, I can tell you that," Maddie said.

"Do you know where she lives?" Max asked.

"Not a clue," Maddie said. "But Charity's boss might know. You can find him easily enough. It's next to the dealership I mentioned." She gave him the name of the business.

"You have been very helpful, Maddie. Can you think of anyone else?" Max asked.

She shook her head. "No."

"I'm sorry for your loss," Max said. "And thank you for your time." He handed her one of his cards. "If you think of anything else you think might help me, give me a call."

CHAPTER FIFTEEN

SARAH SERVED BLUEBERRY PIE FOR dessert. Patches sighed with satisfaction after finishing a delicious piece with a scoop of vanilla ice cream on top. She daintily dabbed at her lips with a napkin just in case any of the blue remained there. Then she took a drink of water. "What a wonderful meal, Sarah," she said with a smile.

"My mother is an excellent cook," Rhett said proudly. "For that matter, so is Susie."

"Would you like to go into the living room and visit with Rhett while Susie and I clean up?" Sarah asked.

She couldn't think of anything she'd rather do. But she said, "I'll help with the dishes, and then I need to get home and compare notes with Dad."

"I have a better idea, Mom," Rhett said with a sly grin. "Why don't you and Susie and the kids go relax. I'll help Patches."

Patches's heart raced. "That would be great, Rhett," she said.

"But, Patches, you are our guest," Sarah argued. "You don't need to slave away."

"Actually I'm an employee," Patches said, glancing at Rhett. "Employees are hired to help."

"But not to do dishes." It was Susie who protested this time.

"We'll talk about the case too," Patches said. "That's final."

The ladies reluctantly rounded up Susie's little ones and left the kitchen. "This is really nice of you, Patches," Rhett said as they began to gather dishes from the table.

She looked up. "I really do want to spend some time with you. And there are some things we need to talk about."

They got busy cleaning up the kitchen. A few minutes later, Patches's phone rang. She was tempted to ignore it. She was having such a relaxing time just being with Rhett. He was such a great guy. But Rhett said, "You'd better take that. It could be important."

"All right," she said reluctantly and plucked the phone from the countertop where she'd laid it earlier. One glance told her it was from her father. She touched the screen, put the phone to her ear, and said, "Hi, Dad. Did you learn anything helpful today?"

"I'll say I did," he said. "I have a lot to report. Are you still at the Ketchums'?"

"Yes," she said. "Why?"

"I need to ask Rhett something."

"Let me find him," she said, glancing meaningfully at Rhett. She called out, "Rhett, it's my dad. He has a question for you."

Rhett grinned, waited a moment, and then said, "Sure, what does he want?"

Patches put the phone to her ear again and said, "Do you need to speak to him, or can I put my phone on speaker?"

"Put it on speaker," her father said.

She did that and then put the phone on the counter near where the two of them were rinsing dishes and loading the dishwasher. "Okay, Dad, go ahead," Patches said.

"You two can keep doing the dishes while we talk," Max said.

"Dad, what . . . how . . ." she stammered.

Her dad chuckled. "Patches, my girl, surely you don't think your old papa is dumb, do you?"

"Of course not," she said as she caught Rhett's eye and grinned sheepishly.

"Your mother and I never raised you to be an actress, and you aren't very good at it."

"I guess not. But how did you know what we were doing?" she asked.

"I'm a detective, and detectives *detect* things. We raised you to be a hardworking, thoughtful girl. I assumed you would have offered. It's how you are, and your mom and I are proud of you for that. And it's not much of a leap to guess Rhett would want to help you," he said.

Rhett and Patches looked at each other sheepishly. Patches could hear a quiet chuckle on the phone. "Show-off," Patches teased. "We thought it would be a good chance to talk about the case."

"This is good timing then. First let me report what I learned in my interviews," Max said. He then named each person he had interviewed that day in the order in which he had interviewed them. "I didn't learn anything worth repeating from all but the last one. So let's talk about the woman who claims she was Charity's best friend. Her name is Maddie Rollinson. After speaking with her, I concluded she is not a suspect in the murder. Her grief is genuine, and so is her desire to assist us. Now," Max said, "I can play the recording I made of our interview while you're working if you'd like."

"Dad, you know we don't need to listen to the interview. Why don't you just tell us since it's all recorded in your brain," Patches said.

"Very well," Max said. "She believes Gene Gaffey and his best friend Bernie are capable of committing murder, of killing Charity. But she does not think they would both be involved—either one of the two, yes, but not both of them together. And let me explain why. After Charity and Gaffey divorced, Bernie tried to date Charity."

"You can't be serious," Patches protested.

"I'm afraid I am. However, Maddie says she knows for a fact that Charity didn't care one whit for the guy. He called her a lot when she refused to go out with him, even stalked her at her work, which was next door to where Bernie sells cars. Anyway, Charity's heart was elsewhere," he said.

"Oh? And where was that?" Patches asked as she placed a plate Rhett had just rinsed off and handed to her into the dishwasher.

"Rhett, I don't mean to embarrass you, but she only cared for one man," Max said. "She wanted you back, and according to Maddie, she had totally changed her life. Charity was going to church and did not drink or take any kind of drugs. She wanted desperately to win your heart."

"I told you and Patches about her calls," Rhett said. Then after a moment's hesitation, he said, "She had really changed?"

"According to Maddie. Would that have made a difference to you?" Max asked.

"Of course it would," he said, not meeting Patches's staring eyes. "But it would not have made me take her back. I would have encouraged her to look for someone else who was the kind of guy she wanted, someone as different from Gene as she could find."

Now he caught Patches's eyes. She blushed. She did that a lot, and it always made Rhett grin.

Max continued. "Maddie told me she tried to get Charity to go meet you in person, Rhett, that maybe that would make you change your mind about her."

"I'm glad she didn't," Rhett said as he rinsed another plate. "That would have been awkward."

"I think Charity knew that," Max said. "She went to your rodeos when they were close enough that she could. She even dragged Maddie off to a rodeo when you were riding here in Salt Lake. And not only that, the two of them found your truck in the parking lot."

"How did they know what I drove?" Rhett asked.

"For all I know, she may have driven by your house sometime. She knew your truck."

"Now I feel like a jerk," Rhett said. "But I didn't love her. I liked her, and I respected her and enjoyed being around her, but I didn't see her as an eternal companion. But because of me, she's dead."

"Please don't, Rhett," Patches said. "You cannot go blaming yourself."

Rhett shook his head with downcast eyes, and Max resumed talking over the phone. "Maddie and Charity were near your truck when a cowboy walked up." He then told them all that had happened and ended with, "Charity told Cal she was a friend of yours."

"I guess that could be true," Rhett mumbled as he handed the last plate to Patches and reached for a bowl.

"The guy said you were a bad person. And he spit a stream of tobacco juice on your windshield," Max reported.

"I remember that night. It was right where I had to look through the windshield to drive. I wondered how that had happened," Rhett said. "I didn't know what it was. I assumed it was just some big bird with bad aim, but I should've known. Cal always has a chew of tobacco in his mouth. His teeth are brown, and his breath is horrendous. That jerk!"

"I'd say you're right about that assessment," Max agreed. "Anyway, he told Maddie and Charity that he was the best bull rider there ever was and that the only way you were able to beat him was by cheating."

"What?! Cheating? I would never cheat. I never have, and I never will. I just ride better than he does," Rhett said as he almost slammed a dish into Patches's hand.

"Hey, I'm not the one who said you cheated," Patches said, but she grinned.

"Sorry," Rhett said. "But cheat? There's no way."

"This rider, Cal is the only name Maddie heard—" Max began again.

"Cal Thurley," Rhett interrupted. "I should have known. He hates me. I don't know how many times he's told me I just got lucky, that he always drew a tougher bull than me. But he never accused me of cheating, at least not to my face," Rhett said.

"That's what he told Charity and Maddie. He said you bribed the judges," Max revealed.

"What? I would never do that. If I were dishonest and stupid enough to even try, I would have been reported and banned from riding for the rest of my life," Rhett said, anger shooting from his eyes. His hands were empty now, so he didn't slam anything into Patches's hands. They had both stopped working and were staring at the phone on the counter.

"Cal told the girls he knew *for a fact* you bribed the judges. But when Maddie asked him how he knew it, he spit on her shoe and he and a tall, large woman who was with him left without another word," Max reported.

"He wouldn't have killed Charity," Rhett said firmly. "If Cal were going to kill someone, it would be me."

"Rhett, criminal minds don't work the way ours do. He knew who Charity was, and perhaps he killed her and tried to frame you just so you would go to prison and be unable to ride again. Who knows? That might have given him more satisfaction than killing you," Max reasoned.

"So we need to do some serious checking on Cal Thurley," Patches said. "He was one of the people on the list you gave me, Rhett, who I never did get ahold of."

"If he was at the rodeo, he couldn't have been in Heber to commit the crime," Max reasoned.

"I just remembered!" Rhett said. "He got disqualified the very first night. And I never saw him around after that."

"In that case, we add him to our suspect list. So far there is him, Gene Gaffey, and Bernie Growfield."

"Why Bernie?" Patches asked. "What was his motive?"

"Charity rebuffed him. That could have been enough motive right there. And he probably knew she yearned for you, Rhett," Max reasoned. "And speaking of Bernie, I feel bad I hurt his knee so severely."

"Why, Dad? He hit me," Patches protested hotly. "You had every right."

"No, I could have put him down without injuring him like that. I shouldn't have done it, and I am sorry I did."

"But he could be a killer," Patches objected.

"We don't know that yet, and we certainly didn't at that time. No, like I told you before, he reminds me of one of the guys who killed Cousin Sammy. I think Bernie got what I would like to give to those guys."

"We need to look closer at his background," Patches said thoughtfully. "Maybe there's a reason he reminds you of that guy."

"I'm sure there is. As soon as we find Charity's killer, I am going to look into that," he said.

"Maybe even before," she suggested. "We need to learn more about all three of the suspects."

"Four," Max said.

"Four?" Patches asked.

"Yes. Are you finished with the dishes?" Max asked.

Rhett quickly grabbed another bowl and began to rinse. "Not quite," Patches said, grinning at Rhett. "Now what's this about another suspect?"

"It's a woman," Max told them. "A very nasty woman."

"It couldn't have been a woman," Patches said. "The shoe size is too big."

"Possibly not for this woman," Max said. "Maddie described her as a big woman. Her name is Angel Affut, and she hated Charity." Max then told them all he'd learned about Angel and her possible connection to Cal, although he emphasized that the connection was mostly conjecture on Maddie's part.

"So she might have been able to carry Charity to the barn," Patches suggested. "But I'm not sure why she would want to frame Rhett."

"Wait a minute," Rhett said. "Max, you said Maddie told you Charity had changed her life and was going to church and not drinking. So how did the killer get her drunk enough for her to pass out?"

"I asked that same question to Maddie. She said whoever killed her must have forced the drink down her throat. Now I have a question for the medical examiner. I am going to call Jay Ackerman as soon as I hang up. I want to know if there were marks in her throat where something was shoved down it, perhaps a tube to pour alcohol into her stomach."

"Oh, the poor girl," Rhett said. Patches looked at him and could see he was hurting.

"I'm sorry, Rhett. It must be awful to hear about someone you cared for going through that," Patches said.

"I just hate to think how she must have suffered and how terrified she must have been."

"It's horrible to even think about," Patches agreed.

"I'm sorry, Rhett," Max said. "There's just one more thing. Patches, how did it go with the cameras? Did you find anything Deputy Lebow missed?"

"Deputy Lebow only checked on a few cameras, and he didn't even bother to get much of the footage copied to a thumb drive. I have a bunch, but I haven't had a chance to go over it all yet. I was going to take it to Detective Davis's apartment so we could go over it together. But then, of course, well, you know . . . Rhett getting shot and all," Patches said. "I need to get home now and study it myself."

"Patches, why don't you get a hotel room and do it right there in Heber. I think it's important we get any information the cameras might be able to provide as soon as possible," Max suggested. "You can work late, and if you have to, finish up in the morning."

"Okay, I can do that," she said. "And, Dad, maybe we should add a fifth name to our list of suspects."

"Deputy Lebow?" Max asked.

"Exactly," she agreed.

"Now that you mention him, I suppose that wouldn't be such a bad idea. I didn't mention this earlier, but according to Maddie he kept pestering Charity to go out with him. And I guess she actually did a couple of times. But she apparently made it clear she wasn't interested. And he constantly belittled you, Rhett. So, yes, he goes on the list, and we'll want to discreetly check into where he was at the time of the killing. And we'll have to do it without alerting the sheriff or his detectives until and unless we come up with something concrete." A moment later Max ended the call.

"Patches, I can help you look at the camera footage if you'd like me to," Rhett offered as soon as the call was over.

"You need to rest. You did get shot today," Patches reminded him.

Rhett shook his head. "It's nothing. I get hurt a lot worse than that riding bulls. I'd like to help, if you don't mind."

Just then Sarah walked into the kitchen. "Did I hear you guys on the phone with someone?" she asked.

"It was Patches's father. He had a lot to report and needed some information from me. We are almost done in here," Rhett said. "Then Patches needs to find a hotel room and do some work on the computer."

"What kind of work?" Sarah asked.

Rhett explained and told her he was going to help. "Two computers will be better than one," he explained. "But I'll need to borrow yours, if I can. Detective Ackerman has mine."

"Of course you can borrow it. Why don't you two work here. We'll keep the kids out of your way, and you can work just fine."

"That would be nice," Patches said. She turned to Rhett and said, "If I could borrow a phone book, I'll make a reservation for a room so I can be sure to get one if we go kind of late."

"Oh my goodness, Patches," Sarah began. "This is a big house. Even with Susie and her little ones here, there are empty rooms. Why don't you stay with us. It will be comfortable. And you can have breakfast with us in the morning."

"Yeah, Patches, that's a good idea. You'll stay, won't you?" Rhett asked with a pleading look in his eyes.

"If you're sure it won't be too much trouble," she said, liking the idea a lot. "I keep an overnight bag in the truck. Dad and I both do that because we never know when we are going to need to stay somewhere."

"It is no trouble at all," Rhett's mother said. "I'll get a room ready for you, and you two can go to work. You can use the dining room table if you want. It doesn't get much use. Or you can work right here in the kitchen if you'd prefer to."

"Probably the dining room," Rhett said. "I'll get your laptop, Mom."

Ten minutes later, Patches and Rhett were seated side by side at the dining room table. Patches quickly burned a second thumb drive for Rhett. "I'll start in the middle if you want to start at the beginning," she said.

"We are looking for a gray sports car with out-of-state plates?" Rhett clarified.

"Since one of our suspects drives a silver Charger, I'd say let's look for both gray and silver. I have the license-plate number of Bernie's car," Patches explained. "If he was in town at the time of the murder, we'll be a lot closer to where we need to be to solve this thing. And even if we get a silver Charger with Utah plates, let's look closer. Who knows? He might have switched plates."

"And the driver will most likely be wearing a gray Stetson," Rhett said.

"A felt cowboy hat at least. I don't suppose everyone wears Stetsons," she kidded.

"Just us real cowboys," Rhett joked back. Then, with a serious face, he looked across the table at her and said, "Cal Thurley wears a gray hat. Just saying."

"That figures," Patches said.

They had barely begun the tedious task of reviewing the camera footage when Patches's cell phone rang. "Hi, Dad," she answered. "Did you get in touch with Detective Ackerman?"

"I did, and he is quite upset with Deputy Lebow."

"He should be. Rhett is helping me review the footage. His mother insisted I stay here. With the two of us working, it should go a lot quicker," Patches said.

"That's good, but is Rhett up to it? He did take a bullet today," Max said.

"He says he gets hurt a lot worse riding bulls. If he gets too worn out, I'll make him quit," she promised.

"I'll talk to you in the morning and see what you found," Max said.

The next hour was spent with almost no conversation between the young private detective and her client. Rhett got up and stretched.

"Are you about done in?" Patches asked quickly.

"No, but when you get bounced around like I do, the joints and muscles need to be stretched occasionally. I'm fine."

"I know this is boring," Patches said. "You'd be surprised how much time my parents and I spend doing tedious work like this."

"I don't mind, but I don't think I could do it day in and day out. I prefer the excitement of bucking bulls and the calming work of the ranch," he responded as he sat back down again.

Patches was looking over at him with a very serious expression on her face. She said softly, "Rhett, would you mind if we have a prayer? I think we'll have better success if we pray."

"Why don't you say it," he suggested.

"Or you could." She smiled at him.

"It was your idea, and a good one. Please, you pray for us," he said. So she did.

For a few more minutes after that, they worked in silence. Then Rhett said, "I've got something here." He slid his mother's laptop closer to Patches's. "It's a gray car, a small one."

"Let's see if we can enlarge it a little," Patches suggested.

"I don't think I can on my mom's computer."

"We can on mine," she said. "Let's mark the spot and slip it into this port here," she said, pointing at an empty one on her computer. It only took a minute to get to the spot on her computer. She zoomed in and said, "I can't quite determine the make."

He leaned so close to her that their heads were almost touching, and she had to fight to keep her attention on the computer. She liked having him so close. She wondered about him, and then she thought about Kori and remembered that Rhett was bringing her flowers when he'd gotten shot, and she felt a wave of sadness. But she concentrated on the picture in front of her and tried to ignore the warmth from his closeness.

Rhett pointed to the screen. "Out-of-state plates," he said. "Can you make it a little larger?"

"I can, but it could begin to get a little fuzzy," she said.

As she enlarged the picture, they both leaned closer until their heads touched. "Okay. There, I think I can make it out now," Patches said as she studied it closely. "California, isn't it?"

"I think so, but I can't make out the number."

"I'll mark this spot," Patches said. "Let's move on a little ways and see if we can get a view of the driver."

But the car simply drove out of the camera's view. "I guess that's all we're going to get. But it probably doesn't matter," Rhett said. "If it were Cal Thurley, it would have Colorado plates. That's where he's from. The truck he drives to the rodeos has Colorado plates; I'm sure of it."

Patches sat back and grinned.

"What?" Rhett asked.

"California plates or not, we know the time that car was on the camera. All we need to do now is see if we can find it on another camera in the same general area at about the same time," she said.

"You can do that?" he asked.

"Of course," she said, and he watched as she began to search. "Here we go," she said a minute later. She zoomed. "It's a woman," she said. "And there is no hat."

"It could be Charity's coworker Angel," Rhett suggested.

"We'll mark this spot too," she said. "Then we'll look for some more in the same time frame."

Ten minutes later the same car showed up in the parking lot of a local grocery store. They watched the driver get out. "Not her," Patches said. "She's no bigger than I am. But we do have the license-plate number. I'll mark this spot just in case, and then we'll begin again where we were."

It was a half hour later when Patches found something of interest. "Hey, Rhett, this car is silver, and it's a Dodge Charger." Once again, she zoomed in. "Utah plates," she said.

Both their heads were touching again, distracting Patches. She wondered if Rhett was distracted. *Probably not,* she told herself. This investigation was very personal to him, and there was no way he would be thinking silly thoughts like she was, while facing the possibility of being charged with murder. It only took her a few minutes to find the same car on another camera, and this time she got the license number of the Utah plates.

"Gotcha," Patches said. They both leaned back, and Rhett looked at her with a furrowed brow. "I know that number," she explained. "That's the car that was parked in the driveway at Bernardo Growfield's home when my dad busted the guy's kneecap. We checked the number, and it is registered to him. He was in town. This is a huge find."

"So that's it?" Rhett asked.

"Not so fast, Cowboy," she said. "I'd still like to see the driver." So once again she searched other cameras in a similar time frame. "Here we go," she said. She zoomed in. "I think it is Mr. Growfield," she said as she marked the spot. "But no cowboy hat."

"It's probably on the seat of the car," Rhett said.

"Or in the trunk. Or it isn't him," she said.

"But it's got to be," he said. "You found your man."

"We're closer," she said. "But we're not there yet." She searched some more and found the same car on several other shots. She marked each one.

"Are we finished now?" Rhett asked.

"If you need to get to bed, go ahead," she said. "But I want to keep looking for a while. I already know there are some other spots with gray cars on them. That's why I copied the ones I did."

"If you keep at it, so will I," he said decisively.

It wasn't long before they had another gray sports car on the screen, but they soon eliminated it. The same thing happened three more times. But the next one was different. This time, when they zoomed in, they discovered Colorado plates. "So is that Cal?" he asked. "Why would two of the suspects be here?"

Patches shrugged. "Anyone can come to Heber. Neither one of these may mean anything. But then again, who knows?" She marked this one and then found the Colorado car several other times. And in one, the driver was getting out at a café.

They leaned forward, and suddenly it was Rhett who said, "Gotcha. That guy right there is Cal Thurley."

They found him on the footage a few more times and marked each one. Then Rhett said, "So now we've got it, don't we?"

"Maybe, but I still have more checking to do," she said.

"Why?"

"Because I saw other gray and silver cars, or I wouldn't have collected this much footage," she said.

"All right, slave driver," he said with a chuckle. "Let's keep working."

Patches became increasingly tired, and Rhett, she could tell, was also ready to get some rest, but they continued to search over the next two hours and finally reached the end. She noted the time on the computer. "It's after eleven," she said. "And we've got all we're going to get."

"So it's down to those two suspects," Rhett said.

"Maybe, maybe not. But I have more work to do in the morning. I need to go back to all the camera locations and see what I can find," she said.

Rhett looked puzzled. "Why?" he asked.

"Your sore neck is why," she said with a tired smile.

"Oh," he said with a drawl. "But what if whoever shot me isn't driving either one of these two cars? I didn't see the car of whoever shot me very well. I mean, I don't think I did. Maybe it was one of the other gray cars."

"This is a process of elimination," she said. "If it was either one of these guys again, and if they were in the same cars we located here tonight, it will help us a lot. And if it wasn't, we'll go back and look closer at those other gray cars. But I am quite confident we will find either Cal's or Bernie's. For now I'm ready for some sleep, and I know you are too. You look like you're about to drop."

Rhett nodded with a tired smile. "I feel like it, too. And thanks, Patches."

"For what?" she asked.

"For praying. It helped."

***

By shortly after six the next morning, Rhett was rested, dressed, and headed out to check his animals. He didn't see Patches but said hi to his mother, who was already working in the kitchen. "Patches is showering in the basement," she said. "I'll tell you what I told her. Breakfast will be ready at seven."

"I'll be back in by then," he said.

He went out the back door, did some chores, petted the dog, and then walked around the front of the house where he had left his truck. Patches's truck was next to it, and beyond that was Susie's yellow Nissan. He was about to head for the house when he noticed that there was a paper taped to the windshield of his truck.

His stomach twisted. He walked over and reached for the paper. He pulled it off and read the words scrawled in ink. The twist in his stomach began to roll around. He felt nauseous, and a chill brought goose bumps to his arms.

He looked all around, knowing he would see no one. Then he walked slowly back to the house. Would this nightmare never end? And, if it did, would he be alive to witness that ending? Bulls were frightening animals, but the fear he felt each time he got down in the chute onto one was healthy fear. It was the kind of fear that helped him to be successful. But the fear he felt now was not that kind of fear. It was gut-wrenching. And he couldn't control the events that were causing it.

CHAPTER SIXTEEN

PATCHES WAS SITTING IN THE kitchen visiting with Rhett's mother when Rhett walked in with a sheet of paper in his hand. Patches took one look at his face and knew something was wrong. But before she could say a word, Sarah said, "Rhett, you are as white as a sheet. What's the matter?"

He waved the piece of paper toward them. "This is the matter," he said, his voice strained.

He collapsed into one of the chairs at the table and dropped the sheet of paper in front of him. Sarah reached for the paper, but Patches said, "Don't touch it."

Sarah jerked her hand back. Just then Susie walked in, her baby in her arms. "What's going on in here? Rhett?" she asked.

Rhett pointed to the paper. Then he looked up at his mother. "I think Patches wants to be able to check this for fingerprints. Mine are on it. I didn't even think. Sorry, Patches."

"It's okay. We can soon eliminate your prints from any others that are on there," she said. "I'm sorry, Sarah. I was rude."

"It's okay. I'm just glad you're here. But I do want to know what's on that paper that has my brave son so shaken," Sarah said.

"I have some latex gloves in my truck," Patches said. "I'll run and grab them and put them on before I touch it."

"I have some right here in the cupboard," Sarah said. "You sit there, and I'll grab a pair for you."

A minute later Patches picked up the note. The others gathered around her as she read it aloud. "It says, *Rhett, your day is coming. I will get you for what you did. It's you I need to kill, not Kori, but if I have to kill her to get your attention I will. Next time you will not see me coming.* It's unsigned. But, as you can see, it is handwritten. This will help us a lot."

"Rhett," Sarah said with a catch in her voice. "You need to leave—go somewhere no one can find you until this guy's caught."

"I can't do that. He'll just go after Kori again," he said.

"Then you both need to go somewhere," Susie chipped in.

"I'm calling Detective Ackerman right now," Patches said. "There is no way anyone is going to get hurt."

A moment later she had Jay on the phone. She quickly explained about the note. "I'll be there as fast as I can," he said. "And I'll call the officer at the hospital and tell him to make sure no one gets near Kori."

In a few minutes Patches, who was watching through a window, saw Jay Ackerman's SUV pass beneath the ranch sign and then slide to a stop behind the other vehicles out front. Before he even reached the door, Sheriff McCoy also arrived. Jay waited while the sheriff jogged up to the porch, but before they could knock, Sarah Ketchum opened the door.

A calm determination had come over her. And she said, "Thank you for coming, officers. We are sorry to bother you so early this morning."

"It's just fine, Sarah," Sheriff McCoy said. "I'm sorry you folks are being harassed the way you are. We will get to the bottom of this, and I can assure you that neither your son nor Deputy Davis will be hurt again. They will be protected."

"Thank you, Sheriff. The note is on the kitchen table."

"I touched it, Sheriff," Rhett said as he looked up from the table where he'd been sitting since bringing the note in. "But Patches made sure no one else did."

"It's not a problem," Sheriff McCoy said. "We can isolate your prints from any others that may be there."

Detective Ackerman had already pulled on a pair of latex gloves. He picked up the note just as Susie's two older kids, both younger than five years old, came running in complaining that they were hungry. Susie said, "We are busy here. Why don't we go into the family room, and I'll put a movie on for you. I'll bring you some toast in a minute."

The detective read the note out loud. The sheriff frowned. "Whoever wrote this certainly doesn't like you," he said to Rhett.

Patches spoke up then from where she was standing near the kitchen door. "Sheriff, Detective, my father and I have developed a list of five suspects. Maybe you already know about them. At any rate, I can explain whatever you need to know about each of them if you'd like me to."

Jay asked, "I don't suppose you've had a chance to look at the camera footage you gathered yesterday, have you?"

"Rhett and I went through it last night. Two of the suspects Dad and I have identified were in town near the time Kori was shot. And I plan to go back and see what I can get from the cameras from yesterday when Rhett was shot."

"I was just nicked," he said, looking up from the table.

"Yes, and an inch or so difference could have killed you," Patches reminded him. Then she turned back to the officers. "Gene Gaffey's best friend, Bernie Growfield, was driving his silver Dodge Charger in town."

"He is the guy your father kicked in the kneecap?" Jay asked.

"That's right."

"Are you sure it was him?" the sheriff asked.

"Absolutely. The license plate was the one that was on that same car in his driveway when Dad and I had our little talk with him," she revealed.

"Silver?" Jay said. "I suppose Polly could have seen silver and thought gray."

"That's what we think. But there was another guy in town. He has a flashy gray sports car with Colorado plates," she said.

"Do you have any idea who he is?" Jay asked.

"His name is Cal Thurley. He's a bull rider who has it in for Rhett."

"Explain," Jay said.

So Patches relayed to the officers what her father had learned from Maddie Rollinson about Cal Thurley.

"And he was in town?" Sheriff McCoy asked. "Are you sure?"

"It was him," Rhett said. "And he could have been here when Charity was murdered. He was eliminated early in the competition, and I didn't see him after that."

"Dad and I will check with the same people we talked to about Rhett being at the rodeo when Charity was killed. They can probably help us confirm that Cal had left," Patches said.

Jay made some notes. Then he said, "Patches, it sounds like you and your father have been busy. Will you bring me up to date on the other people you suspect and why?"

Over the next hour there was a lot of back-and-forth about the various suspects Patches and her father had identified. But she saved the touchiest for last. And it was the sheriff who prompted her to tell them who it was.

He asked, "You said you have five suspects. You've mentioned four. There is Gene Gaffey, the wife-beating ex-husband. And, of course, there is his best friend, Bernie Growfield. Growfield sure seems like one we need to take a serious look at. Then there is the cowboy, Cal Thurley. Why would he be here in Heber, unless this is the way he drives to and from Colorado? Rhett, do you know where in Colorado he lives?"

"I'm pretty sure it's Grand Junction," Rhett said.

The sheriff slowly nodded his head. "So I-70 would be the more likely way he would travel. But he was here in Heber. That makes him a very serious suspect. Okay, then there is the Amazon, the big woman who hated Charity. What did you say her name is?"

Jay, who had written it all down, said, "Angel Affut."

"Right. Okay, so those are four. Who is the fifth?" Sheriff McCoy asked.

Patches looked at Rhett. He shrugged and nodded his head. Then she said, "I know you guys won't like this, but Dad and I worry about Deputy Lebow." She hesitated briefly, expecting an explosion from his colleagues or at the least a strong protest. But it didn't come. So she said, "I suppose you guys must trust him, or he wouldn't be part of the investigative team."

Jay and the sheriff looked at each other for a moment. Jay said, "This is yours, Sheriff. I'll let you tell them."

The sheriff nodded. "You're right. I did team him up with Detective Ackerman. Partly it was because I didn't want to use any of the other detectives because of their current caseloads. But when Lebow came in and told me he would like to help and that he was unbiased and would stay that way, I decided to talk to Jay about it. We agreed that if he was working with Jay, he could keep him on a short leash and have an idea what, if anything, he was up to. In the meantime, he might be able to do some legwork that would save Jay some time."

Patches spoke up then. "As I have proven, Clayson said he'd checked all the cameras and found very little, but he did not check most of them. I checked every one I could find in town, and you already know what I found."

Jay took a deep breath. Then he said, "And Lebow went back out to Polly Weeks's place and interrogated her again. She called me after he left. She was very upset; it sounded like she was in tears. She said Clayson berated her for changing her story from the shooter driving a gray pickup to a gray car. She claims he told her if she didn't straighten that out and tell us it was a pickup that she would be charged with giving false information to a police officer."

Patches asked, "So did she change her story back?"

"No, she did not," Detective Ackerman said. "She says she knows what she saw. Well, let me clarify that. She said it could have been silver, that the colors were pretty close. She asked me if that was a problem. I told her it wasn't. Then she said she knew it was a car, that when Sheriff McCoy spoke with her at the scene she was so upset she couldn't think clearly."

"Which is what she told me," Patches said.

"Yes, but get this: After that she asked me if she was going to be arrested. And I don't mean over the similarity of silver and gray vehicles. She was worried about Clayson and his threat since she was not willing to say it was a pickup."

Sheriff McCoy cleared his throat. Everyone looked expectantly at him. "I guess you all probably wonder what I am going to do about him." No one responded, so he continued. "At this point there is nothing more I can do. I fired him last night. Now I'm short a deputy and someone to help Detective Ackerman."

"I'm sorry, Sheriff," Rhett said. "But I have confidence in Detective Ackerman."

"Despite my being such an idiot after Kori was shot?" Jay asked. "I'm truly sorry."

"Hey, you were just doing the best you could with the information you had," Rhett said. "I don't hold it against you."

"Thanks, Rhett," Jay said. "And I can assure you I will do the best I can to catch whoever is behind all this nonsense. But I guess I'll have to do it by myself."

Sheriff McCoy cleared his throat again, and all eyes once again turned to him. "Seems to me like the best help we've had so far has come from Miss Fisher and her father." He looked directly at Patches. "I know this is unusual, Patches, but if you ever want to go to the police academy and become a deputy, I'll find a position for you in my department." He chuckled. "In the meantime, Jay, even though this is also very unusual, I would suggest you work closely with Short Investigations Agency."

Jay nodded. "We wouldn't be where we are without them. I totally agree."

"I know something I can do, something I already planned to do sometime this morning that might help," Patches said. "I want to check the cameras again. I'll be really surprised if I don't find that either Cal's gray sports car or Bernie's silver Charger were in the area around the time of the shooting yesterday. And I also wonder if it wouldn't be interesting to figure out what Clayson Lebow was doing last night. Sheriff, what time did you fire him, and when you did, did you relieve him of his sheriff department vehicle?"

"Yes, I did. I took his badge, his ID, his department weapons, and his patrol vehicle. He left the office as an unemployed man around eight last night," the sheriff said. "And, Patches, I would personally appreciate it if you would check the cameras and then let Jay know what you learn."

"I'll get right on it. And is it okay if Rhett helps me go through them like he did last night?" she asked.

The sheriff ran his hand across his chin before saying, "Well, it would be, but I think he needs to go somewhere that will be safer than staying in Heber. I also plan to move Deputy Davis someplace where she will be safe."

A stab of jealousy went through Patches when Rhett said, "Maybe I could take her some place and settle her into a hotel. Then I really should go to a rodeo I am signed up for Tuesday night. The last I checked, Cal Thurley had not signed up for it. And I won't advertise to anyone where it is or that I've gone there."

"But you will tell us, won't you?" the sheriff asked.

"Sure, as long as you don't tell anyone else. And I'll also let my mother and the Fishers know," he said. "It's in Des Moines, Iowa."

"Okay, we won't let anyone else know," Sheriff McCoy said. "Kori can be released from the hospital today. I'll provide her with a new cell phone that no one can connect her to and would suggest you get a new one, too, Rhett. I know you already did, but I mean another one. Just keep in touch with Detective Ackerman on the new phone. Let him know where you and Kori are from time to time. My first concern right now is for the safety of the two of you." He gave Rhett a searching look. "Are you sure you should be riding bulls so soon after taking that bullet yesterday?"

Rhett chuckled. "It's still a few days, but I've ridden with far worse injuries. I'll be fine." He turned to Patches. "Sorry, Patches. I'd love to help you, but I don't have much of a hankering to get shot again. And I sure don't like to think Kori is in danger. But, of course, I'll give you my new cell number as soon as I obtain one and leave my old *new* one here at the house."

Patches was fighting to keep her emotions in check. She was glad Rhett would be out of harm's way, but . . . She thrust the thought aside. And then she said, "I have a phone in the car you can use. We keep several inexpensive phones for this very purpose. There's no need for you to buy one. I'll go get it right now, and then I'd better get to work checking all those cameras."

Rhett moved to follow her from the room, but the sheriff stopped him. "Rhett, I think it would be best if you left your truck here. I will arrange for one you can borrow for a few days. It's the least I can do if you are willing to help Deputy Davis."

Patches stopped at the door. "That's a good idea," she said. "Thanks, Sheriff." Then she opened the door. Rhett hurried out behind her, and they walked together to her truck. She got the phone out of a duffel bag that was under the back seat. "Here you go. And here's a charger. The number is taped to the back. You may want to make sure you have all the numbers you need entered into it before you leave."

Rhett moved close to her before he said, "Patches. You are a gem. Thanks for what you're doing for me."

"It's my job," she said with a catch in her voice. "You are paying me to help you."

He touched her cheek and kept his fingers there. "But you are going the extra mile. Thank you. And just in case you would be interested in knowing this, I am your biggest fan." He smiled. She blushed. "You be careful. I'm not the only one in danger. You have put yourself right in the middle of this thing, and I fear our shooter knows it. I would be absolutely devastated if you were hurt helping me."

Patches took a deep breath before she responded. Then she said, "Thank you, Rhett. I'll be very careful. And you are my favorite cowboy, but you are also my favorite client. You be careful too. You may need my services again sometime."

She sort of hoped so. She liked him way too much. "I need to grab my bag and my laptop, and then I'd better get to work," she said.

"Wait," Rhett said. "Maybe we could have another prayer. That sure did help us last night."

"It's your turn," Patches said. After he had finished, they walked back into the house together. After she'd gathered up her things and thanked Sarah for her hospitality, she was ready to leave. But Susie stopped her as she headed toward the door. "Patches, if you'd like, I'll borrow Mom's laptop and help you like Rhett did last night."

"Really?" Patches asked. "That would be great. I'll let you know if I find anything I need to look at closer. If I do, I'd welcome your assistance."

"Then you can count on me."

"Thanks, Susie," Rhett said. "I don't feel so bad about leaving now." He turned to Patches. "Susie is a lot smarter than me. She'll be a big help to you."

***

It was less than an hour later when Sheriff McCoy and Jay Ackerman delivered a loaner truck to Rhett. "No one in the department but the two of us know you have this vehicle or where you and Kori are going. No one even knows the two of you are leaving. Would you like to leave your truck out front here, or do you want to put it in your garage or barn?"

"I think it would be best to leave it here in front. I want people to think I'm home, that I'm hiding in the house or on the ranch. I'll leave the keys with Mom in case she needs it or wants to just move it around to give the impression I am using it. I don't want anyone thinking I've left town," Rhett responded.

"That's best. Now, about Kori Davis," the sheriff said. "I am going to have Jay take her to Park City. She will go into the lobby of a hotel there. She won't check in. She'll let you know which one she's at, and she will wait there. Then you can pick her up and head east toward Iowa. Just to be on the safe side, you might want to meet her at a back entrance."

"I can do that. Jay, how soon are you leaving to pick Kori up?" Rhett asked.

"As soon as I get back to the office," Jay said. "And I will head straight to Park City with her."

"What if someone follows you?" Rhett asked.

"I'll stay out of sight and watch for anyone who might try to follow me. And I think I'll hide my SUV and wait with her in the hotel until you get there. I kind of want our shooter to think we are trying to hide her there if they do happen to see me with her. It will make it easier for you to hide her somewhere else without being discovered."

"In that case I think I'll leave now. I'll hang around Park City until I get her call," Rhett said.

It was barely an hour later when Kori called him. "I'm ready to go," she said. She told him which hotel she was at, and he told her he could be there in five minutes and that he would like to meet her inside the back door.

"As soon as we are in the loaner truck, Jay can go."

"Okay," she said. "And, Rhett, thanks. You don't have to do this."

"I don't mind at all. I want you to be safe."

CHAPTER SEVENTEEN

RHETT CARRIED KORI'S SUITCASE FROM the hotel and placed it in the back seat of the truck after helping her into the front. Then he climbed in and buckled his seatbelt. "Well, Deputy Davis, I guess we're off."

She looked at him, scrunching her eyebrows. "The sheriff told me that you would tell me where we're going after we were on our way."

"I know where I need to end up, but I'm not sure where I'll leave you. My rodeo is in Des Moines, but I don't know what route we'll take to get there. And when I leave you somewhere I want to be sure it isn't someplace anyone might be able to figure out. It will probably be near where I'm staying in Des Moines just in case you need me. I might even pick you up when my rodeo is over and move you someplace closer to home, unless your bosses catch the guy who's after us first."

"Or woman," Kori said. "While we were driving here from Heber, Jay filled me in on what's going on with the case. I've got to hand it to Max and Patches Fisher. They are outstanding investigators."

"So are you. I wish you could have stayed on this case," Rhett said. "I think you would have figured things out. I can't help but wonder if you were shot because you were getting too close to the truth."

Kori smiled over at him. "That's sweet, Shorty, but I have a lot to learn. I don't know that I was close, but I was able, with the help of others, to show that it wasn't you. I was really looking forward to learning from Jay on this case, but I guess it is what it is," she said.

"I ride Tuesday evening and then again Wednesday. We have plenty of time before I need to be there, so we'll take a roundabout route. We will have a few chances to eat together." He grinned. "We might think of this as a date."

"That's nice. But Patches—I know you like her," she said wistfully.

Rhett chuckled. "I like both of you. At this point, Patches and I are just friends."

"Then I guess I'll enjoy your company while I can," Kori said. "I do like you, a lot."

He smiled.

"You shouldn't be riding bulls, Shorty. You got shot too," she said a moment later with a worried expression entering her eyes.

"The sheriff said something about me taking a bullet. But I did nothing of the sort," he said with a grin. "The bullet only nicked me as it passed through my truck. It didn't even break any glass since I had my windows down. I'm fine."

"Are you sure?" she asked. "You had to have stitches."

"I wouldn't ride if I wasn't up to it," he said. "Don't worry about me. Now you, you did get hurt badly. It'll be good for you to be able to rest up and heal without having to worry about Cal or Bernie or . . . or . . ." He looked over at her.

"What?" she asked. "Who else were you thinking?"

"Well, there is also Gaffey and that woman, the one the sheriff calls an Amazon," he said.

"Yes, but the ones we know were in town are Cal and Bernie. What is that woman's name?" Kori asked. "Jay didn't tell me."

"Her name is Angel Affut—doesn't fit in the least, does it?"

"Seriously?"

"Yeah and I guess she's quite a piece of work. Maybe she was cute when she was born. But if so, she grew out of it," Rhett said. "She is certainly no angel."

"Jay mentioned another suspect," Kori said. "What about Clayson Lebow?"

"I hate to even think it," Rhett said.

"Well, think it. I certainly feel he's dangerous," Kori said with a touch of bitterness in her voice.

"I've been thinking about the note on my windshield, Kori. I wonder if it could have been him who wrote it. Patches is going to see if he shows up on any of the cameras after the sheriff fired him last night."

"What did you just say?" she asked with a look of shock on her face.

"Oh, I'm sorry. Maybe I wasn't supposed to say anything. I just assumed the sheriff or Jay told you."

"Sheriff McCoy fired him?" she asked. "Why?"

"Please don't tell them you heard this from me, just in case they didn't want you to know yet," Rhett said. "But Lebow stepped way over the line. You knew he was going to talk to Polly Weeks, didn't you?"

"Yes, and it made me mad. Patches had already talked to her, and she had it right. Jay admitted that to me," Kori responded. "He said Polly told him she was so rattled she simply didn't remember things clearly until later. Shorty, did something happen when Clayson talked to her?"

"You could say that. He did everything he could to get her to say it was a gray truck rather than a gray car. She refused, told him she knew what she'd seen. So he threatened to have her arrested for giving false information to a police officer," Rhett explained.

"Oh no. How did the sheriff find out he'd done that?"

"Polly called Jay and asked him if she was going to be arrested. That was the straw that broke the proverbial camel's back. He's finished with law enforcement. And in a way it's a shame. He could have probably made a decent officer. But the sheriff did what he felt like he had to do and fired him. He took his weapons, badge, vehicle, the works."

"He must be livid," Kori said.

"I would guess," Rhett agreed. "So that's the main reason I wonder if he left the note. It was handwritten, which was stupid of him, or of whoever wrote the note."

"Good grief," Kori said. "Whoever it was, the handwriting can be compared and matched."

"Probably," Rhett said.

"Or someone could have done it for him."

"Or her. We still don't know what Angel Affut drives. Maybe she's been in town too. Maybe it's one big conspiracy."

Kori gave him a questioning look, cocking one eyebrow. "You don't mean that, do you?"

"No, I was just trying to be funny. But someone, and I think it's one of the five people Patches and her father have identified, killed Charity and shot you and me," Rhett said. "But I don't think we should rule out any two or three of them working together."

"I suppose there could still be someone else out there we haven't figured out yet," Kori countered.

"That's possible, I guess. I'll tell you one thing, Kori. If it is someone else entirely, Max Fisher will figure it out. He's one sharp guy."

"His daughter is sharp too, Shorty."

"I can't disagree. I'm lucky my attorney steered me in their direction."

"She's pretty," Kori said.

"Angel Affut? I don't think so."

"No, you idiot. You know exactly who I mean. Patches is pretty."

"So are you," Rhett said, causing Kori to blush.

They rode in relative silence after that, and when they did talk it was about their families or memories from school or the state of the nation—generic things.

***

While Max began to dig deeper into the lives and backgrounds of some of the suspects, Patches worked hard at the cameras. She found that both Cal's car and Bernie's may have been in town again around the time someone had shot Rhett. Patches would have to check the images closer, enlarge them, to be sure. But she thought it was strange. She wondered why it couldn't just be one of them she kept seeing. It would make things easier if they could narrow their focus. They had too many suspects. *Poor Rhett,* she thought. How could such a nice guy have so many enemies?

What was most disturbing to her was that Clayson Lebow had been out and about until well after midnight. Patches called Susie and told her she would be there as soon as she'd eaten lunch.

"You will eat lunch with us," Susie said. It was not a question. "Mom has been keeping herself busy cooking. There is plenty."

"Are you sure? That's too nice."

"Yes. We'll expect you in a few minutes."

"In that case, I'll be there."

After lunch Sarah took her grandkids to town for ice cream, and Susie and Patches went to work on the computers. As soon as they were sure the cars in question were indeed the same ones that had been there around the time Charity was killed, Patches called Jay and reported what they'd learned.

"Good work, Patches. You are saving me a lot of time. I've been to the crime lab again. It took me a long time earlier today, but I found the bullet that creased Rhett. It was lodged in that pine tree in front of Kori's duplex. I took it in to the lab to have it compared to the one that hit Kori; I want to make sure we only have one shooter," he said.

"That would be good. I was just thinking how frustrating it is to have so many suspects. It would be nice to be able to narrow it down," Patches said. "I don't suppose they have anything back yet on the ChapStick, do they?"

"That's going to take a little longer," he reported. "It takes time with DNA, although it's a lot faster than it used to be. As we feared, fingerprints on it were out of the question."

"I figured that. My dad is planning to talk to Angel Affut this afternoon, if he can find her. He's been doing some background and trying to determine the movements of Gaffey and Growfield yesterday. I don't know what he's learned yet, but when I do I'll let you know. Anyway, he plans to find a way to get something that has Angel's DNA on it."

"That would be helpful. As soon as I get back to Heber, I'm going to try to find out if Cal Thurley stayed in a motel in town. It's a long shot, but perhaps I could find something that might have his DNA on it as well."

"If he stayed last night, maybe the maids haven't cleaned his room yet," Patches suggested.

"That's what I'm hoping for," Jay told her. "I wish now I would have done that before looking for the bullet. There's just so much that needs to be done. I want you to know I really value your help and your father's."

"I'm just glad we can help, Detective," Patches said sincerely.

"I also took the note from Rhett's truck so it could be compared to Clayson's handwriting,"

"Dad is working on that too. He was going to visit the places where Bernie and Gaffey work. He will have some handwriting for you from both of them," Patches reported.

"That's great. I suppose he'll find handwriting of Angel's too."

"I'm sure he will."

"Great. Well, I'm heading back to Heber now," Jay said. "I am anxious to find out if Cal stayed in town. As I think about it, it won't take me much longer to find out if Bernie stayed in town too."

"Do you have a picture of Angel?" Patches asked. "Maybe you could ask about her as well."

"That's a great idea. I have her driver's license picture, along with Cal's, Bernie's, and Gene Gaffey's. People here know him since he's from here, but I think I'll show all four pictures at the various motels in town," Jay said.

Susie had taken a break while Patches was on the phone. She returned as soon as she heard Patches finish her call. They both sat down at the computers again and documented the places—lots of them—where Clayson's blue Dodge Charger had been picked up by cameras. They even put the shots in order of time to get an idea of where he was going. As it turned out, his driving around was quite erratic. It was like he was looking for something or someone. When they'd finished that, Patches was troubled about where Lebow had been. "What would Clayson be doing parking at a couple of bars in and near Heber and going inside?" she asked herself as well as Susie.

As Rhett had told her, Susie was a smart woman. She said, "I was just thinking. Maybe someone wrote the note for him. Perhaps there is someone he knows from his work as an officer who would be willing to help him for a price or because they owed Lebow a favor."

"Good thought," Patches said. "It looks like I've got more work to do." She grinned at Susie. "I think I'll go barhopping. And I'll let Detective Ackerman know what you said about the note. He'll be pleased."

Fifteen minutes later Patches entered one of the bars Lebow had gone into the night before. She shuddered as she stepped inside. This wasn't the first time her work had required she enter such establishments, but it didn't get any easier. She felt out of place and, well, dirty whenever she had to spend time in a bar. She wasted no time inside. It was midafternoon, and there were not a lot of patrons yet, but most of the ones who were there leered and wolf-whistled at her. One guy even invited her to join him at his table and offered to buy her a drink. She forced a smile in his direction and said, "Sorry, but I don't have time."

He frowned and invited her to give him her number and said he'd call her later. This time she just ignored him and walked to where the bartender was filling a glass. "Hi, are you old enough to be in here?" he asked. "You look kind of young."

She smiled at him and said, "Thank you. I take that as a compliment. I am of age, but I am here on business." She laid one of her cards in front of him.

He glanced at it and said, "Really?"

"Yes, I am what it says," she replied.

"Give me a minute. This drink is for the young fella who wants your number." He leaned close to her and said very softly, "If I were you, I would steer clear of that guy. He's lazy and, well, you get the picture."

"I do, and thanks. I will," she said as the bartender moved toward the end of the counter. She watched him as he took the fellow his drink. The bartender was probably in his forties, she guessed. He was less than six feet, was barrel-chested, and had huge tattooed arms. He seemed nice enough.

When he came back, he said, "Why don't we slip out of sight while we talk. I guess you have something to ask me."

"That would be nice," she said.

He led her to a hallway barely out of the room but close enough that the bartender could hear if anyone approached the counter. "I'm Frank," he said. "So what would a pretty little thing like you need from me?"

"Do you know Clayson Lebow?" she asked.

"The deputy? Of course. He's been in here a few times helping the city police with some problem or other. What about him?" he asked.

"Did you work last night?" she asked.

"Oh yeah. I put in lots of hours."

"Then maybe you could tell me if Deputy Lebow was in here last night at about eleven fifteen," she said. She knew exactly when he had been there, because the time had been shown on the camera from across the street that had captured his picture.

"That's being exact," Frank said with a grin. "Yeah, he came in about then. He looked around and talked to a couple of patrons. Then he left. He must have been working undercover on something, because he was out of uniform."

Patches didn't tell Frank that Lebow had been fired. But she asked, "Did you notice if anyone wrote anything on a sheet of paper for him?"

Frank slowly shook his head. "No, I don't believe so."

She leaned toward him. "Could you by any chance tell me the names of the people he talked to?"

"Why are you asking about Deputy Lebow?" he asked, looking suspicious now and stepping back a little.

"I just need to know who he talked to. It's for my client," she said.

"Well, okay, but I probably shouldn't be doing this," he said. He told her two names. She didn't quite have her father's memory, but hers was well above the average person's. She didn't need to write the names down. She would remember them if she needed them later, or if she wanted to give them to Jay, which she probably should. She thanked Frank and hurried out of the bar just as the fellow at the table who had asked for her number called out to her and reminded her that he still needed her number.

She was relieved when the door shut behind her and the wolf whistles that had followed her were silenced. But she had to do this again. There was a second bar she knew Clayson had been in. She hoped she would get a positive result there because if she didn't, it would mean she would need to check in other places, ones with no cameras near enough to capture pictures of the people who came and went. And, in addition to that, she would have to try to find the guys whose names Frank had given her or give them to Jay to locate.

She carried the smell of the first bar with her as she entered the second one. This bartender, Jim, was a thin fellow, about six feet tall, probably in his fifties, and had his long hair pulled back into a gray ponytail. He wasn't friendly like Frank had been, but luckily Patches wasn't in there for very long before she learned something that might be helpful. Yes, Lebow had been in there, Jim the bartender told her. And yes, he had spoken to two or three people. Patches asked Jim who Lebow had talked to.

"I really don't see where that is your concern, young lady," Jim said.

"I just need to know if any of them wrote something on a piece of paper for him," she said. This guy was disgusting. She wasn't used to being treated so rudely. And it wasn't just what he said, but the demeaning way he said it. The guy made her skin crawl.

"Hey, I'm sure the deputy was in here on police business. I've never seen him in here when he wasn't on duty. He was in plainclothes, but that's not so unusual for any cop. I would suggest you ask Deputy Lebow for yourself. It ain't my business to tell some cute little PI his business," he said, leering at her in a way that was most offensive, but she persevered.

"Please, Jim, this is important," she said, careful not to allow the disgust she was feeling to show.

"Like I already said, talk to Lebow. Maybe if you waggle those long eyelashes at Lebow and wiggle those cute little hips of yours, he'll tell you who followed him out of the bar after they'd had a little talk. He is a bit of a ladies man, Lebow is. I bet you could learn what you need from him and maybe even get a date with him out of the deal," Jim suggested. "So get along, little gal."

Patches got along, thinking of how awful the guy made her feel while at the same time hoping that she had possibly learned something important from Jim without him realizing it. Lebow had spoken to someone who had followed him from the bar. The question was who. She needed to look closer at the piece of video she had that showed him. She would have to check the thumb drive again for that.

She tingled at the thought that maybe, just maybe, she was on the verge of getting something on the disgraced deputy who was so anxious to get Rhett into trouble.

CHAPTER EIGHTEEN

PATCHES SAT IN HER TRUCK in a large parking lot and studied the material she had gathered that morning. She knew exactly what location on the thumb drive she needed to access. It only took her a minute or two to bring up the video on her laptop screen of Clayson Lebow as he arrived at the bar. She watched as he disappeared inside the bar and fast-forwarded to the point where he came back out. She slowed the video down as a second man exited a minute or two behind Lebow. She watched as the two men got together and spoke briefly.

The two of them soon headed for their respective vehicles. She could not be sure what the second man was driving. It was an older sedan, dark in color and very dirty, but because of the distance of the camera from the bar, it was impossible for her to zero in enough to get a clear picture. She could not make out a license plate. The man was wearing a hat of some kind, but she couldn't tell what his clothes looked like. She would not have been able to recognize Lebow if it weren't for the fact that she had him and his car in closer shots and had been able to watch the car drive to that location.

She watched as the second car followed Lebow's Charger onto the street and drove east behind him. They were soon out of sight. She exited the video and pulled out her thumb drive. Then she reconsidered, put it back in, added a second thumb drive and copied the contents of the first one onto the second for Detective Ackerman. Maybe, with the resources he had, he could have the picture enhanced and perhaps identify the other guy. For that matter, there was a very good chance that he, with police authority, could get the name from Jim in the bar.

Patches called Jay, explained what she had, and agreed to meet him at the sheriff's office. When she was there, she gave him the names of the two men

Frank told her Lebow had talked to in the first bar. Then she handed over the thumb drive. Jay said, "Thanks, Patches. That's good work." He grinned. "I can get the information from Jim. I know the guy. He'll tell me who followed Lebow out of the bar. He won't dare give me the guff he gave you. And as soon as I know who it is, I'll have a talk with Lebow's contact. And I'll talk to the other two guys, too, if needed. I'll let you know what I find."

"All three of them are probably guys Lebow knows from police work. I would guess that some of them have spent time in your jail," Patches said. "And maybe he did them a favor or two that he shouldn't have."

"I agree," Jay said. "So what are your plans now?"

"I'm going to call Dad. If he needs me to help him this evening, that's what I'll do. I'm anxious to learn what he has found out today. And I'll let you know," she said.

***

Patches got home in time for dinner with her parents. But Max assured her that they had work to do that evening. "I know where to find Angel Affut. You and I are going to have a serious talk with her if she is where I think she'll be, which is at her apartment."

Over dinner Max told his wife and daughter what he had learned that day about three of their suspects. He had followed up on calls to the people Patches had called the first day of the investigation, folks who'd verified that Rhett was in Reno during the time Charity was murdered. Those same people were able to back up what Rhett had said about Cal Thurley. Cal had left Reno the first night after being disqualified, and he could easily have been in Heber at the time of the murder.

Patches drew a deep breath. She was sick of looking at so much video from such an assortment of cameras at all sorts of locations. But she had established a rapport with both business people and government employees during the time she'd spent searching for helpful video footage. Reluctantly she said, "Should I go back and start reviewing video of the timeframe in which the murder occurred? Perhaps the killer will be on them again. Maybe it would help narrow down our search."

Max smiled. "I know you must be tired of it, but yes, I think we need to do it again. Hopefully the places you've been will still have a record from that far back. Some people have it recorded over every three or four days. Some do it weekly, and the good ones have their systems programmed to keep the video for at least a month."

"Okay, Dad, if you think I should, I'll go back to Heber. Some of the people I need to contact won't be available tonight. So I would need to go back tomorrow morning," she said.

"Tomorrow is good. Like I told you, we have an interview tonight that could prove to be very delightful," he said with a grin. For a moment the little family ate in silence. Then Max put his fork down and said, "Clearly, until we can locate family or friends of Cal's in Grand Junction, and your mother has confirmed that he is from there, we aren't likely to be able to check on an alibi for him. Of course, maybe you will be able to find something tomorrow that shows he was in Heber."

"I hope I find something that will give us the answers we need," Patches said.

Her mother smiled and said, "If it's there to be found, you will find it. I am proud of the work you do."

"Thanks, Mom," Patches said. "I have the best teachers in the world."

Again they ate in silence. The next time Max spoke he said, "I didn't succeed in narrowing down our list of suspects today. Gene Gaffey claims he was either at work or at home during the time period in question. There's no way to tell if he was at home since he lives alone. But I talked to a couple of people at his place of employment. He was not at work. He lied about that. But they did give me a sample of his handwriting, which we need to get to Jay. Maybe you could take that tomorrow along with samples I got of Gene Gaffey's handwriting and Angel's. All three had cooperative employers, although I didn't tell them why I needed the samples."

"I can take them to Jay tomorrow. Did you get any DNA from Angel while you were at her new place of employment?" Patches asked.

Max grinned. "They showed me where she works, and I managed to find some stray hairs she left behind on the chair she uses when she files for them. They were all the same color, and I was assured the chair was new and had not been used by the person she replaced, as that woman had broken her chair. Angel has only been there for a short time, but her new boss didn't hesitate to be helpful and seemed concerned over the matter. When I explained to him why I couldn't divulge the reason I needed the samples of her hair and her handwriting, I could tell he was disturbed."

"You're good, Dad," Patches said. "But I haven't seen Gaffey's vehicles on the video segments I recovered," Patches said. "I didn't see any silver Corvettes like the one we saw in his driveway. And I was able to rule out any silver or gray pickups I spotted."

"He could have rented a vehicle," Max said. "We'll check rental places if it is necessary. I know that's a lot of checking to do, but we will if we have to."

"Perhaps I could get on the phone tomorrow and do that, Max," his wife said.

"That's a good idea, Hallie. Please do. And at the same time check for the other suspects—see if they rented any cars. At least it won't take any additional calls to do that," Max said.

"All right, it looks like I have my work cut out for me," Hallie said with a smile. "I'm glad to be able to do something more to help."

"That leaves Bernardo Growfield," Max said. "I contacted him today. He was easy to find. I did check at the dealership where he works, as I mentioned, but I found him at his house recuperating." Max's face was grim. "I still think I overreacted, but I didn't tell him that. In fact, I didn't tell him much of anything. He was not at all happy to see me and wouldn't give me the time of day."

"No surprise there, so we don't know if he has an alibi or not," Patches said.

"Not for sure. But I ruled out any likely ones I think he might try to use. I learned at the dealership that he had the week off, so he can't claim to have been at work. I checked out a bunch of bars, stores, and service stations in his general area. No one had seen him, although I did learn where he liked to spend his evenings a lot of the time," Max said.

"So once again it's up to me," Patches said, smiling and suppressing a sigh.

"Partly. But I think you and I have some visits to make in Heber," Max said.

"What do you mean?" Patches asked.

"Your mother has discovered that Bernie has a couple of relatives there. I took the information she found and was able to learn that it was on a visit to one of them that he met Gene Gaffey some years ago."

"So maybe he has a perfectly good reason for being in Heber?" Patches asked.

"That's right, or an easy way to attempt to fabricate an alibi," Max told her. "We will find out. But first, as soon as we finish here, we need to go locate an *angel* of a lower order."

***

Rhett and Kori had stopped for lunch earlier in the day, but they had spent most of the day on the road. Kori had been in some pain, but the seat leaned back on her side, and Rhett had stopped and bought a couple of pillows and a blanket to help make her comfortable. It had worked, and she had slept much of the time after that.

She took the pain pills the doctor had prescribed, when she needed them. They had an address for Cal Thurley, which Hallie had found and which Patches had passed on to them. It was Kori who had suggested they might want to drive by his home to see if his car was there.

Rhett had smiled at her suggestion. But it turned out to be more difficult than just driving by. Like Rhett, Cal lived on a ranch. It was some distance out of Grand Junction. And the county road that went through the area passed a lane that led to the ranch house where Cal lived. But even though the top of the house and some surrounding outbuildings could be seen from the county road, there was no way they could see if there were any vehicles there without driving clear into the yard.

They'd pulled off to the side near a mailbox that had the name *Calvin Thurley, Sr.* on it. "He must still live with his parents," Kori noted. She grinned. "Like you do. But I don't think we should take a chance of you being recognized by driving into their yard."

Rhett thought about it for a minute and then said, "Let's go back to Grand Junction and get something we can use to make a disguise for me."

"I don't know," Kori said. "It could be dangerous. Maybe we should just forget it."

"You are a police officer, Kori. Surely you have your handgun with you," he said.

"It's in my purse, but what does that have to do with anything?" she asked.

"You can protect me if you need to. You'd do that for me, wouldn't you?"

Kori grinned again. "Of course I would."

"Then it's decided," Rhett said firmly.

An hour later they drove slowly up the lane. Rhett wore a blond wig that covered his longish dark hair, which he'd pinned up with bobby pins. He had a red ball cap over the blond wig, he wore dark glasses that hid his eyes, and his rodeo gear and black cowboy hat were stored beneath a blanket on the floor in front of the back seat. His suitcase and Kori's were both on the back seat. He didn't worry about the license plates on the truck the sheriff had provided for him. They were Wyoming plates, and the sheriff had assured him that if an officer checked, they would come back to a fictional character; the truck was one his officers occasionally used for undercover work.

Rhett had worried about that. "What if I get pulled over?" he'd asked Sheriff McCoy. "The name on the registration wouldn't match my driver's license."

He'd been told, "In the unlikely event of that happening, have the officer call me." But the sheriff had grinned and added, "I would suggest you don't speed or run any red lights or stop signs, and then you won't get pulled over in the first place."

So, feeling fairly secure, they entered the large yard, where they spotted several vehicles, one of which was a small gray Toyota '86 sports car with Colorado plates that matched the ones Rhett and Patches had discovered the previous evening on the video. He and Kori turned and headed back out the lane before anyone came out of the house.

Neither one of them said a thing until they were back on the county road driving toward the highway. Then Kori said, "So Cal must be here. But so are we. We know how long it takes to get from here to Heber, so he could have easily been there, shot at you, and hustled home with time to spare."

"Yeah, he could have. The pickup we saw in his yard, the brown Silverado, is what he always comes to rodeos in," Rhett had explained. "That begs the question: why did he leave Reno in his pickup, return home, and then drive to Heber in his car?"

"To kill Charity and frame you is the most likely answer," Kori responded with more than just a touch of bitterness in her voice.

By the time they sat in the little café that night on the outskirts of Pueblo, four hours or so from Grand Junction, Kori said her wound felt reasonably good.

As they waited for their food, Rhett said, "You know, Kori, I've been thinking about Cal. I wonder if he might have driven to Heber in his Silverado for the murder and then returned to his home, changed vehicles, and drove his Toyota when he came back to shoot at you."

"And you," Kori said.

"We don't know if he was in town when I got shot yesterday," Rhett said. "But I can soon find out." He pulled his phone from his pocket and dialed the number he'd entered for Patches.

She answered very quickly. "Rhett, are you all right?" she asked.

"Of course I am," he said.

"Have you left Kori somewhere yet?"

"Not yet. We are having dinner right now," he said.

There was a pause before Patches spoke again. When she did she asked, "How is Kori? Isn't traveling rough on her?"

"I'm sure it's not easy. But she has slept much of the time. And she has her pain pills. She's doing okay, all considered."

"I'd ask where you are, but you probably wouldn't tell me, would you?" Patches asked.

"I can't afford to. What if you get kidnapped and tortured? You might give me away," he said with a chuckle.

Kori said, "That's mean, Shorty."

Patches asked, "What did Kori say?"

"She says I'm mean. Here I am trying to keep her safe, and she says I'm mean," Rhett said soberly.

Kori chuckled, and Patches said, "Well it sort of was, but I promise you, no one will take me alive. And if they did, they'd have to kill me before I told them where you were or where you are going, which I already know."

"Okay, enough of the scary stuff," Rhett said. "You be careful, Patches."

"I will," she said. "Now, I suppose you called me for a reason."

"Kori and I did a little sleuthing of our own today," he said. "We happened to pass through Grand Junction, and we took a little side trip."

"Rhett, you didn't do what I think you did, did you?" Patches asked, sounding alarmed.

"Probably, but I was disguised. No one saw us, that we noticed, so it didn't matter, but both of Cal's vehicles were in his yard," Rhett said.

"Really? That's interesting," Patches mused aloud. "He was in Heber around the time you were shot."

"That's why I called you. Was he in his Toyota '86 or his brown pickup?"

"His car. So he had to have driven all the way back there after that."

"That's not a problem. Since Kori and I have driven from there to Grand Junction, we now have a pretty good idea of how long that takes," Rhett reminded her. He went on. "There is something I think we need to know." He explained his theory about Cal killing Charity and disposing of her body in the barn and about him driving his truck after leaving Reno but before going back to Grand Junction. "So here's the thing. We were wondering if someone could check the cameras again and watch for his Silverado. Kori has the license-plate number. Let me hand the phone to her for a minute."

Kori read off the number, and then she said, "I'm doing okay, Patches, really I am. But Shorty is right—you need to watch yourself."

There was a pause, and Kori smiled and handed the phone back to Rhett while saying, "Patches wants us to get out of Grand Junction."

Rhett chuckled and then said into the phone, "Not to worry, Patches. We're far from there now. So what have you learned?"

"Cal and Bernie were both in Heber last night. And after Lebow was fired, he was out and about town in his Dodge Charger. He visited a bar where he spoke to a guy who followed him outside. It looked like they spoke again, and then they both left, the second guy following Lebow," she said.

"Were you able to figure out who the other guy was?" Rhett asked.

"No, the camera that caught them was quite a ways away, and when I enlarged it, it was grainy. But Detective Ackerman says he'll find out who it is," Patches reported. Then she gave him a brief overview of what her father had learned, and they ended the call.

"Okay, so now we know Cal was in Heber yesterday, but so was Bernie," Rhett said.

They talked about other things and then ate mostly in silence when their meals came. When they were finished, Rhett said, "I think we'd better find a hotel. You need rest."

"So do you, Shorty," Kori told him.

"I can't argue with that," he said with a yawn.

An hour later they were in a hotel in Pueblo in rooms that were close to each other. Rhett made sure Kori was comfortable before he went to his own room and headed for the shower.

CHAPTER NINETEEN

PATCHES AND MAX WERE SITTING in Max's old pickup on a street a short distance from the apartment where Angel Affut lived. "I hope she's home," Patches said. "We have got to start narrowing down our list of suspects."

"I have a description of her car and her license-plate number," her father said. He recited the number, and Patches stored it in her head.

They walked to the parking lot and among the cars. It was a large apartment complex, so there were a lot of vehicles. But they finally found the one they were interested in. "That's it right there," Max said, grinning while pointing to a bright-pink Hummer. "She must have special-ordered that thing," he said. "I guess she thinks it's what an *angel* would drive. Let's go have a visit with her."

Patches paused for a moment and then resumed walking when she said, "I wonder if that could be the pink vehicle I saw when I was looking at the videos."

Max nodded. "Something else to watch for when you review the videos again," he said as they reached Angel's apartment number. He knocked, and they waited.

The woman who answered the door towered over Max and Patches, and when she glowered at them, those muddy-brown eyes radiated anger and hatred. The smell that surrounded her was almost overpowering. Her face was rather plain. Her fists, on the ends of strong, thick arms, were clenched, and she had stringy hair.

Patches and Max exchanged dismayed glances. She looked like she would be a tough nut to crack.

Max spoke first. "Ma'am, we're looking for Angel Affut." Then he looked expectantly at her.

Her glower didn't shift. "You are not welcome here, whatever you want. Get out before I throw you off the balcony."

Patches couldn't help herself, even though she knew her dad would scold her about it later. She said, "You don't even know what we want. No wonder Charity Gaffey was promoted over you."

Veins in Angel's forehead swelled, her face went red, and those muddy eyes narrowed. "You little witch. What do you know about that worthless woman?"

Max and Patches again exchanged glances. Max shook his head almost imperceptibly. Then he looked at Angel and said, "We really would like to speak to you for a moment. We are private investigators and have an important matter to discuss." He thrust his ID at her.

She nodded after examining it very closely. "About what?" she asked. "Does this have something to do with Charity Gaffey?"

"It does," Max confirmed. "We have been hired to look into her death."

"Then come on in, I guess. But if you want to see me cry about Charity's demise, you will be sorely disappointed. I hated that woman, and I had good cause. Someone did me a favor." She guffawed at what she apparently believed was humorous and stepped back, holding the door open.

Patches thought she was going to die. The smell was horrible. She couldn't think of a word to describe it, but she followed her father inside, fighting to keep the bile that was rising in her throat from erupting all over the big woman's fairly clean tan carpet and large pink-toed feet.

As they were directed to sit on a sofa in her living room, Patches wished she didn't have to breathe; every time she did, the awful stench nearly made her gag. Her father seemed not to suffer from the smell of Angel's apartment like she did. Patches hoped he would make the interview short and to the point so they could get out of there as quickly as possible.

To her relief he said, "We don't want to take much of your time, so we'll get right to it. You already indicated that you knew Charity Gaffey, that she was a former coworker of yours."

Angel laughed heartily again. "Oh, I get it. You want to know if I killed her?" she finally asked after wiping her eyes with the back of her hand. "I didn't do it, and I couldn't have done it. I'm not saying I liked the woman, because I certainly didn't. She used her *femininity* to influence our boss's promotion decision." She'd used the word *femininity* as if it were a dirty thing. "The only reason he passed over me in favor of Charity was the way she batted her eyes at him all the time and swung her hips back and forth seductively. She was constantly flirting with him. But I would never kill someone over such a trivial thing. The very thought is ridiculous to the extreme."

Max told her the day of Charity's murder and then asked, "Where were you that day?"

"I was at work," she said. "I got my revenge against Charity and our boss by quitting my old job and getting a new one. That left Charity with more work to do until someone else could be hired to replace me, and it left our googly-eyed boss with shoddy work—that's all Charity ever did. I wouldn't be surprised if he killed her when he found out I was the one doing all the work while she did all the flirting."

Max got quite serious now. "Angel," he said. "I've checked with your new place of employment already. They said you did not come to work at all that day. Why are you lying to us?"

Anger flared in her eyes, but then she grinned and looked quite sheepish for a moment. Finally she said, "Okay, I lied. But it's not like you think. I really don't like my new boss much better than my old one, and I can do a lot more than a little silly filing like he had me doing, so I was out looking for another job that day."

"I see. I suppose you can give me the names and addresses of the people you spoke with," Max said.

Angel's muddy eyes drew narrow. "I did not kill Charity. I owe someone a box of chocolates for doing it. I'm tired of this nonsense. I invite you two to leave now, before I have to throw you out."

"Very well," Max said as he and Patches rose to their feet. "But you might want to reconsider your lack of cooperation. We are working closely with the officer in charge of the investigation, and we promised to let him know everything we learn. He won't take your attitude lightly." Max pulled out a card and held it out to her. "Take this. If you come to your senses, give me a call."

"I ought to thrash you two," Angel said.

Patches spoke up then, half ill with the smell of the apartment and of Angel. "I don't think you should try that. The last person who attempted to assault us got a broken kneecap for his troubles. You would be wise not to underestimate us."

"Get out!" Angel shouted.

They moved to the door, but as they walked out, Patches called out, "By the way, Angel. That's a really cool Hummer you have."

Then she shut the door before Angel could respond. Back in Max's old truck a couple minutes later, Max said, "That went well. She is still a suspect, I'm afraid. I'd really hoped to be able to eliminate her."

***

Rhett rested well. Kori not so much. He had intentionally let her sleep late because he felt she needed it, and he was in no hurry anyway. She told Rhett at their late breakfast she had been in pain for most of the night. She chuckled and said, "It would be nice if we could find a hotel with a hospital bed for me to spend the next few days in."

Rhett worried at what she said, and he offered, "I'll get you to a hospital if you need me to."

She smiled at him and gently touched his arm. "That's sweet of you, Shorty, but don't worry about me. Despite the pain, I'm really doing pretty well. When we get to wherever you decide to leave me while you do your rodeo thing, I'll have them bring me a bunch of pillows. I'll be fine."

"If you're sure," he said, as her hand lingered on his arm.

"I'm sure," she replied with a shy smile.

They were only partway through their meal when Rhett's phone rang. He pulled it out and answered quickly. "Hello, Mom, is everything okay there?" he asked.

"I don't know," was her worrisome answer.

"What's going on?" he asked urgently as his eyes met Kori's. Her eyebrows were drawn close together.

"We had a visitor a few minutes ago, and he worried Susie and me," she said. "Do you remember Charity's older brother, Brandon Simmons?"

"Of course I do. He was gone from home long before I dated Charity, but I met him several times," he said. "What did he want?"

"He was looking for you. He said he had something to tell you that he wouldn't tell anyone else," Sarah said. "I explained that you were out of state, and he wanted to know where you were. When I told him I didn't know, he got angry and acted threatening."

"What did you say to get him to leave?" Rhett asked. "I assume he's gone."

"He's actually still sitting outside in his car," she said. "But I told him I would call you and have you call him."

"Did he give you any idea what he wanted to talk to me about?" Rhett asked.

"Not exactly, but Susie and I both think he knows something about the murder. He said whoever did it was going to pay dearly. He said he'd heard it was probably you that killed her."

"Did he say what gave him that idea?"

"He said the lead officer working the case told him he was pretty sure it was you. I can't imagine Jay Ackerman telling him that, but maybe he did. It's more likely he's been talking to Clayson Lebow," Sarah concluded.

"He didn't give you the officer's name?" Rhett asked

"No," Sarah responded. "Clayson clearly didn't tell Brandon he'd been fired. Rhett, Clayson is seriously out to get you hurt."

"Did Brandon say he would hurt me?" Rhett asked.

"Brandon or Lebow?" Sarah asked.

"Brandon," Rhett clarified.

"Not exactly. But he kept saying he would find out, and whoever it was, he'd get him. He wants to talk to you personally and see what you have to say for yourself. He saw your truck and told us he knew we were lying about you not being here."

"Other than me, did Brandon say if he or the officer had any idea who else could have killed Charity?" Rhett asked.

"No. But he was pretty angry. Susie and I are worried. I'm not sure we're safe here."

"Mom, take Susie and the kids and go to her house," Rhett said with some urgency. "And do it now."

"What about the chores here?" Sarah asked. "I can't just leave. And what about the dog?"

"Take the dog too. And I'll take care of the chores—you guys just go."

"But you can't come back and take care of things," Sarah said.

"I'll call Evan Whitney," Rhett promised as he noticed Kori awkwardly trying to make a phone call. "He'll help us out. Just go."

"But Brandon is sitting outside," she reminded him.

"I'll have him taken care of," he promised. "Give me his number, and then as soon as he leaves, you guys do the same."

After entering Brandon's number into his cell, he said, "I love you, Mom. You be careful."

"I love you, too, Rhett. I'm sorry you are in such a mess, but the Lord will help us," Sarah said.

After ending the call with his mom, he listened to Kori as she talked on her phone. She was saying, "Rhett told his mother and his sister and her kids to leave. But Brandon is apparently sitting out front, and they don't dare go out to their cars until he's gone."

Kori listened for a moment, and then she said, "Yes, please do, Jay."

A moment later she finished her call. "Jay's heading out to your ranch right now," she said.

"Good. Thanks for calling him. Now I need to call Charity's brother and find out what he's up to," he said.

"Did I gather that someone accused you of killing Charity? To Brandon, I mean?" Kori asked.

"He told my mother a deputy accused me."

"We both know that would be *former* deputy Clayson Lebow," she said darkly. "Why don't you ask Brandon when you talk to him."

"I'll do that," he said as he tapped on the number he'd just entered and put the phone to his ear. "Brandon, this is Rhett. I understand you want to speak to me."

"Tell me where you are, and I'll come meet you. I know you aren't far, because your truck is here. We need to talk about this in person." Rhett was pretty sure the voice on the phone was Brandon's, even though it had been a long time since he'd last spoken to him.

"That's not possible right now, Brandon. Why don't you at least give me an idea what this is about."

"It's about the murder of my little sister, you idiot," Brandon said.

Rhett ignored the insult and asked, "What exactly about it?"

"Like why you did it," Brandon said.

"Brandon, I did not kill your sister. I would never have hurt her."

"Then why didn't you take her back after she finally got the courage to leave that creep Gene Gaffey?"

"I wasn't in love with your sister, Brandon, but I didn't dislike her," Rhett said. "I only dated her in high school, and that was years ago."

"But she loved you," Brandon said as if that were enough reason for Rhett to have loved her back. "Although, for the life of me, I don't know why."

"Brandon, I was out of state when she was killed. That's been proven. But the cops and my private investigators are working hard to figure out who did kill her," Rhett said. "And if you know something that might help them find who it was, then you need to call the detective on the case right away. His name is Detective Jay Ackerman. I'll even give you his number."

"I know who he is, but I talked to his partner already," Brandon said. "And he made it pretty clear that you are the main suspect. Until he told me that, I didn't really think you would have done it. I thought it was her ex-husband. She told me he was really angry when she left him."

"You talked to Detective Ackerman's partner?" Rhett asked as his eyes met Kori's. She was shaking her head, and anger was shooting from her eyes. "When was that?" Rhett asked.

"It was about an hour ago. Detective Lebow says the investigation is focused on you and only you. I asked him about Gene Gaffey, but he just laughed," Brandon said. "Then he told me Gene had an ironclad alibi, that there was no way he could have done it."

"Gene does not have an alibi. So it could be him who killed her," Rhett said, quickly tiring of this conversation, even though he was relieved he had managed to get the guy talking.

"Not according to the detective," Brandon said. "If you didn't kill Charity, how did her body get into your barn?"

"Brandon, please, contact Detective Ackerman. He can explain all of this to you. And don't hassle my family anymore."

"I was just looking for you," Brandon said defensively.

"I'm not home, so why don't you leave my ranch and go talk to Ackerman," Rhett said, working hard to control his temper.

"You aren't listening," Brandon said angrily. "I already spoke to the chief investigator, and he says you killed her. And you have the gall to deny it?"

"Of course I deny it. I didn't touch her. I was in Reno. And who told you Lebow was the chief investigator?" Rhett asked.

"He did. He called and asked me to meet with him. That's why I came to Heber," Brandon said. "But once I found out you were the suspect in the case and you weren't in jail, I decided to confront you."

"Well, you wasted your time," Rhett said.

"Oh no. I gotta go," Brandon said and abruptly ended the call.

Kori asked, "Did he talk to Lebow, then?"

"Yes. He claims Clayson called and asked him to come to Heber to talk," Rhett said. "And Clayson told him he was the chief investigator on the case and also told Brandon I was the only suspect in the case."

"We need to call Sheriff McCoy," Kori said. "Should I, or do you want to?"

"Let's leave that to Jay. I have a feeling he just drove into my yard, because Brandon was all of a sudden awfully anxious to get off the phone," Rhett said.

"He'll call me back after talking to Brandon," Kori said. "You told your mother Brandon was older than Charity. He must be a lot older, because I never knew him."

"He's eight or ten years older. He left Heber for college right after high school, and I don't know what he's been doing since. He's a beanpole of a man. At least he was back when I knew him," Rhett said.

"Could he have carried Charity across the fields to your barn?" Kori asked.

"I doubt it. But he might be bigger and stronger now," Rhett said.

"Could he have killed his sister?"

"I would never have thought of him as a violent person. But who knows? Maybe he's changed for the worse. He does seem angry with me, and not just because Clayson told him I was guilty. He thought I should have taken Charity back," he said. "That's crazy, I know, but maybe he got mad at both of us."

Rhett's phone rang at the same time Kori's did.

"He's gone now," Rhett's mom said when he answered. "And Susie and I are leaving. Will you call Evan? And tell him I have the dog so he won't have to worry about feeding her."

"I will. Why did Brandon finally go?" Rhett asked. "Did Jay Ackerman come?"

"He did, and the two of them were talking out there for a little while," Sarah said.

"I wonder what Detective Ackerman said to him. Let me know when you get to Susie's, and if you still don't feel safe, then go someplace where no one can find you."

"I'll be fine at Susie's," Sarah said. "You don't need to worry about us."

"Thanks. Keep your doors locked there," Rhett cautioned. "I love you, and I want you to be safe. I'll call you again, and if you need me, don't hesitate to call. Goodbye, Mom," he said.

He listened for a moment as Kori spoke on her phone. It seemed she was talking to Detective Ackerman and might be a little longer, so Rhett called Evan Whitney's home. Evan wasn't home, so Rhett talked to Maggie Whitney. Rhett explained about needing someone to do the chores for a few days.

"All right," Maggie said. "I'll have Evan call you in a little while."

"He doesn't need to do that. I just need someone to take care of the animals while I'm gone, except for the dog—she's with my mom."

"I'm sure Evan will be happy to help. You take care, Rhett."

Rhett could hear the motherly concern in her voice. "Thanks, Maggie. You too."

His call ended about the same time as Kori ended hers. She said, "That was Jay. He told Brandon to follow him to the office. Jay is hopping mad. He wants the sheriff to let him arrest Clayson for impersonating an officer."

"What do you think the sheriff will say to that?" Rhett asked as he took one last bite of his toast and pushed his plate back.

"I think he'll agree," Kori said as she looked at her mostly full plate and pushed it away. "Jay also asked me to have you call Brandon back. He hopes that maybe now that Brandon knows Clayson lied to him about being an officer he might loosen up and tell you more about why he first suspected Gene. Apparently he told Jay that much. Mostly he thinks if you talk to him you might feel better about your mother and Susie being safe."

"Why don't you try to eat a little more while I call Brandon again," Rhett suggested as he again called Brandon's number.

Kori shook her head. "I don't feel all that great. I'd better not."

Before Rhett could express his concern, Brandon was back on the phone.

CHAPTER TWENTY

Patches had been working on her assignment to get more video footage from the many cameras around the area. Some of the folks she spoke with, ones she'd spoken to before, pressed her to tell them why she was so interested in the cameras. She had simply told them she was assisting the sheriff on the investigation of the murder of Charity Gaffey. That had seemed to satisfy them.

She was looking now for any of the suspects' vehicles that might have been in or around Heber at the time the medical examiner believed Charity to have been killed. Some of the surveillance systems had already automatically erased the video from the day of the murder, so she didn't have a lot to go on and was drawing a blank. She called her father and told him it didn't look like she was going to be able to find anything.

"Patches, can anyone get to Rhett's ranch without going into town?" Max asked.

"I thought of that too." She explained how easy it would be, that there was more than one way to avoid the cameras in town and still get to Rhett's place.

"I expected that would be the case. Why don't you report to Detective Ackerman," Max told her. "If there's something else he would like you to do, go ahead and help him. Otherwise, why don't you come back here and help me. I was hoping to look deeper into the backgrounds of our suspects. But I had another matter come up, and I got delayed."

A few minutes later, at the station, Patches was allowed to go back to Detective Ackerman's office. He was not alone, and she told him she'd wait and talk to him when he wasn't busy. But he said, "No, come in." He waved a hand at a blond-haired man who was seated in front of his desk. "This is Brandon Simmons. Charity Gaffey was his sister." Then to Brandon, he said, "Brandon, meet Detective Patches Fisher. She and her father are also investigating your sister's death. We are working together to find and apprehend her killer."

Brandon turned toward her. He did not seem very happy, but he said, "It's nice to meet you, Miss Fisher." Then he turned back and faced Jay.

Patches sat down in a chair next to Brandon. Jay said, "It appears we have a big problem. Former Deputy Lebow called Brandon and asked him to come and meet with him this morning." He then went on to bring her up to date on what had transpired between Lebow and Simmons. "So Brandon was convinced Rhett Ketchum had killed his sister. He knows now that Rhett was out of state at the time and that Lebow has his own agenda."

Brandon turned toward Patches. His blue eyes bore signs of sadness. "Lebow didn't tell me he had been trying to get my sister to date him. And Charity didn't mention it either. She and I were fairly close, but she didn't tell me everything about her life. And I didn't expect her to. But we talked occasionally on the phone. I had encouraged her to get away from Gene Gaffey and told her his beatings would only become more severe if she stayed. I knew she desperately wanted to, and after she finally did, she told me she wanted to get back together with Rhett, even though it had been years since they'd dated."

Patches felt anger burning in her heart. Her anger was not directed toward Brandon. She felt sorry for him. She was angry at the disgraced deputy, Clayson Lebow. He was determined to force the arrest of Rhett for murder, even though it had been firmly established that Rhett had no motive and had a firm alibi backed up by multiple credible witnesses.

Jay turned his attention to Brandon and said, "As I was saying before Detective Fisher arrived, I need to have you explain where you've been and what you've been doing since the day before the murder."

"I didn't kill my sister," he said angrily, coming partway out of his chair.

"Settle down, Brandon. I'm not accusing you of it, but someone is trying very hard to frame Rhett Ketchum for the crime," Jay said. "That isn't going so well for whoever it is. They might consider you another possibility to frame, so I'd like to be able to cut that off at the pass by determining that you were elsewhere and could not have done it. Then, if and when the real killer attempts to frame you, we will have saved ourselves a lot of time and effort and you a lot of trouble."

"In that case, I'll tell you whatever you want to know," Brandon said.

"Good. Let's do that right now," Jay said. For the next few minutes, Brandon gave them the information they needed. Then, before he left, Jay said, "Now, Brandon, you are not to attempt to contact Rhett or any of his family about this matter. Are you clear on that?"

"Yes, sir, I am. I'm sorry. But your man Lebow had me convinced about Rhett," Brandon said.

"He's certainly not my man, but I see that. You may go now. Thanks for coming in," Jay said.

After Brandon was gone, Patches said, "I came up empty on the cameras this morning. I'm sorry. But there are, as you know, plenty of ways the killer could have reached Rhett's ranch without coming near any of the cameras we know of."

"I didn't really expect too much to come of this," Jay said. "But I appreciate your efforts."

"Is there something more I can do to help?" Patches asked.

"There is, if you don't mind," the detective told her. "Would you mind following up on Brandon's claims of where he's been and what he's been doing? I really don't think he could be our killer, but I won't rule him out until we know for sure where he's been."

"I will work on that today," Patches said. "So what happens to Lebow now?"

"I haven't seen the sheriff yet. He's out of town, but I want Clayson charged with impersonating a police officer and obstructing an official investigation," he said. "And I am determined now that we need to find out where he was and what he was doing when Charity was killed," he said. "I am going to do some snooping around. I'll let you know what I find out, and I'd like an update on what you learn about Brandon's movements."

"You got it," Patches said as she rose to her feet to leave. "Thanks for letting us help. It is rather refreshing."

"It is to me as well," the detective said as he too rose to his feet. "And, Patches, you be mighty careful out there. We are dealing with a dangerous person—or dangerous persons. And as much as I regret having to say this, I include Clayson in that. He has an agenda, and I wonder if it's only jealousy over Charity's affection for Rhett or if there could be something more."

***

Rhett and Kori drove farther east during the day Friday but made frequent stops to let Kori move around a little. She was in more pain than she had been before they left, and he tried to be very solicitous of her. As they strolled slowly around a large rest area on I-70 in Kansas, she said, "Thanks for looking after me, Shorty. I just hope I'm not holding you up."

The rodeo Rhett planned to ride in was to be held early the next week in Des Moines, Iowa, so he was not concerned about making good time. Mostly he was interested in keeping Kori safe, and he believed they were both out of danger for the time being. He said, "We have all the time in the world."

"I understand that, but since we are headed for Des Moines, why aren't we up on I-80?" she asked, puzzled.

"Like I told you, there's no hurry. And anyway, I don't think a direct route is a good idea," he explained.

Rhett had spoken with Jay and Patches, so he was up-to-date on the investigation. But he had a niggling worry in the back of his mind about Brandon Simmons. As far as he knew, Brandon was an okay guy, but Rhett didn't like the fact that he'd shown up the way he had. He said to Kori, "I hope Brandon Simmons is telling the truth about being summoned to Heber by Clayson."

"Is there any reason to think he wasn't?" she asked.

"I don't know. I'll be glad when Patches and Max get back with me on his background and movements over the past few days," he said. "Why would Lebow have called him, and how did he know how to get ahold of him when Brandon hasn't lived in Heber for years?"

Kori chuckled. "There are lots of ways to locate people."

"Really? I guess I've never had to try to find anyone," Rhett told her with a grin as they approached his truck where he'd parked it at the west end of the parking area. "But I guess that's the kind of thing you would know about. All I know is ranching and rodeo."

They were still several feet from the truck when Rhett stopped short. "Kori, there's a note on the truck windshield."

"Oh, Shorty! Have they found us?" she asked with a quaver in her voice. But then she shifted the sling that held her left arm, and said, "If so I guess we'll just have to find them too."

"The cop in you is showing." He chuckled. "We may have to do that." Taking hold of her arm, he said, "Let's not go directly to the truck in case whoever left the note is watching us. I think we should walk around a little longer."

"And look for suspicious vehicles and people?" she asked.

"Are you okay to do that?"

"Of course," she said. "I do pretty well when I'm moving around like this."

"Good. But we will also want to kind of keep an eye toward where we are parked to see if anyone moves around it. They may be long gone, but I want to be sure."

"Sounds good to me," Kori said.

"Where is your pistol?" he asked.

"It's in my purse in the truck," she said, her face white but determined. "I screwed up, didn't I?"

"Hey, it's my fault too," he said as they strolled back the way they'd just come from, watching all around them.

"But now we're like sitting ducks," she said. "And we have no way of defending ourselves. We'll have to be extra watchful. I wish I weren't so forgetful."

"Kori, can you keep a secret?" Rhett asked.

"You know I can, Shorty," she said. "Why?"

"I wasn't going to tell you this," he said. "And maybe I still shouldn't. You might have to turn me in."

Kori stopped walking and faced him, concern etched onto her pale face and in her eyes. "What is it, Shorty?"

"Promise you won't turn me in?" he asked.

She studied his face for a moment, but when he grinned she relaxed and said, "Sure, I promise."

"I have a concealed carry permit," he said. "And I have my pistol in my boot holster right now. But I don't know if it's legal in Kansas."

Kori let out a sigh of relief. "Shorty, I am so glad. I don't care if it's legal here or not. I'm just relieved to know that you have it." They started walking again.

They spent ten minutes rambling around the area. They went into the restroom building, even though they had already been there a few minutes ago. They studied every face they saw. Back outside, having seen nothing suspicious, they headed for the truck again. They hadn't noticed anyone moving in its vicinity. "I guess we may as well see what that note's all about," Rhett said as they cautiously approached the truck from a different direction.

When they were close enough, he leaned in and read the note. It said, *Smart move, Rhett. Keep going, and don't come back, either of you. I won't warn you again. If I see you again, it'll be bam, bam, and then it's over for you two.*

As expected, there was no signature. "This isn't the same handwriting as on the other note," Rhett said as his heart hammered in his chest. "How in the world did anyone find us?"

Kori had her phone out. "I don't know," she said as she tapped a contact. "I'm calling Jay."

"Wait," Rhett said. "Let's think about this for a minute. Who knew we were in this truck?"

"Apparently someone knew besides Jay and the sheriff," she responded.

"Okay, so Jay and Sheriff McCoy knew. But they assured us no one else did," Rhett said as he continued to stand beside the truck and scan the parking area and beyond.

"Are you suggesting one of them is not to be trusted?" Kori said with a frown. "I don't believe that for a minute."

"I don't want to either, but I think we need to proceed right now without letting either of them know what's happened," he suggested. "Once we figure it out, then we can talk to them."

Kori continued to frown. "If we can't trust them, who can we trust?" she asked. "But I'm not saying I don't trust them, because I do."

"We can trust my private investigators," he said.

"Wait, Patches knew we were in a loaner truck from the sheriff. So can we—"

Rhett cut her off midsentence. "Kori, she knew we were getting a loaner vehicle, but she didn't know which one or what it looks like. Anyway, I would trust her with my life, just like I would trust you with my life."

Kori hung her head for a moment. Finally she looked up and asked, "Should we call Patches or her father for advice?"

"Yes, I think we should," he said. "Are you okay with that?"

"Shorty, I trust you," Kori said. "We are both in danger and running for our lives. So, yes, if you say it's safe to call them, then do it."

"First let's get in the truck and get moving," he suggested. He moved to grab her door handle, but then he stopped abruptly when Kori grabbed his arm.

"Wait, maybe we'd better check the truck over first," she said.

"For a bomb?" he asked as her worry frown grew deeper.

"Yes," she said.

So before he unlocked the doors, he got down on his stomach and looked under the truck as carefully as he could while she kept a sharp eye on the surrounding area. Then he went around to the back and ran his hand along the underside of the bumper. He felt it touch something. He then looked under the bumper, and what he saw he recognized instantly. Relieved that it was not a bomb, he got a grip on the small object and pulled. It came loose. He stood up with it in his hand.

Kori was watching him as he looked the small object over. "It's a bug," she said. "Someone put a tracking device on this truck. But that can't be. Only Jay and Sheriff McCoy know about this truck. So one of them—"

Rhett held up his empty hand. "Don't say it," he said. "We both think we can trust them, so let's consider this some more. Maybe they were observed delivering the truck to me."

"And in that case, you could have been followed to Park City," she said. "And right to the back of the hotel where I was waiting."

"True," Rhett agreed. "And even though I only left the truck for a very short time to get you from the hotel, I did leave it. Jay was in the hotel keeping an eye on you, so he wouldn't have seen anyone approach the truck. This thing has a magnet on it. That's how it was attached to the underside of the bumper. Someone could have put it there, and then they could have followed us at a much larger distance."

"And whoever that is will be around somewhere now," Kori reasoned as she again looked around.

"I'm afraid that's true," he agreed. "I don't believe there is a bomb. Whoever it is just wants to see where we are going. Let's get on the road, and then I'll call Max or Patches."

"What about that thing, Shorty?" Kori asked. "We sure don't want to keep it with us unless we disable it."

"Maybe we could just put that in the garbage or throw it out in the weeds or something," Rhett suggested.

"Or something," she agreed, and then she smiled. "Yes, definitely *or something*." She pointed over to where the semis were parked. "That semi, the one with the purple cab and the flatbed trailer. It pulled in here when we first approached our truck. I watched the driver go into the building. And it came from the east, so it's going west. Maybe whoever is following us would like to follow him for a while. That would get them farther from us."

"Would it be dangerous for that driver?" Rhett asked.

"I can't imagine why. The killer's beef is with us, not with that guy," she reasoned even as Rhett turned and headed for the semi. He fastened the tracking device to the trailer, near the back, and then hurried back to the truck.

"I have another idea," Kori said. "Let's talk to a few people before we go. Maybe someone saw the note being taped to the windshield."

"Are you up to it?" he asked.

"I'm hurting, but I can do it," she said.

So back to the building they went. Rhett pointed out his truck to several people and asked if anyone had seen someone near it. Finally an older couple told him they had seen someone stop on the far side of his truck. They described a middle-aged man wearing a black pullover shirt and blue jeans. He was wearing dark glasses and gloves. They both said they wondered why someone would be wearing gloves on a warm day like this one. They said the guy had gotten out of his car, looked around, and then affixed the paper to the windshield.

Then they dropped a bombshell. They told Rhett and Kori that the guy ducked down on the far side of their truck, out of their sight, and was doing something. They even wondered if he'd gotten inside Rhett's truck and messed with something. When he stood up again, he dove into his car and drove off, right past them. Rhett asked them if the man's car had Utah or Colorado plates. They didn't have any idea about the license plates. However, they both described it as a gray sports car.

Rhett thanked them and led Kori back to the truck. "Okay, should we go now?" he asked.

"We might as well," she said.

He opened the door for Kori and helped her get in and get settled in her pile of pillows. He took a quick look in the truck. His rodeo gear was all there, as was their luggage and Kori's purse. Then he got in and drove out of the rest stop and back onto the freeway. "I wonder if the man the couple told us about did get in this truck. The doors were still locked, and I can't see anything missing. I'm pretty sure it wasn't Cal's car. But I wonder if this sporty gray car was the one our shooter was driving. It's certainly suspicious."

Kori nodded. "Very suspicious," she agreed. "I'm glad you found that tracking device."

"Now I'll make that call," Rhett said. "I think I'll try Max first. He's more experienced in this kind of thing."

CHAPTER TWENTY-ONE

PATCHES WAS AT HOME WITH her parents. They were all working at computers. Patches had made several contacts to confirm Brandon Simmons's alibi and was now compiling all the information on him she could find online. She was convinced he had been where he said he'd been during his sister's murder. Nothing Patches had found had given her any cause for alarm. His story about Clayson Lebow calling him to arrange a meeting looked solid. She thought about calling Jay but decided not to. This information could wait.

Max was doing more research on their list of suspects, looking deep into their pasts. Hallie was working on some company paperwork. She had already contacted all the rental companies in a wide area and determined that none of them had rented a vehicle to Bernie or any of the other suspects.

Max's phone rang, and he picked it up from beside the computer. "Blocked caller," he said as he answered it.

Patches stopped what she was doing and looked at her father as he said, "Hello, Short Investigations."

He listened for a moment, and then he said, "My wife and daughter are in the room with me. I'm going to put this on speaker, Rhett."

"Kori also has this phone on speaker," Rhett said.

"I wonder what he wants," Patches said as her father put his phone on speaker and then laid it back beside his computer. She moved closer and asked, "Are you two okay?"

"Of course we are," Rhett said, sounding light-hearted. "I just hope the guy driving the purple semi is okay as well."

"Rhett, what are you talking about?" Patches asked.

"Someone left another note on our windshield and put a tracking device underneath our rear bumper, a tracking device that is now on the back of a semitrailer being pulled by a purple Kenworth."

Patches and her parents exchanged worried glances, and then Max said, "Okay, Rhett and Kori. Let's have the whole story. Clearly someone knows where you are, and that's not good."

"They know where we *were*," Rhett corrected.

"Are you sure of that?" Hallie asked.

"As sure as we can be. They now only know where the semi is. We're on the road again. As you guys know, the sheriff provided me with a loaner vehicle. Supposedly only he and Detective Ackerman knew we had this particular pickup."

"Stop right there for a moment, Rhett," Max said. "Are you suggesting they are tracking you or that at least one of them is?"

"I hope that's not the case, and I honestly don't think it is," Rhett responded. "But we're calling you for advice rather than them, just to be on the safe side."

"If not them, then who?" Patches asked.

"Let me tell you what I think," he said, and he explained how he thought someone might have seen them giving him the truck and then planted the device on it at the hotel where he'd picked Kori up. "If that's the case, then our shooter or shooters know we were leaving the area together. Kori will read you the note."

After Kori finished reading, Max said, "So it's a warning, and it's a threat if you don't heed the warning."

"It sounds that way to me," Hallie said.

"That's certainly the way Kori and I interpret it," Rhett agreed. "There is one more thing you should know about the note. Kori and I believe it was not written by the same person who wrote the first one; the handwriting looks different."

"And we nosed around the rest stop here and found a couple who saw a guy put the note on the windshield," Kori said. "He was wearing dark glasses, a black pullover shirt, and blue jeans."

"And get this," Rhett added. "He was driving a sporty gray car."

"That brings up something else," Max said. "We just talked to Detective Ackerman on the phone. He finally tracked down the guy who, according to the video Patches located, followed Clayson Lebow from the bar the evening he was fired. The guy at first denied anything to do with Lebow, but after Jay showed him the video, he finally confessed to writing the note for Clayson."

"But you two are convinced that the handwriting on the second note is different?" Patches asked.

"Yes, we are quite certain, so we need to figure out who wrote and left the one on our truck," Kori said.

"Yes, we do," Max agreed. "The fellow who wrote the first note told Ackerman that Clayson threatened to turn him in for some dope he found on him a month ago. He said at the time that Lebow had given him a break. But now we know he used that information to blackmail the fellow into writing the note."

"So I wonder if the guy who was tracking us is someone else who owed Lebow a favor," Kori suggested. "I can't believe what Clayson is up to. It's despicable."

"But the one you have now was left by someone in a gray car," Patches said.

"That's correct. And one thing we know now is that Clayson Lebow is in this whole criminal episode up to his pointy little ears," Rhett said with some venom in his voice.

"There is no question about it," Patches agreed angrily.

"And I can't help but wonder what Lebow did with the dope he confiscated, unless he let the guy keep it," Kori suggested.

"That will all be figured out. We'll work with Detective Ackerman on this matter," Max said. "But first, I do have some advice for the two of you. Keep going, wherever you are. But I think you should do something about what you are driving."

"I can't just abandon this truck," Rhett said. "It's not even mine."

"No, but you can rent a car, and I do mean a car, not a pickup. You can carry your rodeo gear in a car, can't you?" Max asked.

"Yes. There is nothing in the bed of the truck, and besides my gear we just have our luggage."

Just then Kori cried out, "My pistol! Rhett, it's gone. Whoever was tracking us must've broken into the truck somehow and taken it from my purse."

"This isn't good," Max said as he saw alarm on the faces of both his wife and daughter. "They probably saw your rodeo gear."

"Oh, shoot," Rhett said. "That means they know I'm headed to a rodeo and if that's the case, they probably know which one. And this was a rodeo I really wanted to ride in; I needed to. Whoever this is can find me eventually. They'll only be fooled into tracking the semi for so long. This rodeo is toast for me. A few phone calls would be all it would take to know where I'm signed up to ride, if they haven't already done that."

"Rhett," Patches said, "I'm sure Kori will agree with this. You'd better not change your mind and ride in that rodeo, wherever it is. It's far too dangerous. You guys aren't even armed anymore."

"Actually I have a pistol with me," Rhett said.

"That's something, but even then, you shouldn't take any chances," Patches continued forcefully.

"I concur, Rhett," Max said. "Rent a car somewhere soon, and then drive someplace far from the rodeo. "Hopefully there will be an arrest made soon, and you can both come back."

"Or arrests," Patches said. "We still haven't ruled out that there could be more than one person involved."

"What about Brandon Simmons?" Rhett asked. "Do you know any more about him now?"

"I'm working on that right now," Patches told him. "But his alibi holds up, and I haven't found anything negative on him."

"Then hopefully we don't have to worry about him," Rhett said.

"Rhett, you and Kori need to take care of yourselves while we figure things out here. So get a car and then drive," Max said sternly. "Where are you guys now?"

Rhett told them as nearly as he knew. "We are headed east."

"Max, what should you have them do about the sheriff's truck?" Hallie asked.

"Good point. So what about the truck?" Rhett asked.

"Leave it somewhere safe. Maybe a police department near where you now are would keep it for you. Ask the sheriff, if you want to. I'm sure he and the detective are fully on our side. In fact, Patches and I will be contacting Jay as soon as we end this call. I'll get back with you. For now, you need to let us worry about the suspects. I'm sure you will be fine, but you do still need to be very cautious. It would be a mistake to underestimate your enemies," Max said.

"We'll be careful," Rhett said. He heaved a sigh. "I was sure earlier that we were fine. That may not be the case now."

For the next couple of minutes, the Fishers discussed the latest developments, and then they made plans for what they needed to do next.

***

Patches's father placed a call to Detective Ackerman and put the phone on speaker. "Hey, guys, what's wrong?" Jay asked. "I take it you haven't missed the sound of my voice from when we talked a little while ago."

"Yeah, well, something has happened you need to know about," Max said. "Rhett and Kori have been discovered. They were followed, and someone put a note on the windshield."

"But . . . but, how can that be?" Jay asked, sounding puzzled.

Patches told him about the tracking device, the missing weapon, and the description of the car. Then she told him what Rhett's theory was. "And Jay, this note referred to the first one, the one Lebow put on Rhett's truck at the ranch."

"Same handwriting?" the detective asked.

"They are pretty sure it's not, but it is handwritten," Max said.

"That's what I was afraid of. I haven't found Clayson since he talked to Charity's brother. When I do, the sheriff wants him arrested. But maybe he's headed to meet whoever followed the tracking device," Jay reasoned. "He may be planning to meet the guy in that area."

"Could be," Max said. "But I think they got the best of whomever it is for now."

"But they still know what they are driving," Jay said. "I worry about that." He paused for a moment, and then he said, "I'm pretty sure Lebow has driven that truck on an assignment in the past. I wonder if he had a key made for it. With what we know about him now, he may have done that. That could explain how it was broken into without doing any noticeable damage."

"Yes, I can see that being possible. Rhett's going to rent a car; he's not going to the rodeo, in case they simply go there and wait for him," Max said. He explained why Rhett couldn't go to the rodeo. "They were worried about the truck. I suggested he leave it at a police department somewhere near where they are now."

"Do you know where they are?" Jay asked.

"Approximately," Max informed him. Then he told Jay what Rhett had said about their location and direction of travel.

"Good. I'm sure the sheriff will be fine with what they're doing. Right now, I'm going to see if Clayson is in town, but I frankly doubt it. If I don't find him soon, then we'll have to assume he's out of town, and we'd better let Rhett and Kori know," Jay said. "He could be after them."

After that call, the Fishers worked at their computers again. An hour later Patches said, "I am certain now that Brandon Simmons isn't a suspect. He doesn't have any red flags in his background. I think Clayson Lebow was trying to get him involved in harassing Rhett."

"I think it's time to talk to Bernie Growfield again," Max said. "And his relatives in Midway and Heber. If he's not the shooter, that could explain his being in Heber—he could've been visiting family. I want you to come with me, though." Max grinned at his daughter. "Since I am the one who broke his kneecap, he may be more willing to speak with you than with me."

"I doubt he'll respond to me any better than to you," she said. "But I guess it's worth a try."

"If we get nothing from him, we'll go ahead and interview his relatives in the Heber Valley. In the meantime, I hope Ackerman finds Lebow."

The visit to Bernie's went about as expected. The man was totally belligerent. Patches didn't do any better with him than Max did. Of course, he'd hit her the last time, so even though they'd hoped he'd be more forthcoming, it was not a surprise when he wasn't. Bernie told them to leave, but he kept his distance on his crutches. As they left he said, "I'll get you two one day for this."

Max stopped before Bernie had shut the door. "Why do you hate us so much?" he asked, his eyes narrowed dangerously.

Bernie snorted. "My father told me short people like you always try to push your way around to make you feel tougher." Patches began to back away, wishing her father would follow, but he wasn't moving. "He also told me I shouldn't ever let anyone of any size try to bully me. Not that you two are tough enough to bully anyone," Bernie sneered.

Patches said, "Dad, let's go. He's just trying to get you to break another kneecap."

Her father ignored her. "Bernie," he said. "I know your kind. You are the worst kind of bully."

Patches knew he was restraining anger and hoped it didn't boil over.

"No, I just don't like to be pushed around. My dad and uncle destroyed a couple of guys like you a few years ago because they stole their fishing hole and thought they could get away with it. Well, I'll tell you this, when my knee heals, I'm going to do the same to you," Bernie said. "You can't just come barging onto my property thinking you can do as you please since you're PIs."

Patches grabbed her father by the arm and tugged. "Come on, Dad. We have work to do."

For a moment Max stood like he was rooted to the ground. But finally he said, "Yes, we don't have time for scum like Bernie." He turned, and the two of them hurried to Max's old green pickup.

He had the truck on the road before he spoke again. When he did, he said through clenched teeth, "I am going to get them."

"Who?" Patches asked.

He turned and looked at her. "I'm going to get Bernie's father and uncle."

"Why? You don't even know them."

"Oh, I know them all right. I knew Bernie reminded me of them. I've wondered until today, but now I know. They are the men who were angry because Sammy and I were having good luck fishing and they weren't. They are the ones who killed Sammy and put me in the hospital," he said.

"Dad, are you sure?" she asked.

"Absolutely. The bit about the fishing business sews it up," he said. "Bernie couldn't have been plainer about who killed Sammy."

"Oh, Dad!" Patches said. "You must be right."

"I know I am. As soon as we finish this case, I will find them, and when I do, I'll turn them over to the police. They'll stand trial for what they did to us and they'll be convicted," he said.

"So maybe Bernie really is Charity's killer," Patches said. "He sounded like he thought killing people he didn't like was his right. He grew up with a killer for a father. He's full of hate. And I would think being rejected by Charity is all the motive a person like him would need." Patches knew her father was right. He'd finally solved the crime that had led him to the profession he now practiced. And she had no doubt he'd bring his attackers to justice.

"I guess it's time to visit some of Bernie's relatives in Heber Valley," Max said. "And while we try to learn why Bernie might have been in Heber, who knows, we might get lucky and learn more about his father and uncle."

The address was in a very nice home in Midway. The people who lived there were cousins of Bernie's, or the husband was. Unlike Bernie, he seemed like a decent sort of fellow, and his wife was a pretty woman with a big smile and an infectious laugh they could hear before the door even opened. They invited the Fishers right in and introduced themselves as Norman and Lexie Growfield without even asking for the Fishers' identities or the purpose of their visit.

"Can I get you a soda?" Lexie said with a wide, white smile.

"Thanks, but that's not necessary," Max said. "My name is Max Fisher, and this is my daughter, Patches."

Lexie was maybe an inch taller than Patches, with short blonde hair and sparkling blue eyes. She laughed, but it was not at all a mocking sound. "Patches," she said. "What a quaint name. I like it. Don't you think it's a cute name?" she asked her husband.

"A cute name for a cute girl," Norman said with a smile. "Are you sure you wouldn't care for some refreshment? We don't drink alcohol, but we have pop in the fridge."

"Really, we're fine, but thank you," Patches said as she studied Bernie's cousin. She could see a faint resemblance to Bernie. Had she not been specifically looking for the resemblance, she would probably never have noticed it. He was several inches taller than his wife, with curly hair as dark as hers was light. His eyes were brown and shone with intelligence.

"Then we'll all sit, and you can tell us what you have to sell," Norman said.

"I'm sorry," Max said after they were all seated in a clean and comfortable living room, the kind that looked like it had either never seen children or had an excellent housekeeper. "We are not salespeople." He stood and handed a card to Norman and then sat again. He watched while Norman studied the card and handed it to Lexie without a word.

Lexie also studied it and then gave a short version of her infectious laugh. "Private investigators. Who would have guessed? I always pictured PIs as big burly men with hairy arms and chests." She laughed again. "So funny you should come. We were just talking about seeking someone out to help us."

Patches and her father exchanged quick glances, and then Max said, "What kind of help are you referring to?"

Just then two children who resembled their parents entered the room, quietly and almost, well, reverently, Patches thought. The little girl had hair as dark as her father's, and the little boy had hair as blond as his mother's.

They stopped, with surprise on their little faces. Their mother said, "Daddy and Mommy have company. Why don't you go back to the playroom until we finish here."

They each smiled, said they would, and left as reverently as they had entered.

"What beautiful children," Patches said. "Are they twins?"

"They are," Norman said with a proud smile on his face.

"How old are they?" Max asked. "I would guess about five, but I'm not very good at guessing."

"They're seven," Lexie said with a smile. "Our pediatrician says they'll always be a little small, though they are perfectly healthy."

"I believe it," Patches said. "They're adorable."

"They will probably not be a lot taller than you when they are grown," Norman said to Max. "Maybe as tall as Patches."

"I am almost five feet," Max said with a chuckle as he stretched his body as far as he could. Everyone laughed. "Neither of you is small," Max observed.

"That's true, but the genes are in our family. You remind me a lot of my grandfather on my mother's side, Mr. Fisher," Norman said. "A kinder, more intelligent man never existed."

"There's nothing wrong with being short," Max said. "No more so than being tall. God meant for us to be all sizes and to be the best we can be no matter our physical stature."

"That's why we're so glad to meet you folks," Lexie said. Her smile had vanished, and there was no longer a sign of laughter in her voice. "We want someone to investigate Norman's cousin."

"What's his name?" Patches asked, although she thought she already knew the answer.

"Bernardo Growfield. He goes by Bernie," Norman said, his eyes growing hard. "He hates people who aren't as big as he is—along with a lot of others for who knows what reasons."

CHAPTER TWENTY-TWO

PATCHES HAD LEARNED FROM HER father to mask her surprise in situations like this, but she had a hard time doing it now. "What do you want to investigate him for?" she asked, the act of speaking helping to hide her astonishment.

"I don't know if it would be safe for you folks since he hates smaller people with a passion, something he learned from his father," Norman said. "He's been hanging around here lately, stalking my family, and we fear for the children. He is a cruel man, and we're afraid he might hurt them or he might even hurt us. He might hurt you two as well. No offense, but maybe you could recommend someone."

"We'd hate for you two to get hurt trying to help us. And you are probably very busy anyway," Lexie added.

"Don't worry about us and our safety. We can take care of ourselves. And we are busy, but let's talk about this a little more before any decisions are made. Have you seen Bernie lately?" Max asked.

"Oh yes, he drives by every few days. He always slows down, sometimes stops, when he passes our home. We don't dare let the children play outside at all," Norman said. "I work from home, and my wife is a stay-at-home mom, so we've been able to keep track of them. But we think Bernie is up to no good."

"Have you seen him outside of his car?" Max asked, his face serious and his eyes intense.

"Well, yes, he did park across the street just a couple of days ago. He got out and leaned against his car," Lexie said. "He had one leg in some kind of a cast or a splint or something."

"Broken kneecap," Max said.

"You know him?" Norman asked, his eyes wide with surprise.

"You could say that. He is the reason we are here to speak with you folks," Max informed them.

"But why?" Lexie asked. "Did you know he was harassing us?"

"No," Max said. "But he is the subject of a case we are working with the sheriff on."

"I wouldn't get too close to him if I were you," Norman said. "Even with that cast, he wouldn't hesitate to attack you if he thought he could get away with it."

"Oh, but he would hesitate, I can assure you," Max said.

"How can you be sure?" Lexie asked.

Patches looked at her father, and he nodded. "Bernie hit me, so Dad broke his kneecap."

Norman and Lexie both looked surprised and glanced at each other for a moment. Then Lexie began to laugh. "I'd loved to have seen that," she said. "But how did you manage to do it?"

"Let me tell you a story," Max said. "Ten years ago my cousin Sammy and I went fishing on the Provo River. Sammy was the same size as me, around five feet. We were having pretty good luck fishing, but a short ways from us were two men. They weren't catching anything. They eventually moved closer and told us we were fishing in their hole and that we should leave. We didn't agree, and they attacked us. We fought back, but, well, we lost the fight. Luckily for me, some other fishermen came along and found us. Our fish and our gear had been taken."

"Oh, that's horrible," Lexie said.

Patches and Max nodded, and Max continued. "I was injured pretty badly and was in a coma for several days. When I finally woke up, I asked about Sammy. He had died of his injuries."

The color was slowly draining from Norman's face.

"I promised myself then that I would never be vulnerable like that again, nor would my wife and daughter. So we learned self-defense. Bernie found that out the hard way."

"Were the guys who hurt you caught?" Norman said.

"No, but I have a rather good memory, and when I see them again, I will know them," Max said. "I'd even know their voices if I heard them."

Norman was nodding his head, but he seemed preoccupied. He asked, "Max, if I showed you some pictures, would you be able to tell whether or not the men in the photos are the men who attacked you?"

"Of course," Max said. "Why do you ask?"

"My grandfather was murdered. I have always believed two of my uncles were responsible, but they denied it, and there were no witnesses. The cops never did make an arrest. My grandfather was about the same height as your daughter, but it was not just about size. They accused Grandpa, their father, of stealing some property from them. Of course, it wasn't true. The property in question was Grandpa's, but they thought he should give it to them. The dispute went on for a while before they actually started to spread the word that Grandpa was a thief. Grandpa confronted them about it, and they beat him to death. At least, we believe it was them. The cops could never prove it. That property went to my father, and it is this very place where Lexie, the twins, and I now live."

"Oh my," Max said. "So maybe Bernie wants the property?"

"Maybe, or perhaps he just wants to punish us because we have it now. My father sold it to us for a low price, which Bernie and my uncles probably objected to. Lexie and I don't know for sure, but we feel that Bernie is very dangerous to us and our children. Of course, we fear most for the children because they could never defend themselves if he caught them alone," Norman explained.

"Isn't there a chance your uncles might decide to try to take the property from you?" Patches asked.

"That's possible, but both uncles moved out of the state shortly after my grandfather's murder. And to my knowledge they have never returned."

"Is one of them Bernie's father?" Max asked.

"Yes. He and his other brother are as cruel as Bernie. My father was the youngest of the three, and he was as different from them as it's possible to be," Norman said. "But are you sure you'd be able to identify them after ten years?"

"Dad has a photographic memory," Patches told them. "He'll know them; I can promise you that."

"Give me just a minute," Norman said and exited the room.

"Bernie's dangerous," Lexie said after her husband had stepped out. "That's why we fear for our children. We're afraid that he wants to do something to them to hurt us. For that matter, he could easily hurt us directly if he got the chance. That's why we need someone to help us. And after what you've been telling us, I think you two are perfect for the job."

"We have to bring the case we are working on to a conclusion," Max said. "But perhaps since we are already quite acquainted with Bernie, we will be able to help."

Norman returned with a photo album. "The pictures in here are from beyond ten years ago, probably more like fifteen. Would you look through it and tell me if you see the two men who attacked you and your cousin?"

He handed the album to Max, who began to thumb through it. Suddenly he stopped. He put his finger on a picture that had three smiling men in it. "Right here. These two," he said and thumped his finger on the picture of the two men he had waited all these years to identify. "The third man I have never seen before."

"He is my father. The others are my uncles," Norman said. "So they are the ones who killed your cousin?"

"Oh yes. They are the ones," Max said as he ground his teeth in anger. "Will you give me their names and addresses?"

"I would be happy to," Norman said. "But there is one condition."

"Oh? What would that be?" Max asked.

"You must agree to help us stop Bernie from harming our family," he said.

Max thrust out his hand. "We will," he said. "Now, we have a few questions for you about Bernie."

For the next few minutes, they established the dates and times Norman and Lexie knew Bernie had been in the area. Then Max and Patches told them of the death of Charity Gaffey, why Bernie was suspected, and why they hoped to learn if he was in the area at the time of the murder.

Norman and Lexie shook their heads. "I can't positively say what he was doing during those hours, even though I followed him several times for several hours," Norman said.

"Norman was following Bernie to keep his family safe," Lexie interjected.

Her husband nodded. "I wasn't following him during the time frame you mentioned. But I do know this: he is certainly capable of killing people, just like his father did."

"Have you spoken with him at any time in the past few days?" Patches asked.

"No," Lexie said.

As the story unraveled, Patches excused herself and went out to the truck. She returned with her laptop and a thumb drive. She explained about the various surveillance cameras and how she had isolated pictures of Bernie and his Charger. She put the thumb drive into the USB port on the side of her computer. Five minutes later Norman said, "There, that's him, and see that car back there?" He pointed out a blue Nissan sedan. "That's me," he said.

They continued to examine each place on the video where Bernie's car was seen and were able to spot Norman's car in the general vicinity as well. Norman said, "I kept track of each time he drove out here to our house. Twenty times that I know of, but none of them coincide with the date of the murder."

"Now, there are two more situations we're worried about," Max said. "Someone shot and injured a sheriff's detective and later the man in whose barn Mrs. Gaffey's body was found. The video you have just looked at was taken during and near those times. You couldn't say you knew where he was when the murder took place, but what about when the two shootings occurred? We know from the videos that he was in town both of those times. So we wonder if he could have been the one who made those attacks."

Norman verified that on those occasions he had been following Bernie. They went back over the video very carefully. Norman was certain he'd had Bernie in sight during the times of both shootings.

"So he couldn't have been the one who shot the officer and the other man?" Patches asked.

"That's right. It couldn't have been him, even though I believe him to be capable of such a thing," Norman said firmly.

Max sat back and pulled his phone from his pocket. "I am going to call the detective handling the murder case and the shootings. I'd like him to talk to you. Do you have any objections?"

"At this point, if you are going to help us, then no, I guess we can let the authorities know of our concerns," Norman said.

Max made the call. "Detective Ackerman, this is Max," he said. "We have just eliminated Bernie Growfield as the person who shot Kori and Rhett. But he is still a suspect in Charity's murder. Would you be able to meet us in Midway so we can go over it and introduce you to a couple of witnesses?"

Jay promised to be right out. When he came, Patches and Max met him in front of the Growfields' home. Jay told them then that the lab had been able to verify that both the bullet that hit Kori and the one that hit Rhett had been fired from the same weapon. But he had no idea whose weapon that was. "We know it wasn't Clayson Lebow's service revolver. The sheriff had me take it to the lab and it didn't match."

"But he could have had other pistols," Patches said.

"Yes, he almost certainly does," Jay agreed.

"And do you know yet where he is?" she asked.

"I can't find him. I'm afraid that he may have gone to meet the person that followed Rhett and Kori," he said. "Now, why don't you introduce me to Bernie's cousins?"

***

Later in the day, Max and Patches were able to put a tracking device on Bernie's silver Charger in the parking lot of a bar in Provo. The tracker was a high-powered device, and even if Bernie was as far as a hundred miles away, they would be able to keep track of his exact location. Hallie Fisher was designated to keep track of the vehicle. Each time Bernie's car moved there would be an alert, and she could then watch where he went. If he headed into Heber, she was to let Patches, Max, and Detective Ackerman know.

Once that was done, Max and Patches drove down to the Provo police station, where they met with an older detective by the name of John Gravitt. After introductions and shaking hands with Max and Patches, Detective Gravitt said, "You're lucky to have caught me here. I just got back from vacation today. How can I help you?"

"I know who killed Sammy Kist ten years ago," Max said. And he pulled out the picture of the Growfield brothers that Norman had given him. "This one here is not involved," he said, indicating Norman's father. These are the two who attacked us."

"Let me get the case file," Detective Gravitt said. He returned with it a few minutes later and extracted the drawings that had been made at the time by a police artist based on Max's descriptions of the two men. Without a word he laid them on his desk. He looked back and forth between the picture and the drawings. Smiling, he said, "You're right, Max. These are the guys. Can you tell me how you figured it out?"

Max took him through the story of Bernie and what he'd said and then explained how Bernie was stalking Norman and Lexie and their young children.

When their meeting with Detective Gravitt was over, Max and Patches left the police station hopeful that after so many years the two killers would soon be brought to justice.

Max would have liked to be with the officers who would arrest the two men, whenever that occurred, but he'd told Detective Gravitt that he was involved in a case that made it very important that he stay in the area.

Returning their attention to the murder of Charity Gaffey, Max suggested, "Let's make another visit to Angel Affut's former employer, Patches. I mean her second employer, not the one she and Charity shared. I'm hoping we'll find someone else we haven't already talked to who might be able to help us." They drove north.

Luck was with them that day. They learned a cowboy had come in looking for Angel just a few days before the murder. The informant did not know who it was, but when shown a picture of Cal Thurley she indicated that he was the guy looking for Angel. But she had no idea what they had talked about.

Back in the old green pickup, Max said, "I guess we need to visit with Angel again. She has some explaining to do."

They spent much of the afternoon searching for Angel but were unable to locate her. Finally they went to the place where Charity had worked up until her death. They showed the picture of Cal to the other employees there. No one there had ever seen the cowboy.

As they left that location, Hallie called to tell them the silver Charger had left a bar shortly before and was driving on Interstate 80 in the direction of Heber. Max sent Patches to follow the Charger while he continued to work in the Salt Lake area. "I am going to talk to Gene Gaffey again," he told his daughter. "I'm hoping he will tell me more about Bernie. I'd like you to go back to Heber."

Late that evening Max received a call from Detective John Gravitt in Provo. "The Growfield brothers are in custody in Idaho. They resisted arrest, but our officers managed to take them in without anyone being injured badly. The Growfields are refusing to waive extradition, so it will be a while before we can get them back to Utah," he said. "If you get time, it would be nice if you could go up there and identify them in person."

"That will depend on this case," Max said. "Is there a chance they will bond out of jail?"

"None," Detective Gravitt told him. "They are being held without bond. We've reopened an older cold case and have found evidence they were the killers in that case as well."

"Would that be the murder of their father?" Max asked.

"That's the one."

***

Karen Wilton was the dispatcher on duty again on Saturday morning. She called Sheriff McCoy. Upon hearing her report, he asked urgently, "Where is Detective Ackerman?"

"He checked out at the office just a few minutes ago," Karen said.

"Thanks. I'll get him, and we'll head out there," he said. "Did the caller say anything else?"

"No," she said. "He just said, 'There's another body in the barn and hung up."

"It was a male voice?" Sheriff McCoy asked.

"I think so. It wasn't a terribly deep voice, but it sounded masculine," she reported.

"Make a copy of the call as quickly as you can."

"I'll do that, Sheriff," she said.

"No indication which barn?" he asked.

"It sounded like the same caller as before, so I assume it's the Ketchums'."

"We'll know soon enough." The sheriff had his hat on his head and was already headed for Jay's office. "Don't send anyone else until I tell you to," he instructed Karen.

When the sheriff got to Jay's office he saw Jay leaning toward his computer, studying something on the screen. "Hello, Sheriff," Jay said, looking up. "What's up?"

"There was just another call about a body in the barn. No specifics," he said.

"Rhett's barn?" Jay asked as he closed the screen on his computer and grabbed his hat.

"That's what we need to find out," McCoy said. "Let's take separate vehicles."

"Should I notify the Fishers?" Jay asked as they jogged from the building.

"I guess it can't hurt," the sheriff responded. "They have certainly been a big help so far."

They reached their SUVs and got in, and with the sheriff in the lead, they headed for the Ketchums' ranch.

CHAPTER TWENTY-THREE

PATCHES WAS SHOWERED, HAD EATEN a light breakfast, and was ready to go. But she was not yet sure where she was going. She met her dad in the living room, and he said, "You were late getting in last night. Do you have anything to report on Bernie Growfield?"

"I followed him around for hours," Patches said. "He went past Norman's house several times and past Rhett's ranch once. But finally he returned to Salt Lake," she said as her phone began to ring.

A moment later she heard Detective Ackerman's voice. "Patches, is your father there with you?"

"He is," she said. "Would you like me to put you on speaker?"

"Please do," he said.

"Okay, all set. What's up this morning?"

"The sheriff and I are heading for Rhett's ranch. Dispatch got another call claiming there's another body in the barn," he said grimly. "I'll let you know what we find, but you may want to head this way, just in case it's for real and not a joke of some kind."

"We'll be on our way right now," Max said. "I hope it's a false call, but this whole business is getting crazier by the minute."

"That's for sure. We'll see you when you get here," Jay said and ended the call.

They took Patches's truck. While she drove, Patches made a call on her synched phone.

"Hi, Patches," Rhett answered.

"Are you guys okay?" she asked.

"Of course we are," he said.

"I need to know where you are," she said, packing as much urgency in her voice as she could.

"Patches, what's the matter? Why do you need to know where we are?" Rhett asked.

"Is Kori still with you?" she asked.

"She is. Please, what's going on?"

Max spoke next. "There is a situation here."

"Is there some reason to think it might not be safe to tell you where we are right now?" he asked.

"Oh, no. I'm sure it's safe to tell us," Max responded.

"Okay," Rhett said, and he chuckled. "Even if I tell you, how will you know I'm not pulling your leg? These phones we're using don't have GPS, and neither does this rental car."

"This is serious, Rhett. Tell us where you are," Patches said. "And then stop someplace close by and take a picture with you in it that identifies the area."

"For real?" Rhett said. "You're scaring us. Kori is white as a sheet."

"Just do it," Patches said, her voice almost angry.

"We're at a hotel in Memphis, Tennessee," Rhett said. "We're just having breakfast. I know we're slow getting moving, but what else do we have to do? Frankly, I'm ready to come home. So is Kori."

"Get a picture or two and email them to me," Patches instructed. "You do have your laptop, don't you?"

"It's in my room," he said.

"Why don't you hurry and get it," Max suggested. "Your phone does take pictures, doesn't it?"

"It's your phone, and yes, it does," Rhett answered. Patches could hear him as he spoke away from his phone. "Kori, make sure no one snatches my breakfast. I'll be right back." Then to Patches he said, "I'll take care of it right away. Can you tell me what's going on now?"

"It may be nothing, but the sheriff's dispatcher got a call a few minutes ago. The caller claims there is another body in the barn."

"In my barn?" Rhett asked, sudden alarm in his voice.

"The caller didn't say, but Jay and the sheriff are on their way there right now," Patches informed him. "We're on our way too. Be sure you get both of you in a picture showing where you are."

"So you're saying I need an alibi," Rhett said. "This is nuts. I'll bet someone is conning the sheriff."

"I hope so," Max broke in. "But just in case, let's document where you are."

"You got it. I'll get right on it."

A few minutes after ending the call with Rhett, Jay called. "Patches, as hard as this is to believe, there is a dead man in Rhett's barn," he said. "We can't tell yet who it is. I hope it's not Rhett."

"It's not. I just talked to him. He and Kori are in Memphis," Patches said.

"Oh good," Jay said, and Patches could hear him exhale in relief. "In that case, call Rhett and make sure he can prove where he's at. Kori too."

"He's sending us pictures. I expect them any minute now," Patches informed him.

"Good. We just need them to be able to prove their location so there will be no question that Rhett isn't the killer or the deceased, for that matter. We're going to see if we can figure out who the victim is. We'll see you when you get here."

"I wonder how the victim died," Max said as Patches sped up.

"The body, at least the face, must be messed up, or they would have known it wasn't Rhett," Patches reasoned.

Just then her phone indicated an incoming email at the same time Max's did. "I hope this is Rhett responding," Max said. "You keep driving. I'll check." A moment later he held his phone out for Patches to glance at.

"Kori looks white, like Rhett said," Patches observed. "All this travel can't be good for her."

"But it is good evidence they are where they say they are," Max observed.

The photo showed Rhett and Kori standing with two people with the hotel's name embroidered on their shirts, in front of a sign that identified the hotel. The text that accompanied the picture read, *I hope this will do. Do you know anything else about the body?*

"I'll call him," Patches said, and she verbally directed her phone to dial the last number she had called.

"I wish my truck could do all the stuff yours does," Max said.

"It would if you wouldn't be so stubborn and refuse to buy a new one. You can afford it," Patches said. She grinned over at her father and added, "Or you can buy me a new one, and you can have this one." Then as Rhett answered the call a moment later, she said, "Hi, Rhett. Thanks for the picture. It's just what we needed. I suppose you got the names and contact information of the people in the picture with you."

"I'm traveling with a detective," Rhett reminded her. "We not only got their information but also that of the guy who took the picture for us. We have several more, but we figured we needed to send only the one for now."

"Yes, that's great, Rhett," Patches said.

Max broke in. "Finish your breakfast, and then check out. I'm pretty sure no one can figure out where you are from our conversation, but just to be on the safe side, get on the road again as soon as you can."

"Will do," Rhett said. "Did you find out if there really is another body in the barn?"

"Unfortunately yes. We don't know who it is yet," Patches answered. "Jay and the sheriff were afraid it was you."

"But that's ridiculous. Surely they know what I look like by now."

"Apparently the body isn't that easily identifiable," Patches said. "We don't know anything else yet."

"Is Clayson Lebow back in town yet?" Rhett said.

"Not that we know of," Patches said. Then she reported on her activities of the evening before. "So depending on when it happened, the body probably isn't Bernie's. And for that matter, I'll probably be able to provide his alibi since I was following him around until late last night. Are your mother and sister and the kids still at Susie's place?"

"They are, thank goodness," Rhett said. "But with them and the dog not home, someone could've taken the body right to the barn from my lane."

"Good point," Patches said. "We'll be there soon. I'll let you know when we know more."

"I wonder if the dead guy could be Clayson Lebow or the guy he had following us," Rhett said.

"I hadn't thought of that," Patches said. "I suppose it's possible."

"This is creeping us out," Rhett said. "I'd better get off the phone so we can hurry and eat and then hit the road."

"You guys be careful," Patches said before hanging up.

A few minutes later, Patches pulled into the yard at the Diamond Bar Ranch and parked next to the two sheriff SUVs. She and her father hurried past the house and to Rhett's barn, where they entered slowly. Patches called out, "We're here."

"Come on in and join us. It's the same stall as the one Charity's body was found in," Jay called back after stepping out of the stall.

They hurried to the stall door and looked in. Patches gasped. There was blood all over the floor and the walls, and the victim's face was obliterated. "He was killed in here," Jay said. "He was shot several times. He has no ID on him. We have no idea who it is."

"Could it be Clayson?" Patches asked as she fought a suddenly squeamish stomach.

"We hadn't thought of him, but I suppose it could be. We need to figure out how tall the body is," Jay said. "We can't even be sure of his hair color at this point." He backed out of the stall, and the sheriff followed him. "His height may not help us identify him, but it will enable us to eliminate some people. We have some folks coming to help Jay process the scene. Hopefully we'll be able to identify the body by fingerprints or dental information—if we can find some teeth."

"Rhett suggested that if it's not Clayson maybe it's one of the people he's had helping him," Patches said.

"That's a thought, for sure," Jay said.

The sheriff said, "So there are plenty of people it could be. Now, Rhett's family went to his sister's place. We already checked to make sure they were there and safe. But we wonder if the neighbors, Evan or Maggie Whitney, might have heard or seen anything."

"We can ask them if you'd like," Patches suggested.

"Yes, please do," Sheriff McCoy said.

Maggie answered the door. "Well, hello, Patches," she said brightly. "And this is your father, I assume."

Patches nodded. "Maggie, meet Max Fisher. He's the head of our agency."

"It's a pleasure to meet you," Maggie said as she waved them in. "You sure have a wonderful daughter. I'll bet you're very proud of her."

"I sure am," Max said with a smile. "Is your husband home?"

"He's outside somewhere. Let me call his cell phone." A moment later Maggie said, "Dear, the Fishers are here to talk to us."

A couple of minutes later, the tall, slender farmer rushed in the back door. Following quick introductions Max said, "Maybe we should all sit."

"Of course," Maggie said. "Where are my manners?"

"Your manners are just fine," Max said. "But we have something serious to discuss."

After they were all seated, Max said, "I understand you have been taking care of the Ketchums' chores."

"I have. Is there a problem over there?" Evan asked as alarm crossed his weathered features.

"I'm afraid so. It's not anything you are in any way responsible for. But we need to know if you heard anyone entering or leaving the Ketchums' place during the night," Max said.

The Whitneys studied each other for a moment. Then Evan said, "As you know, it's a ways over there, but now that I think of it, there might've been a car near there when I got up to use the bathroom and get a drink." He looked at his wife as he spoke. "I didn't see any lights, but the window was open, and it was still night. I think I heard a motor. I didn't think anything of it."

"Do you know what time that was?" Max asked.

"I looked at my watch while I was up. It was around two thirty," Evan said. "I did look out the kitchen window, but I couldn't see anything. So I didn't think any more of it and went back to bed."

"Did someone break into Sarah's home?" Maggie asked. "That would be just awful if they did. They have enough trouble to deal with already."

"No, there was no burglary," Max said. "But I'm afraid there is a problem in the barn."

The elderly couple's eyes opened as wide as saucers. "What kind of trouble?" Evan asked.

"I'm afraid there has been another killing," Max said.

Maggie let out a strangled cry, and her husband put an arm around her shoulders and pulled her close. "Are you all right, Maggie?" he asked.

"A body," she murmured. "I wonder who it is." Then she gasped and went whiter than Patches thought was possible. "Is it Rhett?" she asked, her voice trembling. "I know he was shot just the other day, that someone wanted to kill him."

"No, he's safe," Patches assured her as she stood, crossed the room, and joined the old couple on the sofa. "I talked to him a few minutes ago. He and Deputy Kori Davis are out of state." Despite her best efforts, a twinge of jealousy passed through her. She was afraid all this time together was all it would take to make Rhett fall for Kori. She thrust the thought away and listened as Max spoke.

"We know it isn't Rhett, but we don't know who it is," Max said. "There's no ID on the body, and his face is unrecognizable."

Maggie moaned again, and both her husband and Patches held tightly to her. "The sheriff and detective will figure out who it is," Patches said.

"Or you will," Evan said. "They wouldn't know as much as they do and would probably still be blaming Rhett for the girl's murder if it hadn't been for you, Patches."

"They would have eventually figured it out," Patches said. "Anyway, Rhett was out of state then, as he is now, and we have proof."

"So no one will try to blame him this time since they know he's gone," Evan said hopefully.

"Actually, other than you folks, us, his family, and the sheriff and detective, no one knows he's not home," Max said. "So I think whoever committed the murder is probably hoping to pin it on Rhett."

Maggie finally had regained her composure and was sitting up straight on the sofa. "I'll be fine now. I'm such a baby," she said.

"You are no such thing, Maggie," her husband said soothingly.

"I'm relieved no one can blame Rhett. But I still think that nasty deputy Clayson Lebow will probably try," Maggie said.

"If anyone else knows Rhett was out of town, it could be Clayson or a friend of his," Max said. "But if he does know, we don't know how he found out about it. He was fired by the sheriff. He is no longer a deputy. Evan, we thank you for your help. At least we now have a better idea of when the killing may have taken place." They didn't mention the threat Rhett had found on his windshield hundreds of miles away. The Whitneys didn't need to worry about that too.

"I hope it helps," Evan said.

"It does," Patches said as she and her father rose to their feet. "We need to get back to Rhett's place and see what else we can do to help the sheriff."

When Patches and Max walked back into the barn, Jay was leaning against the stall across from the one containing the victim. He was speaking to someone on the phone, and from the look on his face, the subject being discussed was grim.

A couple of other officers were at work in the cell, measuring, taking photos, and collecting bits of evidence. Jay pushed away from the wall when his call was finished. "That was the state lab," he said. "DNA results are back. The ChapStick you found was used by Clayson Lebow."

"Oh my," Patches said.

"There is still more from the lab," Jay said. "Clayson's DNA was also found on the boots in the back of Rhett's truck. There was none of Rhett's."

The sheriff's face darkened. "So Clayson could be the killer," he said. "One of my own deputies." He slammed his fist into the other hand.

As much as she hated to come to the former deputy's defense, Patches spoke. "I suppose he could have lost the lip balm when he came in and first found Charity's body."

Jay nodded his head. "Yes, that's possible, but at this point, I'm having serious doubts about our former colleague. The balm can be explained, and I'm sure he will try to use that as an excuse. But the boots in the back of Rhett's truck? They not only had his DNA but there was also dirt that matched the samples from Evan's cornfield. I am certain Lebow planted them there, but he was careless for leaving his DNA on the boots." Jay was thoughtful for a moment, and then he said, "He probably was arrogant enough to think he would never be a suspect." He turned to his boss. "Sheriff, I would suggest we put out an attempt-to-locate on him."

"Yes, I agree," McCoy said. "We need to have him arrested as a suspect when he is found. I'll leave you and the others here to continue to work the scene. I'll go meet with the prosecutor and present what we have against Lebow. If he thinks it's enough, we'll get a warrant. Keep me apprised."

"Before you go, Sheriff, there is one more thing I learned from the lab. The bullet that was taken from Kori's shoulder and the one that grazed Rhett's neck were fired from the same weapon," Detective Ackerman said. "Would a search warrant for Lebow's apartment and his vehicles be in order?"

The sheriff rubbed his chin thoughtfully. "Yes, at this point I think it would," he finally said. "You go to work on that. With all that we have, I think we can get a search warrant. And as soon as you get it, we'll serve it, whether we find Lebow at home or not." With that he left, anger and frustration evident in every step.

"What would you like us to do?" Max asked Jay.

"First call Rhett and Kori. Then if you could work on alibis, or the lack thereof, for our other suspects, that would be a great help," Jay said. "We have got to narrow this thing down and make an arrest as soon as we can. This killing today has to be by one of them. I just don't think we've missed any other possible suspects."

"Okay, so we'll check on Bernie Growfield, Gene Gaffey, Cal Thurley, and Angel Affut," Patches said. "Although, I can vouch for Bernie until a little while after midnight."

"We don't know when this occurred," Jay said.

"We haven't yet told you what we learned at the neighbors' place," Patches said. "Evan Whitney was up at two thirty this morning. He heard a vehicle over here. He looked out his kitchen window, but he didn't see any lights. It could have been someone going past the house to the barn. So that is something to consider."

"All right. So we cannot eliminate Bernie at this point," Jay said. "I also think we need to check on the whereabouts of Charity's brother, Brandon Simmons. If we happen to have Lebow's body here in the barn,

Brandon would have had a motive. He could've been angry with Lebow for misleading him about Rhett being a suspect. Simmons as Charity's killer just doesn't feel right to me. But we have to consider it at this point."

Patches flipped her bangs. "I wish I'd have stayed on a stakeout at Bernie's place," she said regretfully. "He might have left right after I saw him go into his home. I didn't stick around there."

Her father said, "Don't blame yourself, Patches. You were keeping our new clients and their children safe. And remember, if his car went back to Heber, the tracking device would have told us. But despite that, I think we do need to go have a talk with him. Should we go now? We have a lot of ground to cover."

"Go ahead," Jay said. "And thanks for all you two are doing."

Back in Patches's truck a few minutes later, Max said, "Before you call Rhett, let's talk about what we have to do today. I think we need to split up to save time. Who would you like to take?"

"Well, since I kind of feel responsible for Bernie, I'll go talk to him about last night," she said.

"Okay, but don't mention Sammy's killers or the twins," Max cautioned.

"Right," she said. "And I'll follow up on Brandon Simmons if you want me to."

"Do that," he said. "I'll contact Gene Gaffey and Angel Affut. Now, go ahead and call Rhett."

CHAPTER TWENTY-FOUR

AT THE TIME RHETT'S PHONE rang, he and Kori were westbound. Rhett had already told Kori he felt like he needed to return home. "I'll leave you in a large hotel somewhere not too far out," he'd said. "This trip has been rough on you."

Kori admitted she needed to rest, that all the driving was hard on her. "I hope that's someone calling about who the dead person in your barn is, if there really is someone."

Rhett answered the call, and Patches said, "My phone is synched with my truck, so you're on speaker. Dad's with me."

"What's the verdict?" Rhett asked despondently.

"It's not good," Patches said. "There is a dead man in the same stall Charity's body was found in."

"Who is it?" Rhett asked as Kori watched his face anxiously.

"We don't know," Patches responded. "He's been shot several times. His face is unrecognizable, and he has no ID on him."

"Was he killed in my barn?" Rhett asked.

"Oh yeah," Patches said. "Your stall is a bloody mess."

"What's it going to take to identify the victim?" Rhett asked.

"Fingerprints are our best bet at this point," Max responded.

"Can you at least give us an idea of who you think it might be?"

"We all wonder if it's Clayson Lebow or the guy he had following you. Clayson hasn't been seen since the stunt he pulled with Brandon Simmons," Patches responded. "For that matter, Brandon was the last person to see him." She then told him all about the lip balm, the boots from the back of Rhett's truck, and about the bullets used to shoot Rhett and Kori being from the same weapon. "Charity's killer could be Lebow, unless he dropped the ChapStick when he was there investigating."

"But the boots," Rhett said.

"Yeah, there is that," Patches agreed. "Dad and I are going to follow up with the suspects now." She filled Rhett in on what she, her father, and Detective Ackerman were doing.

After she had done that and the call was over, Rhett said, "That does it, Kori. I'm definitely going back."

"I pieced together some of what Patches told you, but why don't you tell me everything," Kori suggested.

After he'd finished, Rhett said, "I wonder if they'll find the gun used to shoot us when they search Lebow's apartment."

"Would he really try to kill us?" Kori asked sadly. "I knew he was a jerk, but a killer?"

***

Patches knocked boldly at Bernardo Growfield's door. As near as she could tell, his car was parked right where it had been when she'd last seen it shortly after midnight. There was no answer for a time, and she wondered if someone had picked him up and taken him somewhere. But then she heard movement inside. She knocked again, stepped to one side, and waited.

When the door finally opened, Bernie glared and said, "You again!"

"We need to discuss some things," Patches said, refusing to shrink at his look of intense hatred.

"Like what?" he asked insolently. "Like why my dad and uncle have been arrested?"

"They have?" she asked. Of course, she already knew that, but she didn't tell Bernie that. "What were they arrested for?"

"As if you don't know," Bernie said, stepping out of the door with a crutch under one arm. She couldn't see the other crutch. "They should have killed your old man as well as your uncle."

Bernie seemed to know all about Sammy's murder. She wondered why he didn't try to deny that it had happened or, at the least, that his father had anything to do with it. "I guess their time ran out," she finally said.

"You scummy people," he said. He limped closer to her as he spoke. She resisted stepping back. She was pretty sure she could take him down if she had to. "Get off my property," he snarled.

"Not until you answer some questions for me," she said, still holding her ground.

"I ain't got no answers for the likes of you." He lifted his crutch and swung it at her.

Patches ducked, and as the crutch swung harmlessly above her head she stepped in and hit him so fast and powerfully in the face that he tried to step back. But his bad knee failed him, and he went down. Patches grabbed the crutch and wrestled it away from him. Blood was gushing from his nose, and his lip was bleeding.

"I'll kill you," he threatened.

"Where were you last night?" she asked, undeterred by his threats.

Patches was aware of several people coming across the street. She glanced at them, gave a withering stare, and they all stopped several yards away. "I've got things under control here," she said. "Why don't you people return to your homes."

They grumbled, and one of them said the cops would be coming, but they stepped back to the edge of the road. Ignoring them now, Patches said, "I asked you a question, scum."

"I was home all evening and all night," Bernie said as he tried to wipe the blood from his face with the back of his hand.

"That's a lie, and you know it. What did you do after you returned from Heber a little after midnight?" she asked.

That got his attention. "What? How did you know that?" he asked as he attempted to sit up.

"I know a lot of things about you. You are no better than your father and your uncle. Where did you go after you got here?" she pressed.

"Okay, so I was in Heber. I got family there. I got the right to visit them," he said.

"After you got home, did you leave again?" she insisted.

"No. I stayed here and minded my own business."

Patches could see she wasn't going to get anything else from him, so she said, "Stay away from Heber."

She was back in her truck and half a block away when she heard sirens wailing in the distance. She kept going. Bernie would tell the cops whatever he wanted. She had other things to do. She had the address of Brandon Simmons. That was where she headed next, even as she phoned Detective Ackerman and advised him of what had just happened.

"I'll have someone swing by the Growfields' home in Midway occasionally to make sure they're okay," Jay said.

***

Max had started by looking for Gene Gaffey. He wasn't at his home, or at least his Corvette wasn't, and he didn't answer the door. So Max drove to Gene's place of employment. He wasn't there either. And his boss told Max that Gene had been missing way too much work and that, when he did return, he would probably be fired. Max shrugged, thanked him, and left. He then drove to Angel Affut's apartment. Neither she nor her bright-pink Hummer was there.

He knocked on the apartment door to the left of hers. There was no answer. He tried the one to the right. An elderly man answered the door. He had wisps of white hair that hung long around the sides and back of his head. The rest of his head was shiny but dotted with age spots. He was only a little taller than Max with white, shriveled skin. "Hey, sonny, what can I do fer ya?" he asked in a scratchy voice.

"My name is Max Fisher. I'm a private investigator. I was looking for your neighbor, Miss Affut," he said.

"It's nice to meet you," he said with a genuine smile on his face. "I am Irvin Ingram. Now, why anyone would want to speak to that woman next door is beyond me. I swear her odor seeps through the wall between us. Please, come in. I don't get company very often."

"Thank you," Max said as he entered. Contrary to what Irvin had said, Max couldn't smell a trace of Angel in Irvin's apartment. But there was some potpourri that was steaming a pleasant odor, so perhaps it masked Angel's smell.

After they were seated in Irvin's immaculate living room, Irvin said, "Can I get you a cup of tea?"

"No, thank you. It's just information I'm after," Max responded. And before Irvin could say anything else, he went on. "I am trying to trace the activities of Miss Affut for the past day or so."

Irvin's barking laugh filled the room, and he raised a blue-veined, very thin hand and pointed toward the wall that separated his apartment from Angel's. "She is almost certainly up to no good," he said.

"Oh, really? Why do you say that?" Max asked.

"She is the meanest person I've ever met. And she has strange company."

"Strange in what way?" Max pressed. He had the feeling he was about to hear something important.

"Not strange if seen alone, I suppose. I mean, I don't consider cowboys strange, but one who is friendly with her is strange, especially when he's so much cleaner than her," Irvin said.

Max leaned forward, anxious to hear more. "Tell me about the cowboy."

"She called him Cal. I never got a last name. But they seemed very friendly with each other. I heard her call him *cousin* once, so I guess that explains their association. He's been to her place several times in the past month or so," Irvin said. "For that matter, I saw him here before, just not so often."

"When was the last time he was here?" Max pressed as he considered this enlightening new information.

"That would be last night at about eleven o'clock or so. I was sitting right here reading when I heard steps outside. My blinds were open, and the only light I had on in here was this reading light, so when the cowboy walked past the window I could see him clearly."

"And he went to Angel's door?" Max asked.

"Yes. But I don't like to call her Angel. I am a God-fearing man, and I believe in angels. To call her Angel is blasphemy to me. I know I shouldn't judge so harshly, but the language I hear from that woman at times is certainly not angelic," he said.

"Tell me about last night," Max requested.

"Oh, yes. So he walked past the window, and she met him outside her door. I heard her say, 'You're late. We have a lot to do tonight,' and then they went inside."

"How long were they there?" Max asked.

"Not long. I don't think I read even a whole chapter before they both came out. She was dressed all in black. I heard her say something about leaving her car here and going in his truck," he said.

"What was he wearing?" Max asked.

"He had a cowboy shirt, a black one, and a gray cowboy hat. I couldn't see more than that. But he always has the hat," Irvin said.

"Did you hear them say where they were going?"

"No, I wish I would have. There have been a lot of robberies in the city lately," he said. "I wonder if that's what they are up to."

Max nodded. "I don't suppose you saw them come back."

"Well, this is strange. But the cowboy came by himself about an hour later, around midnight. I didn't see the woman. He went in the apartment, and that was the last I saw of him," Irvin said.

He was thoughtful for a moment. Max waited patiently without making any comments. Finally Irvin spoke again. "When I got up this morning, I could hear her rattling around over there, and when she left about an hour ago, she was alone. Strange, huh?"

"Very," Max agreed. He stood up and handed Irvin a card. "When Miss Affut comes back, would you please call me right away?"

"I sure will, Max," Irvin said. "Are you sure you wouldn't like some tea? Or maybe a soda? I don't drink anything stronger."

"Nor do I," Max said with a smile. "But I need to go. Perhaps I'll be able to stop by another time."

After he was back in the truck, he called Patches. "I learned something interesting from Angel's neighbor. It seems Cal Thurley was with her late last night and that they are probably related—cousins," he said and filled her in on the rest. "How are things coming for you?"

"I had a little trouble with Bernie. He was in a bad mood. He'd apparently just learned that his dad and uncle had been arrested," she said.

Max let out a short hoot and then said, "They will get what's coming to them now. Are you on your way to Brandon's home?"

"I am," she said.

"He doesn't live too far from here. I'll meet you there," he told her. "I don't know where to go to look for Gene or Angel. Neither his vehicles nor her Hummer were at her apartment complex. Angel's neighbor promised to call me if she shows up."

CHAPTER TWENTY-FIVE

PATCHES WAS THE FIRST TO arrive at Brandon's home. There were no vehicles near it. She waited until her father arrived to go to the door.

They rang the doorbell and knocked twice before the door opened just a crack and a young woman with long, stringy blonde hair and bloodshot green eyes peered out. "What?" she asked, sounding groggy or high or both. "I don't need anything. Go to somebody else's house."

She shut the door in their faces.

"Well, I guess that's that," Patches said, feeling very discouraged.

"I don't think so," Max said as he put his finger on the doorbell again and left it there for a long time. Then he knocked again.

Once again the door opened and the lady looked out. "I told you I didn't need anything."

Max nodded at Patches to take the lead, so she said, "We aren't selling anything. We need some information." She produced her ID. "We are Max and Patches Fisher, from Short Investigations. We need to speak with Brandon. Is he at home?"

"No, he got a phone call late last night and left," she said as she opened the door wide. "If it's about Brandon, I guess you can come in. I can't get him to answer his phone this morning. Why are you asking about him?"

"It's about his sister," Patches said as they stood in the hallway. "Are you Brandon's wife?"

"Yes, I'm Kathy," she said. "I don't know why you want to know about Charity. She's dead, and no amount of mourning will bring her back. I keep telling my husband that." Kathy absently ran a hand through her long, unruly hair.

"We are trying to help the police figure out who killed her," Patches said.

"Brandon is obsessed with her death. I keep telling him he needs to let the cops figure out what happened to her, that he should stay out of it," she said. "He's driving me crazy. But he won't listen to me. I'm afraid when he finds whoever did it, if you don't find Brandon first, that he will do something he'll regret. He gets in a rage whenever he talks about her murder."

"Kathy, was he angry with Charity over anything before she was killed?" Max asked.

"No, he doted on her. Surely you aren't saying you think he killed her?" she asked as the dimness in her eyes turned fiery.

"No, but we did need to rule it out. Has he recently mentioned an officer by the name of Deputy Clayson Lebow?" Max asked as he and Patches stood uncomfortably just inside the door, which remained open behind them. It didn't appear they were going to be invited to sit down.

"If you mean *Detective* Lebow, then yes. He is really angry with him. The detective called him a few days ago and told him to come to Heber and meet with him," she said. "The officer told him an old boyfriend of Charity's had killed her, but it turned out he wasn't even in the state at the time. Brandon almost got himself in trouble for believing the detective. At least that's what he told me. Anyway, he started poking around after that, trying to figure out who else it might have been. Brandon's smart. He could have been a detective himself. He thinks it might have been her ex, Gene Gaffey. He was brutal to her."

"Did he mention any others he suspected?" Patches asked.

"Not by name, but I know there were others. Frankly, I've quit paying much attention to his tirades. I'm afraid he's been making a nuisance of himself."

"When he comes home, please call us," Max said as he offered her a card.

She took it and looked at it. "He didn't come home last night," she said. "I've been trying to call him. I'm afraid he's gone and done something that's got him thrown in jail," she said, as she began to wring her hands.

"Kathy," Patches said as a worrisome thought entered her mind. "What was he wearing last night when he left?"

"What he always wears," she said. "A button-down shirt. I don't remember the color he had on last night. And blue jeans."

"Did he have boots on?" Patches asked.

"Why are you asking me this?" Kathy asked as she began to tremble.

"Just being thorough," Patches said evasively.

For a moment the young woman just stared at her, but she finally said, "He had on his snakeskin cowboy boots. He's quite proud of them. He could have bought a dozen pairs of shoes for what they cost."

"Are your kids at home?" Max asked.

"We don't have children," she said.

"Are you feeling okay?" Patches asked in genuine concern. "Why don't you let us help you to a seat, and I could get you a drink of water."

To their surprise, Kathy complied. Max's phone rang. He looked at it and said to Patches, "I need to take this."

He stayed near the open door as Patches helped Kathy settle into a loveseat in the living room. Then she went into the kitchen and searched for a clean glass. She finally found one and filled it with cold water from the refrigerator and took it to Kathy, who drank it slowly, holding the glass with trembling hands. "Thank you," she said at last and handed the half empty glass back to Patches.

Patches put the glass on a cluttered end table and then sat next to Kathy. "Do you need a doctor?" she asked as she looked at the woman's glazed eyes.

"No, I'm just very tired and worried," she said. "I'll be fine now. I hope Brandon comes home soon."

"So do I," Patches said as she stood up. Her father had stepped outside and still had his phone to his ear. "I guess I'd better go, but you call if you hear from your husband or if you need anything." Her father's card was lying on the loveseat beside Kathy. She extracted one of her own from her purse and handed it to Kathy. "Call me, please, if you need to," Patches said.

She started toward the door, but Kathy stopped her when she said, "He had his gun when he left."

Patches turned back and said, "Was he angry?"

"He's always angry lately."

"Did he say where he was going?"

"No, he just said he had to meet someone," Kathy said. "I hope he didn't use his gun. He hasn't been himself lately. I just wish he would answer his phone."

"Can you tell me what kind of gun he took with him?" Patches asked.

"It was a pistol. I don't know anything about guns, so I can't tell you more than that. Well, I do know it's bigger that a twenty-two, but that's all. I hope he isn't in jail for shooting someone."

Back in the truck a minute later, Max, who was off the phone, said, "That was Detective Gravitt, updating me about the Growfield brothers. He's leaving for Idaho now and says he'll call me after he's had a chance to talk to them, if they will talk."

"Dad, I'm so relieved they're in custody," Patches said. "But I'm worried about Brandon's wife. She just told me Brandon took his pistol with him when he left last night to meet someone. She's afraid he might have shot somebody. But, Dad, did you notice the boots the victim in the barn was wearing?"

"I did. Let's call Detective Ackerman," Max said grimly.

Patches spoke to her synched phone. "Call Detective Ackerman," she said, and the phone soon began to ring.

"Detective Ackerman," Jay answered a moment later. "What have you got, Patches?"

"Jay, does Clayson Lebow ever wear snakeskin boots?" she asked.

"No, not that I've ever seen," Jay answered. "Why do you ask?"

"Brandon Simmons does, and he was wearing them late last night when he went to meet someone. He had a pistol with him. His wife has been trying to call him, but he doesn't answer. I'm pretty sure that's who the body in the barn is," she said.

"Oh no. That means the killer is probably Clayson. We just found a pistol in his house that's the same caliber as the one used to shoot Kori and Rhett. I'm still in his house. There's a note on his kitchen counter with Brandon's name and a phone number on it," Jay reported.

"Have any of the bullets in the barn been recovered?" Max asked.

"A couple of them, but we can't tell what caliber they are," Jay answered. "Some are still in the body. They'll be in better shape; it'll be easier for the lab to determine if they were fired by Lebow's pistol. We have a warrant for him now."

Max and Patches were silent for a minute, but finally Max said, "I don't think Lebow killed Charity or Brandon." Patches looked over at him in surprise.

"Are you sure about that?" Jay asked.

"No, but I have a theory," he said.

"Tell me," Jay requested.

Max said, "Let me work on it some more before I say, but I really do have a feeling I know who did it."

Jay said, "Okay, but please tell me when you have some proof. For now we're still proceeding on the feeling *I* have that it is Lebow."

"I understand. I'll let you know when I know more," Max said. "Incidentally, Bernie's father and uncle are in custody in Idaho for killing my cousin."

"I remember you mentioned that to me. But you'll have to give me the details later. Where is Bernie?" Jay asked.

"He was at home the last we knew. He attacked Patches with his crutch when she tried to talk to him. That was a mistake," Max said with a grin. "She hurt him, but she had more restraint than I did. She didn't kick his good knee. All she did was bloody his nose and knock him down. Cops were coming when she left, but I have a feeling he may not still be there. And I'm sure he wouldn't have been arrested. We will check in a few minutes on him. Did you have someone check on Norman and his family? This could be enough to put Bernie over the edge. Those young ones are in more danger than ever."

"We did, and we'll do it again right away," Jay said. "Oh, and there is one more thing. When I called the medical examiner about the body we were sending, I asked him if by any chance Charity's throat looked sore. He told me it looked like something had been shoved down it. That tells me that she didn't drink the alcohol. I think Rhett will be relieved to hear she wasn't drinking, but he will be devastated that someone did that to her. Anyway, I'd better get going."

As they headed toward Salt Lake, Patches looked over at her dad and asked, "Dad, if Lebow shot Brandon, why would he take his gun back to his apartment and leave it there?"

"He's a cocky man, Patches," Max replied. "He probably thinks no one would suspect him . . . *if* he shot Brandon."

"At least now, wherever he is, he's probably unarmed," she observed.

"I doubt it. I'd be willing to wager he has more weapons," Max said.

"But you don't believe he killed Charity or Brandon," Patches said.

"That's right, I don't."

"Then, who did kill them?"

Max smiled over at his daughter. "I want you to figure it out. You know everything I do. Granted, we need more information, but I think if you analyze our information, you'll come to the same conclusion I have," Max said. "So be thinking about it."

They traveled in silence after that, Patches trying to piece together all the information they had on the case. She began to form a picture, but before she could run it by her father, his phone rang. "Hello, Dear," he said. Then he listened for a moment. "Okay, thanks for the information, Hallie. We'll head that way."

"Head where?" Patches asked.

"To Midway. That was your mother. She was just alerted by our tracking device that Bernie is heading that way. We need to hurry," he said urgently.

Shortly they were on the freeway heading east. While Patches drove, Max called his wife back. When he ended the call, he said, "We're not that far behind him. Maybe two or three miles."

Patches hurried as fast as she dared while she called Detective Ackerman.

"Hi, Patches," Jay said. "What's going on?"

"We are headed your way," she said. "Bernie is on the freeway heading east in his silver Charger. Dad and I are two or three miles behind him; my mother is keeping track of him with the tracking device we put on his car. We're just coming into Parley's Canyon."

"Okay, thanks for the heads up. Keep coming," Jay said. "I was just now headed to Norman's house to check on the family again, but I'll head for the freeway and wait for Bernie."

"Thanks. I'll slow down then," Patches said with a chuckle. "I don't need a speeding ticket."

Several minutes later, Jay called her back. "I'm behind Bernie now. He turned off the freeway and is headed directly to Midway. I've got officers watching Norman's house from a little ways away. I'll keep you posted."

"Okay, we are only a couple miles from the Midway turnoff," Patches responded. "We'll be behind you. Did he spot you?"

"I don't think so," Jay said. "My SUV is unmarked. Norman knows Bernie's coming. He and his family left the house and are driving into Heber, so they're safe for now. My officers will wait out of sight. We'll see what Bernie does when he gets there. If you don't mind, instead of coming across from Highway 40, why don't you two go on into Heber and meet Norman and his family and keep them company."

"All right, we'll do that. I have his number. I'll call him and arrange a place to meet him."

"Thanks," Jay said and ended the call.

"I don't have a good feeling about this," Patches said. "Bernie is probably angry and out of his mind."

"I'm afraid you may be right," Max agreed. "But all we can do now is let the sheriff's department handle their end of it, and we'll take care of our clients."

They met the Growfields in the Wal-Mart parking lot. Norman met them in front of his car, and his wife stayed in it with the children. "Please, tell me what's happening," Norman said, his forehead creased with worry.

"Bernie learned that his father and uncle were arrested in Idaho this morning," Max said.

"For killing your cousin?" Norman asked.

"That's right," Max agreed. "And your grandfather."

"He was really angry, as you can imagine," Patches added.

"So that's why we were warned to watch out for him?" Norman asked.

"Exactly," Max said. "Patches and I put a tracking device on his car, and my wife is monitoring it, so we knew when he started heading toward Midway. That's why you were told to leave your home."

"Did he go to our place?" Norman asked.

"We don't know," Patches said. "We haven't heard back yet."

Norman shook his head. "What should we do now?"

"Stay right here with us," Max said. "When we find out what's happening, we'll plan what to do next."

"Are we safe here?" Norman asked.

"I don't think he'll get past the officers," Max said. "But if he does, Patches and I can handle him. We'd like you to get back in your car and wait there. We'll be right here."

The minutes crept by. Patches kept hoping to hear from Jay, but so far he hadn't called. She was getting increasingly anxious. To get her mind off that worry she said to her father, "I think I know who killed Charity and Brandon."

"Okay, so tell me," he said. After she did, he said, "You are fast becoming an excellent investigator. Now all we have to do is find some more proof."

Her phone rang. She looked at the screen. "It's Jay," she said and answered.

"The Growfields are safe now," the detective said. "Norman and his family will need to get a motel for tonight or longer, unless they have friends or family they can stay with," Jay said. "Their place is a crime scene now, and there will need to be cleanup and repairs done."

"What happened?" Patches asked.

"Bernie is dead," he said. "He jumped out of his car, left it running, and hobbled up to the door. He tried to open it, but it was locked. So he pulled a gun and shot the lock out. By then I was there, in my car on the street, and he shot at me before he could get Norman's door open. The sheriff and another deputy were close by, and they joined me. He kept shooting, and he finally went down."

"You shot him?" Patches asked.

"We did. My SUV is full of holes, and much of the glass is gone. He also hit the sheriff's vehicle once," Jay said. "And the Growfields' door is a mess. It will need to be replaced. And there's damage inside the house from bullets that went through the door. And there's a lot of blood on their porch. I'm sorry it turned out that way, but he gave us no choice."

"I'll talk to Norman and his wife, and then Dad and I will come out," Patches said.

"Tell them if they want some of their stuff, they can use the back door. But we don't want them staying there," Jay instructed. "They are not to come until the body is removed. We'll give them a call then."

Max had Norman and Lexie get out of their car and gave them the news.

"I'm just grateful our children are now safe from him," Norman said as his wife leaned into him for support.

CHAPTER TWENTY-SIX

RHETT AND KORI HAD TRAVELED a long way that day, and Kori was about done in. She was waiting in the truck while Rhett got rooms for the two of them for the night. Had he been alone he would have kept driving, but for her sake, it was necessary to stop for the night. He could have left her there, but he didn't feel good about it, so he tamped back his impatience and stopped in front of the entrance.

He had just finished registering and was walking back to his truck with the keys in his hand when his phone rang. "Hi, Patches," he said. "How are you guys doing?"

"We're fine, but a lot has happened today," she said. "How are you two holding up?"

"I'm fine," Rhett said. "But this traveling is getting to Kori, the poor girl. We're stopping for the night."

"Are you enjoying her company?" Patches said with a break in her voice Rhett couldn't miss. He smiled to himself.

He'd stopped just inside the door. He could see Kori in the truck just outside. Her eyes were closed. "I am," he said. "But I'm missing you so much it hurts."

"What?" Patches asked.

"I miss you, that's what I said," he told her, and he was very serious. There was just something about her that appealed to him in a way no one else ever had. He steered away from that topic and said, "You say a lot has happened. Tell me about it."

For the next several minutes she rehearsed the latest events. Then she said, "Bernie is dead, and Jay is getting his gun checked for ballistics against the bullet that killed Brandon Simmons and those that hit you and Kori."

"Wow," Rhett said, his mind running a mile a second. He didn't think Kori had stirred, so he continued to talk inside the hotel entrance. "So if they match all the way around, all the crimes are solved, I assume," he said.

"I wish that were true," Patches said. "But I'm afraid it's not that simple. Lebow could be the killer, according to Jay, but now he thinks it might have been Bernie. Dad and I are still checking some other things."

"I'm coming home tomorrow," Rhett announced. "I'll leave Kori in a hotel somewhere if the sheriff thinks I should. I would have left her someplace before now, but she insisted she stay with me, and I didn't feel good about leaving her here."

"She likes you, Rhett, or should I say, *Shorty?*"

"I like that you call me Rhett. It sets you apart, and that's how I think it should be," he said softly.

"Thanks, Rhett. I miss my favorite bull rider, but I would miss you a lot more if you got yourself killed. Don't come back yet, please. Even though Bernie is dead, there are a lot of others who might want to harm you. Stay away until we give you the all clear."

"Who hired whom here?" Rhett asked with a light chuckle.

"You hired us," she said.

"That's right. So that makes me the boss," he said. "You can't tell me what to do. I'm coming. But I promise I'll be careful. I can't wait to see you."

"That's sweet, but please, don't make me worry more," she said.

"I see Kori's stirring out in the truck. I'd better get her to her room. Please keep me informed," he said.

"I will," she said. "You're the boss, like you just said."

"Is your dad there with you, Patches?"

"Are you kidding me? You know how he feels about us flirting."

"Is that what we're doing?"

"I think so," she said. "I hope it is. But please, don't come back until it's safe."

"Okay, I'll think about it, if it makes you feel better," he said.

"It does. I miss you. Dad's coming now, so I'd better get off the phone. We have some work to do tonight," she said. And just that quickly the call ended.

Rhett looked longingly at the phone, savoring the sweet sound of Patches's voice. Then he put the phone in his pocket and headed out the door. He had to get Kori settled in and bring her up-to-date on the state of the investigation.

"Was that Patches you were talking to?" Kori asked as he helped her from the truck.

"I thought you were sleeping," he said.

"Just resting. Was it Patches?" she repeated.

"What makes you think that?" he asked.

"I could see the smile on your face from time to time. You miss her, don't you?" Kori asked.

"She's a good lady," Rhett said.

"Hey, Shorty, let's get something straight right now. I like you a lot. You're a good friend. But that's all there is between us. Don't let me be the reason you hold back with Patches. You two are made for each other," she said. She smiled, but Rhett detected some sadness in her eyes.

"Thanks, Kori. I like you a lot too," he said. "But you need to get to bed. And before that happens you need food, and you need to hear all the excitement there has been in Wasatch County today."

"I'm serious, Shorty," she said as she let him take her arm and walk her toward the hotel entrance. "Let your heart go. Don't let her down."

***

Patches and Max had barely pulled up in the parking lot where Angel Affut's pink Hummer was now parked. "Looks like she's home," Max said. They had participated in the search of Bernardo Growfield's house earlier. There was nothing found there that was of importance to the murders, but there was plenty of evidence that he was full of hatred. Not that it mattered now. He was no longer a threat to anyone.

The phone rang beside Patches. She had not yet shut the engine off, and the phone was still synched to the truck sound system. "Hello, Jay," she answered, glancing at her father.

"Are you sitting down?" he asked.

"I am," she said. "And so is Dad. We just arrived at Angel's apartment complex. She's home now, but we're still in the truck. We can both hear you. It sounds like you must have some pretty heavy news for us."

"That's for sure. The lab did a rushed job for me," the detective said. "The ballistics are completed. Bernie's firearm did not fire the bullets that killed Simmons or the ones that hit Rhett and Kori. Nor did Lebow kill Simmons."

"Why did we need to be sitting for that?" she asked. "I would have been surprised if there were any other result."

"Bernie's ruled out as a suspect," he said. "Lebow is not, as he could have more firearms. The news you need to be seated for is that the shots that hit Kori and Rhett were fired from Lebow's gun. And I failed to mention it earlier, but we found a black face covering in Lebow's apartment."

Patches felt like someone had just punched her in the stomach. For a moment she couldn't speak. Max did not have that problem. He said, "So he's still out there somewhere, and he is, I assume, wanted for attempted murder."

"Exactly. Would you like to inform Rhett and Kori, or would you like me to?" Jay asked.

Max answered. "You do it. Patches and I need to talk to Angel right now."

"I'll do that in a little while. And let me know what you learn with Angel. But remember, I still haven't ruled out Lebow, Cal, or Charity's ex, Gene."

"We'll let you know when we know," Max said.

Patches ended the call and looked over at her dad. He had a very small smile on his face, and he said nothing. "What?" she asked.

"I know you would have liked to call Rhett yourself, wouldn't you?"

"Yes, but that's okay," she said.

Max's smile broadened. "I hope we have this matter wrapped up pretty soon. Then if you want to let him know how you feel, you'll have my blessing, mine and your mother's."

Patches felt her face flush, and she fingered for a moment with the blonde bangs that hung in a curl just above her eyebrows. When she spoke she said, "Thanks, Dad. Let's go see what Angel has to say for herself."

They got out of the truck and started to walk toward the apartment complex. Suddenly Patches stopped. "Dad, isn't that Cal Thurley's car?"

Max smiled. "It is," he said. "That's his license number." He stopped walking and pulled his phone from his pocket.

"Who are you calling?" Patches asked.

"Detective Ackerman," he said. "Our theory is right." He signaled her to step back to her truck.

"Detective, this is Max. Are you still in the city?" he asked.

He listened to a response, and then he said, "I think you should come meet us at Angel's apartment. And hurry, if you can." He listened for a moment, his eyes on his daughter. Then he said, "The killers are here." He listened again. "That's right, Jay, *killers*. Cal Thurley and his cousin Angel are both here. Would you like us to wait for you?" He listened some more. Then he said, "So you haven't called Rhett yet?" Another short wait. "Okay, I'm sure she'd be glad to do that."

When the call ended, he said, "Jay wants us to wait and make sure they don't leave. I think he finally understands what's going on with the murders."

"I hope so," Patches said. "And what is it he wants me to do?"

"Call Rhett. Jay hasn't done that yet."

***

"Hi, Patches," Rhett said when he answered the phone. He sat on the bed in his hotel room.

"Dad and I are at Angel Affut's apartment complex. I have news," she said.

He smiled to himself. "Is it good news? Miss me, do you?"

"No and yes," she said.

"No, it's not good news and yes, you miss me?" he asked.

"That's right." She paused. "Lebow didn't kill Charity or her brother," she said. "I suppose that's good news. The bad news is that he shot you and Kori."

Rhett suddenly felt faint. "You're kidding," he said after a moment spent gaining his composure.

"I'm afraid not. Ballistics proves it. At least it proves the bullets match the gun found in his apartment. Detective Ackerman's team also found the face covering Lebow was most likely wearing. It was also in his apartment."

"And I take it he's not in custody."

"He's not. No one knows where he is. So you and Kori have got to be doubly careful."

"So who killed Charity and Brandon?"

"We still aren't positive, but we should know in a little while."

"Who do you think it is?"

"We found out your nemesis and Charity's are cousins. They're together right now, in her apartment. Jay's on his way."

Rhett was silent for a moment, thinking. Then he said, "Cal is with Angel?"

"That's right. Cal is jealous of you, and Angel is jealous of Charity. That seems to be their motive. We figured out they were the killers when we found out they'd been together a lot. Go tell Kori, and again, be doubly careful. Lebow is still out there somewhere," she said.

"What about Gene Gaffey?" Rhett asked.

"Apparently he's a wife beater but not a killer," she said. "I'll talk to you later."

"Patches," he said.

"What?"

"You be careful. Please. I can't wait to see you again."

"You have my word," she said before hanging up.

For a moment Rhett just sat there. But he wasn't being idle. He was praying that the Lord would protect Patches and her father. Then he left his room and tapped on Kori's door.

CHAPTER TWENTY-SEVEN

Jay knocked on the door while Patches and Max stood to either side as they waited. Angel answered the door. "What do you need?" she asked after Jay identified himself.

"We need to talk," he said.

"I have nothing to say to you," she said.

"I think you do, both you and Cousin Cal Thurley."

At the mention of the bull rider's name, he appeared and darted past Jay, who made no effort to stop him. But the same could not be said of Patches. She collared him and had his right arm twisted behind his back so tightly he screamed for her to let him loose. She even held tight when one of his boots connected sharply with her shin. She angrily cinched him down tighter. He quit kicking as he screamed in pain.

In the meantime, Angel apparently decided she needed to do something. Unfortunately she did the wrong thing. She hit Jay with her fist, right in the mouth, knocking him back. She followed up for another punch, but Max intervened. He had her down so fast Patches had to blink. Jay recovered from the blow he'd taken and handcuffed Angel behind her back. He pulled her to her feet and shoved her against the wall.

"Patches, we'll handcuff the cowboy while you frisk Miss Affut," Jay said.

**

"Hi, Rhett, did I wake you up?" Patches asked.

"It's one in the morning, Patches. So, yes, you woke me up. But it's a pleasure to wake up to your voice. It's like music," he said.

"I'm sorry, but I had to call," she said.

"The last I talked to you, you were waiting for Jay at Angel's apartment," he said. "Did something happen there?"

"As a matter of fact, we hadn't accused them of anything before Cal's flight instinct kicked in," Patches said.

"Did he get away?" Rhett asked.

"Of course not," she said. "He had to get past me, and that wasn't going to happen. He did kick me in the shin though. I'll have a bad bruise, but that's all. As for Angel, she made the bad decision to choose to fight. She punched Jay in the face. He has a black eye now."

"And did you take care of her too?"

"I was holding Cal, so Dad took care of Angel," she said. "And we hadn't even accused them of anything yet. But when I frisked Angel, she had a pistol tucked in the waistband behind her back. Jay frisked Cal. He had a pistol in his boot."

"I suppose it's too early to have any ballistics testing on them," Rhett speculated.

"It is, but Cal already blamed Angel. He said she kidnapped and killed Charity and Brandon."

"I'll bet Angel liked that," Rhett said.

"They were questioned separately, so she didn't hear him," Patches said with a chuckle. "But she was quick to say that Cal forced her to help him get rid of both of them. A little searching, by the way, turned up the boots Angel wore when she carried Charity through your neighbor's field."

"What about Lebow's boots? The ones found in the back of Mom's truck?" he asked.

"He apparently smeared them with dirt from the field. Just more of his attempt to frame you," she said.

"So Cal and Angel are the killers?" Rhett asked.

"She is the killer, but he's an accessory and will be charged with murder right along with her," Patches said. "And, Rhett, Cal certainly does hate you. The reason he wanted you framed is because he could never outride you. We think Angel wanted to just kill you, but he thought if you were framed, that you would spend your life in prison. Apparently he wanted to know you were suffering. If he ever gets out of prison, which is doubtful, you'll need to watch out for him. He made that clear."

"I'm not worried, but I am coming home," Rhett said.

"What about Lebow?" she asked. "Aren't you forgetting about him?"

"No, but I promise, Patches, I'll be careful," he said.

He listened to her musical chuckle. Then she said, "I'm messing with you. He was arrested in Georgia a few hours ago. We just learned about it. Jay is pretty sure he was angry with Kori for messing up his efforts to frame you. And he was still angry with you because Charity didn't want anything to do with him. When he could see that someone wanted to frame you, he simply took advantage and tried to help make a case against you. When that didn't work, I guess he decided to shoot you. Anyway, please come back now. I miss you. And since your innocence is proven, you don't need Short Investigations anymore."

"I still need a full report from you. But then, if I flirt a little, your dad won't do to me what he did to Bernie, will he?"

"You'll be safe," she said. "Oh, Dad said something funny. He said if he'd known what Bernie wanted to do to those kids and their parents, he'd have broken both his kneecaps."

"And he would have been justified," Rhett said.

"I'll let you go now, but I can't wait to report to you in person," Patches said before ending the call.

EPILOGUE

THE FOOD WAS GOOD. NORMAN Growfield did a masterful job throwing a backyard barbeque. His guests all seemed to be enjoying themselves. Jay and the sheriff and their wives had been invited and graciously accepted. Max and Hallie Fisher were in a deep conversation with the grinning twins, four people from different generations who had already forged a lasting friendship.

Earlier the adults had talked about the murders. A lot had been learned following the arrests of Lebow, Angel, and Cal. The gray car with out-of-state plates Polly had seen belonged to one of Lebow's criminal friends. He'd borrowed it to commit his crimes. It was also one of them who had written the note found on the truck Rhett and Kori were using while it was parked in the rest area in Kansas. Lebow's helpers were now also sitting in jail awaiting trial. And the voice on the dispatch recordings reporting bodies in the barn was identified as Angel Affut's. She was also proven to be the owner of the unknown Facebook account and was the one who had hacked into Rhett's and Charity's accounts.

Kori Davis was feeling much better now, and she was seated on a folding chair on the lawn, following the discussions. From time to time her eyes drifted to where Rhett and Patches were holding hands, looking at each other and laughing at something one or the other had said. She sighed. She had come to terms with it. She was glad Shorty was happy.

ABOUT THE AUTHOR

CLAIR M. POULSON WAS BORN and raised in Duchesne, Utah. His father was a rancher and farmer, his mother, a librarian. Clair has always been an avid reader, having found his love for books as a very young boy.

He has served for more than forty years in the criminal justice system. He spent twenty years in law enforcement, ending his police career with eight years as the Duchesne County Sheriff. For the past twenty-plus years, Clair has worked as a justice court judge for Duchesne County. He is also a veteran of the U.S. Army, where he was a military policeman. In law enforcement, he has been personally involved in the investigation of murders and other violent crimes. Clair has also served on various boards and councils during his professional career, including the Justice Court Board of Judges, the Utah Commission on Criminal and Juvenile Justice, the Utah Judicial Council, the Utah Peace Officer Standards and Training Council, an FBI advisory board, and others.

In addition to his criminal justice work, Clair has farmed and ranched all his life. He has raised many kinds of animals, but his greatest interests are horses and cattle. He's also involved in the grocery store business with his oldest son and other family members.

Clair has served in many capacities in The Church of Jesus Christ of Latter-day Saints, including full-time missionary (California Mission), bishop, counselor to two bishops, Young Men president, high councilor, stake mission president, Scoutmaster, high priest group leader, and Gospel Doctrine teacher. He currently serves as a ward missionary.

Clair is married to Ruth, and they have five children, all of whom are married: Alan (Vicena) Poulson, Kelly Ann (Wade) Hatch, Amanda (Ben) Semadeni, Wade (Brooke) Poulson, and Mary (Tyler) Hicken.

They also have twenty-five wonderful grandchildren and a great-granddaughter.

Clair and Ruth met while both were students at Snow College and were married in the Manti Utah Temple.

Clair has always loved telling his children, and later his grandchildren, made-up stories. His vast experience in life and his love of literature have contributed to both his telling stories to his children and his writing of adventure and suspense novels.

Clair has published more than thirty novels. He would love to hear from his fans, who can contact him by going to his website, clairmpoulson.com.